Bonds of Fate

Samuel Buckland Chronicles
Book Two

Jason P. Crawford

DEDICATION

This book is dedicated to my wife, Cherrie; to my first and greatest fan, Sara; and to one of my best friends and supporters, Nolan. You are all the reasons that I do what I do. Thank you.

ACKNOWLEDGMENTS

Thank you to Alejandro Palomares and Aaron Fors for their excellent photography and modeling for my cover. Also, thank you to my beta readers for helping make this book even better than the first was.

THE INVADERS

Jambres crowed, his laughter and jubilation echoing over the luminescent landscape of the Heavenly city as he flew through the air. He pointed his swarthy hand at the retreating backs of the defeated Archangels—bleeding golden light, their radiance flickering as they withdrew—and dark energy began to swirl about his fingers.

"Enough." Another hand closed about his, with the same skin. Both men's robes flapped in the warm breeze of the celestial sky. "They are defeated, brother. Do not forget why we are here."

There was a moment of silence; Jambres stared into his brother's determined eyes, and the only sounds were the tinkling of their ensorcelled amulets in the wind.

"...You're right, Jannes." Jambres lowered his gaze back to the two Archangels, who had stopped their flight and landed near the stairwell leading upward into the realm. "We have more important things to do."

Jannes clapped his brother on the shoulder and pointed upward. Amongst the stars of the Heavenly sky, a subtle ripple distorted the twinkling lights. Jambres nodded and the two raised their hands, drifting upward toward the disturbance. Each man clasped his hand around one of the pendants at his neck as they entered the vortex.

There was a shocking sensation, a swimmer hitting an unexpected pocket of cold water, and then they were through. At once, the pair had their hands up in defensive posture, waiting for the inevitable attack.

It did not come.

"Where are they?" Jambres cast his eyes around the new terrain; instead of the levels of city the pair had passed through, they stood in a single, vast room, lit by smokeless candles and effusive sunlight filtering in through the ceiling. Gentle music wafted in through great archways and windows, and there was a small table in the middle of the room, with a steaming pot of tea and setting for three.

Jannes and Jambres approached the table. Jambres ran a hand over the hardwood of the chair in front of one of the settings.

"What kind of trick is this?" Jannes put one arm in front of his brother. "Touch nothing."

Jambres pushed the other's arm aside. "It's a *chair*, Jannes. We have fought *angels*. Why should we fear a chair?"

"Indeed."

The voice echoed off the walls and floor, a deep, sonorous sound that startled the two Egyptian sorcerers.

"Who are you?" Jambres's hands flared once again with magic. "Show yourself!"

"Of course."

Standing across the table from the brothers was a slight figure—beautiful, as all angels were, but lacking the stature and magnificence of the defeated Archangels. He wore a soft, shimmering robe of samite cloth trimmed with golden and silver embroidery. His lips curled in a gentle smile, and he extended a hand towards the two men.

"Please, sit." Two spirits resembling winged children materialized and stood behind the other seats, pulling them out from the table and waiting. "I think we have many things to discuss. It is not often that Heaven is graced with powerful sorcerers such as yourselves."

Jannes sneered. "Do not think to deceive us, angel. We will not be fooled by your flattery."

The angel shook his head and took a seat. "I do not flatter. Deception is impossible in Heaven. It has been made apparent to the Father that force of arms will serve no further purpose." He laced his fingers together and leaned back in his chair, eyes appraising the two standing before him. "As you can see, I have no weapons. Please, sit. I know you are thirsty."

There was another pause as the two brothers looked at each other. Jannes licked his lips and his head turned just a bit from one side to the other. Jambres cocked an eyebrow at his brother, then threw himself into the seat before him, grasping the mug of steaming tea.

The angel's smile grew broader, and he motioned with his hand for Jannes to join them.

"How do I know this isn't a trick? The tea could be poisonous, or enchanted in some way." Jannes glared in his brother's direction. "I don't believe that you are simply going to meet our attack with generosity."

"With what would you rather I meet it?" The angel tilted his head. "I cannot lie. Neither can you. The tea is harmless." He motioned toward the other sorcerer. "It has no poison, no enchantment. It is simply tea." He opened his hands. "Can we not simply discuss the matter, as civilized individuals, without bloodshed?"

Jannes pursed his lips, then nodded. "Very well."

The sorcerer moved more slowly than his brother had, easing himself down and breathing in the vapors of the tea before sipping.

His eyes widened.

"This...this is amazing." He took another sip and looked toward Jambres, who had already drained his and was reaching for the pot to refill it. "What is it made from?"

The angel held up a hand and one of the attendants moved in to fill Jambres's cup before he could do so. "Manna. In Heaven, it can take any form, and nourishes both flesh and soul." The angel sipped at his own cup and moved his eyes from one man to the other.

"I suppose it must be asked. Why are you here? Why have you climbed Heaven and fought through Archangels?" He glanced behind the brothers, who followed his gaze to a great opaline stairwell stretching up through the ceiling. "Do you seek audience with the Father?"

Jannes opened his mouth, but Jambres was quicker. "Your prophet, Moses, defeated us in a duel of magic several years ago before our Pharaoh. We have spent those years seeking out lore and spells from all over the world that would allow us to overcome the power he showed that day." The sorcerer sat back, his smile triumphant. "And we have done so."

"So it would seem." The attendants refilled more cups. The warmth of the tea revealed itself in the two men's faces, which began to sweat as they drank. "What does this prove? You cannot defeat the Father. He is beyond worldly challenges, beyond any attempts to overthrow Him."

Jannes's smile was smaller than his brother's, but no less proud. "That is what Moses told us then, about your God and the angels, but we have proven him wrong." He wiped the sweat from his brow. "Your best warriors have fallen before the magics we have learned and mastered. Even if your God destroys us, we have still done what none have done before—reached the throne and challenged His power."

"It has been done, once. The outcome was not pleasant." The angel motioned again and the two attendants stepped up behind the magicians. "Gentlemen, I can see that the tea is making you too warm. If you would hand your cloaks to my servants..."

Both Jannes and Jambres glanced at the children standing behind them, then slipped their hands up to the collars of their red-brown cloaks. Their fingers ran up over the chains of the amulets they wore under their collars, and they reached back to unfasten the clasps.

The angel watched them, his eyes steady, his countenance pleasant.

Jambres took the heavy golden amulet, set with a great ruby and inscribed with mystical symbols, and placed it on the table before him in easy reach. Jannes stretched forth his hand as well...

And his face blanched.

"Jambres! Put it back on! The spells –"

The angel rose, expanding to a full twenty feet in height with giant purplish wings. He waved his hand, and, in a flash of golden light, Jambres was hurled from his seat and through the wall, his screams dwindling as he plummeted through the celestial plane toward Earth.

Jannes held his amulet out toward the monstrous angel, who turned toward him, eyes full of Heavenly fire. His words shook the air and the ground as he spoke.

"Go with your brother, sorcerer. Go now and you may yet save him from your folly. There is only you here, now, and you cannot stand against the Voice." The angel's hand clenched and another golden blast detonated against Jannes. He coughed and blinked his eyes, but his pendant had taken the worst of it, the edges blackening and cracking.

"Go now."

Jannes's eyes danced between the angel and the hole his brother had made. His head dropped, and he nodded, rising into the air and flying along Jambres's path. Angels and spirits watched as the sorcerer fled, and a great cheer went up through the first four levels of Heaven.

The Metatron, the Voice of God, sat back in his chair and sipped his tea.

THE KEEPER

Samuel Buckland rubbed two fingers against the bridge of his nose, took a breath, then addressed the young man sitting across from him.

"All right, Vincent. When you're ready, tell me about...what happened."

The teenager nodded, licking his lips. He glanced at his questioner from behind his unkempt blond hair, smoothing it back, fidgeting, taking a drink of water.

"Well, Mr. Buckland, it went like this." The boy rubbed his hands over his wrists, where the ghosts of several angry, straight-edged wounds were visible. "I...I was just looking out the window, you know, and..." Another sip, a clearing of the throat. "And I saw Ilianna downstairs. She was...was..."

A momentary flash of irritation crossed Sam's face, but he mastered it quickly. The hand that Sam placed on Vincent's was covered in black runic tattoos, a script that a scholar might recognize as reminiscent of ancient Hebrew text. His gaze drifted from the boy's face to his left shoulder as he spoke. "It's all right. Take your time."

Vincent nodded, running his hand across his mouth. "She was just...just making out with this other guy, you know?" He clenched his fist. "She was *my* girlfriend, man. At first, I got mad. Real mad. Wanted to go down there and..." He hesitated, eyes flicking up to the man across the table.

"You wanted to kill them, didn't you?"

Vincent's eyes were wide, gazing into his water glass as if it were a scrying pool. "Yeah. I did. I could see the look on her face as I choked her, man. I could see the other guy turning and running before I smashed his head in with a rock or something." His fingers wrapped around the glass, his knuckles turning white. "I mean, I could *see* it...and, goddamn it, I wanted it so bad."

Sam nodded, his eyes still looking over the teen's shoulder, toward the doorway. "What stopped you?"

Vincent laughed, but did not raise his head. "I'm not sure. I was standing there, seeing it, wanting it and then..." He waved his hand, dismissing the statement. "I don't know, man."

Sam turned his face back. "Did it feel like someone else's idea for a moment? Like someone was whispering in your ear, that they weren't your thoughts?"

Vincent's head jerked upward, his eyes wide, lower lip trembling. "Y...yeah. Yeah, that's what it was like, like a snake in my ear. I freaked out, slammed my hand against the window, cut myself to shit."

"Try again, Vincent."

Vincent nodded, rubbing his upper arm with his uninjured hand. "Cut myself bad. When

I felt the pain, it was like it went right through the anger, and I started crying, man. That's when everyone came running into the class-room."

"I see." Sam reached to his side and grasped a small notebook, taking a few moments to jot down something. He didn't look down at the paper, his eyes still dancing between Vincent's face and left shoulder as his tattooed hand drew the pen across.

God, how many of these are you going to send me today?

He laid the pen down and leaned forward again.

"Vincent, I think that it's important to know that this was not your fault." He put up a finger to quell the start of the teenager's protest. "There isn't anything wrong with you. You'll need some more counseling, someone to help you work through these feelings."

"Mr...Mr. Buckland?" Vincent looked away for a moment, then back. "How can there be nothing wrong with me? You know...you know that this isn't the first time something like this has happened? I've –"

"You've hurt people. I know, I read all of it." Sam gestured with one hand to the file folders on his desk nearby. "But I also know that you won't be doing anything like that anymore." A glance at the clock on the wall. "All right. I know it sounds like the stereotypical shrinks in the movies, but our time is up. I hope I'll see you again next week, but I expect you'll be feeling much better by then." He stood, and the young man followed. Sam extended his left hand.

"See you then, Vincent."

Vincent scrunched his eyes, cocked his head. His hand came halfway up, then paused, quivering, in mid-air.

Sam waited.

Vincent's eyes reopened, but their color had changed to a smoky-red, the whites criss-crossed with blood vessels. "Mr...Buckland...I..."

Sam took another breath, then lifted his right hand, palm toward the boy. "It's okay, Vincent. It's okay."

His face turned to the boy's left shoulder once more.

"*Begone.*"

The demon, the scabrous, four-armed and no-legged imp that was clinging to its host's head and spewing vile poison into his mind, shrieked as its flesh began to bubble and dissolve under the force of the exorcism. It spat and hissed, its ethereal fingers searching for purchase in the flesh of the boy's neck.

With a faint odor of sulfur and a last wail, the creature was gone. Vincent shook his head like something was caught in his nose.

"Vincent? Are you all right?"

Vincent's eyes were their normal brown again. "Yeah." For the first time since he had come into Sam's office, he smiled. "I'm...I'm actually feeling a lot better, Mr. Buckland. I think you're right. I think everything's going to be okay."

Sam returned the smile, but his was wan, weak. "That's right, Vincent. Take care of yourself, and let me know if you need anything else, all right? You have my number and my email."

Vincent nodded, patting the phone in his pocket. With another wave, he was out the door, and Sam waited for the *click* before collapsing into his chair.

He shook his head, rubbing the fatigue from his neck and sighing. A glance into the glass pane of the coffee table revealed the deep black and blue circles under his eyes. "Am I even making a difference?" He cast his gaze upward. "There's just...there are so *many*. Always someone new."

He stood again and dragged himself to the cappuccino machine standing in the corner of the office. He punched in the buttons that would deliver his caffeine-laced nectar and returned to his desk. His email was lit up with new messages—queries about patients, appointments, departmental meetings—but he closed the window and navigated to a folder titled "Journal." With a few clicks of his mouse, he opened up a new document and titled it "October 27th—Day 771."

As he typed, he let himself drift away from his keyboard, his mind translating the press of letters into speech. His office dissolved, faded, until it was replaced by a grassy green field, clear, blue sky, and a gentle summer breeze. He sat on a checkered blanket, talking.

As he spoke, Gabriel smiled, listening, comforting.

I hope you can hear me...well, you know what I mean. Has it always been this bad? This many people? He laughed. *Did Gramma ever have bad days like this? Where she didn't know if she was making a difference or not? I almost hope so. It would help me feel like I wasn't alone.*

Sam stared for several seconds at the blinking cursor on the screen before his fingers moved again. *Would you believe that part of me is wishing for another apocalypse? Another threat? At least then I'd be making a difference.* His typing grew faster, more frenzied. *It's like I'm beating my head against the wall here—I know that small things add up but I'm not getting to see it, I'm not getting to celebrate their successes. They're here and they're gone, and I know it'll be important in ten years or so but –*

The imaginary Archangel's frown brought him up short. *No. That's wrong. It's important now, and this is selfish of me. I just need to keep pressing on.*

Sam's eyes panned back over to the huge list of appointments and conferences that he was due to attend. He closed his eyes and pressed the intercom button on his desk.

"Yes, Dr. Buckland?"

"Greta? Can you bring in the schedule for tomorrow?"

She hesitated. "Dr. Buckland..."

"Thanks."

He released the button and allowed himself to go back into his imagination. *Every one is a small victory. Every one a small triumph for Heaven. I think...*

"Dr. Buckland?"

He opened his eyes again, focused on his secretary's face. Greta held the appointment schedule under her arm, but made no move to deliver it into his outstretched hand.

"What's wrong?"

"Sam? Can I...can I talk to you for a minute? As a friend?" She fidgeted in place.

Sam furrowed his brow and leaned forward. "Of course you can."

"Good." She tossed the schedule on his desk. "You've been booking yourself solid for the last six months, if not more. I can't remember the last time you didn't spend a vacation at the office." She crossed her arms and shook her head. "You even came in for a few hours last Christmas!"

He held up his hands. "You can't fault me for that one. Don't you remember? It was Caesar Rodriguez. He was having symptoms of dissociative—"

Greta slammed her hands down next to his, startling him. "They're *all* special, Sam. I've been at this longer than you have, and I know what it does to people. You start off as an idealist, a crusader, thinking that you can change the world...and then it wears you away until there's nothing left but someone who's coming in and prescribing medicine so they can keep getting paid." She pulled up and sat in the chair, staring into his face. "You're the best damn psychiatrist that I've ever seen, Sam. You have a great success rate. Your patients have nothing but praise for you. You even manage with cases that everyone else has given up on." She reached out, her dark red nails a sharp contrast to her light skin, and took his hand. "But you're killing yourself. I see it, everyone else sees it. You need to take a break." Her hand released his and she leaned back in the chair. "And don't tell me that you're fine. Because I know you're not."

Sam shook his head. "I don't get that luxury, Greta. If I don't help these kids, no one else will."

She barked a laugh. "Who do you think you are, Superman?" He looked up, startled. "Even he took time off, you know."

He bowed his head. *Maybe she's right.*

"So, where do you want to go? I've already cleared it with the other doctors and Social Services; they'll cover your caseload for a week or two."

"You did, did you?" Sam raised an eyebrow. "What if I said no?"

Greta crossed her arms, matched his eyebrow with her own, tapped on her upper arm with her index finger.

"Fine, fine. I'll go." He rocked back in his chair. "You twisted my arm into it."

"What a fantastic idea, Sam. Do you want me to set up the travel arrangements for you, or not?"

He shook his head. "No. I kind of want to play it by ear, just go where the winds take me." He felt a pang as he spoke, and his memory brought forth the image of a creature of mist, with booming laughter and a generous nature.

I miss you too, Sky King.

"All right." The twinkle came back into her eye, along with her stunning smile. "Enjoy your vacation!" She turned and walked out, and Sam sat back in his chair, eyes still shut. His fingers ran across the arms of his seat before settling, and he let out a great exhalation, filled with accumulated stress.

I hope that this helps. I hope that I'll come back and be like I was when I started. I hope that...

He was still listing off hopes when sleep draped a soft blanket over his mind and took him, leading him to a picnic in a grassy field while his cappuccino cooled in the machine.

THE CHILD

"We're going *where?*"

Sam suppressed his irritation as his adopted daughter scrunched up her dark-skinned face like she had just tasted something rotten. "We're going to Jerusalem, Sara, for a visit. To see the sites of ancient religions, like the Holy Temple." He smiled to himself as his mind sketched the itinerary. "We might also head to Mecca and Medina, see the Ka'aba."

Sara scratched her head and flipped off her iPod, removing the headphones from her ears. "Um...why? I mean, not that I mind the time off of school or anything, but it's the middle of the semester. It's not even break time yet."

He sighed as he took his laptop bag from his shoulder, hung it on its appointed place on the wall, and began removing his shoes. A plain, rectangular golden locket slipped out of his shirt as he bent down, and he tucked it back into place. "Do you really want to head to another country over the Christmas break? I figured you'd want to stay home, hang out with your friends, that sort of thing." He crooked an eyebrow in her direction. "If you'll recall, last year I tried to get you to go to Italy and you shut me down." He padded over to the refrigerator and pulled out a carton of orange juice. "So you get to miss school this way, and you won't even get in trouble."

Sara pursed her lips and tapped her foot. "I did *not* shut you down. You just forgot that I had other things already planned." She leaned against the wall, crossing her arms. "Besides, you were going for some sort of meeting. When I asked if we would have time to go see anything, you told me..." Sara brought her hands up to make air-quotes. "And I quote, 'Probably not.'"

"I..." He took a deep breath as he poured his juice. *Patience.* "Well, this time there's no meeting. So, do you already have something planned?"

"Well...no."

"Okay then."

"So it's a real vacation? Like, us going, looking around, seeing new things?"

Sam nodded.

Sara's smile burst forth. "When are we leaving?" She took a seat at the kitchen bar. "All of my friends are going to be jealous when they hear."

Sam winced, his muscles and joints aching as he sat down at the kitchen table. "Our flight is for tomorrow afternoon. Get yourself packed because I'm going to be picking you up after school and we'll be heading straight to the airport."

"Is there a reason we're going?" Sara cast an appraising eye over her adoptive father, who glanced up at her from his downcast face. "Not that we need one, but...well, you don't usually take time off yourself, you know. You're always rushing off to some conference, some event..."

"Yeah." Sam sipped his juice and rubbed the back of his neck. "Maybe that's why I need to go. Been trying to do too much, even for me."

"Oh, please not the 'genius' thing again." Sara rolled her eyes and turned, grabbing a tangerine from a nearby bowl. "I know my friends laugh every time you say that, but seriously. It gets old. You don't need their attention *that* badly."

Sam took a sip of his drink. "Trust me. I'm not looking for the attention of teenage girls."

A moment of silence stretched before Sara spoke up again. "Well, anyway, guess I'd better get packed. I don't want to forget anything I might want while we're in the Promised Land."

Sam nodded and leaned back. *This is going to be good for us.* He closed his eyes and cast his mind back, back to when Gabriel had touched his heart with that moment of divine vision. The overwhelming, desperate love that had engulfed him then echoed back at him now, and tears trickled down his face.

"...Sam?"

Sam blinked his eyes open; Sara was watching him from across the table, her brow wrinkled, concerned.

"Oh, sorry." Sam wiped his face and eyes. "Just remembering something from a few years ago."

Sara got up from her seat. "In the immortal words of Qui-Gon Jinn, keep your mind here and now where it belongs."

"And who am I to argue with Qui-Gon?" Sam polished off his juice and stood up, stretching his arms in front of him.

"So when are you going to tell me about your days in the voodoo cult?" Sara pointed at the tattoos on his hands and forearms.

"When you're old enough to not have nightmares." Sam adjusted his sleeves so the markings were mostly covered.

Sara's eyes widened and her mouth dipped in a scowl. "Fuck you." She stormed off, slamming the door into her room. The sound echoed through the house, a gunshot in the silence.

Sam didn't even look up. Instead, he rolled the glass between his hands.

"That was fantastic, Sam." Light reflected off the moisture beads. "Way to go."

She doesn't need to know. It'd be too much for her. She's just a child.

"And you would have reacted *real* well if Mom or Dad had told you that when you were her age, huh?" He stood and brought his glass to the sink, running water over it and putting it into the dish rack. Wiping his hands on a near-by towel, he turned to face the hallway that led to Sara's room.

A stray thought brought a smile to Sam's face. *Funny how this is harder than facing down the Angel of Death.* He took a deep breath, squared his shoulders, and headed down the hall. Before knocking, he leaned in and put his ear to the door.

Nothing.

He rapped his knuckles on the wood. "Sara?"

Something hard slammed into the door on the other side and thumped onto the ground.

"Right." He sighed, rubbed his forehead, put it against the door and closed his eyes. "Sara, I didn't mean that exactly the way it sounded. You'll hear all about it one day. Just...just not yet. It's not the right time. All right?"

No answer.

"I'm sorry." Sam turned from the door and began his return trip down the hallway, but before he got halfway through, the door opened.

"Apology accepted." Sara leaned against the doorframe, her arms crossed again. "But only because you're bringing me to Jerusalem."

Sam laughed. "Fair enough."

~~~

"I remember when airlines let you check two bags free per passenger." Sam shook his head as he and Sara walked away from the counter, taking a bite of his napkin-clad chocolate donut before continuing. "Now it's fifty per."

"You shouldn't say things like that, Sam." Sara hitched her small carry-on backpack up on
~~~

her shoulders as her eyes roamed the airport. "It makes you seem old."

"I feel old." Sam also took in his surroundings, but what he saw was not the same as what Sara did. To his left, several scuttling spider-demons, about a hand-span in size, scrabbled toward a nearby line. Ahead, a security supervisor berated an employee, holding her in place with his authority as his taunts and insults lashed into her soul. Sam could see the tears leaking down her freckled face...and the barbs on the tongue of the fat man before her.

He paused, watching. The air around the supervisor shimmered, a heat-wave undetected by everyone else, and, as Sam's attention focused in, he could smell rotting flesh and brimstone.

Dammit. Even when I'm trying to go on fucking vacation.

"Sam? What's the matter?" Sara turned around, looking at him stopped in the middle of the walkway, people flowing around him like water in a stream. "Sam?"

"Just a second, Sara." Sam watched a moment longer. *A taskmaster. Hate those bastards. Making abusers out of people.* He set his shoulders, then began walking toward the pair, tossing the donut in the trash, unfolding the napkin, and scribbling on it with his pen.

"What are you doing?" Sara's eyes flicked from Sam's face to the TSA man, whose face was now red with anger. Everyone else in the crowd was doing a fantastic job of pretending to be deaf, turning their eyes away from the spectacle going on in the airport lobby.

"No, Sam, you can't. Just let them—"

"Stay here, Sara. Don't move." Sam put out one hand to block her, then stepped up to the employee and boss. The woman was fully weeping now, babbling apologies, and Sam's heart broke for her.

"Hey, it's going to be okay." He clicked his pen shut and returned it to his pocket, then put that hand on the young woman's shoulder. She looked up at him, her face a war between anger, fear, confusion, and embarrassment, and the big man in front of her rounded on Sam.

"What the hell is your problem, asshole?" The supervisor rose up on his toes, trying to look down into Sam's face. The barbs on his tongue were clearer, now, and Sam flinched at the sight of the sick, green ichor which coated them. "This isn't any of your fucking business! Why don't you just—"

Sam put his right foot back, widening his stance. "You know, you should really watch how you talk to people." His left hand gripped the napkin. "You never know when someone is going to turn out to be more important than you thought."

The TSA man reached out and shoved Sam, rocking him in place but failing to dislodge him. "Shut the fuck up! I don't give a rat's ass who you think you are; there's fucking work to be done and this bitch—"

Sam shoved the napkin into the man's face.

Scrawled on the thin paper was a complex diagram, a series of pentacles, circles, and other symbols. The other man's skin blanched, going from red to white in a moment, and his next word emerged as a whispered hiss.

"Keeper." He tried to withdraw but his muscles were locked in place. Sam stepped up to him.

"No shit, asshole." He brought his right hand up, two fingers extended toward the demon.

"Begone, taskmaster. Your term here is ended. Return to Hell, where your feet bleed and burn and the whip you hold tears open your own flesh." He placed the napkin on the half-bald head in front of him.

"Begone."

The thick thorns on the man's tongue melted into the same green fluid which Sam had seen, pooling, running out of his mouth and up his face, soaking the napkin through until it was a sodden green rag. Sam plucked it from the now-speechless supervisor's face and flicked it into the air, making a sharp gesture with his left hand as he did so.

The napkin burst into flame, eliciting a gasp from the surrounding crowd, many of whom had stopped to watch the interaction between

Sam and the supervisor. Sam glanced around, smiled, and touched the girl's shoulder again.

"Wh...what's going on?" The supervisor rubbed his head, as if he still felt the wet napkin on it. "I...I...Greta, are you okay?" He moved toward the young woman, who recoiled from him.

Sam shook his head, and turned to walk away. The onlookers whispered as he went past them back to where Sara stood, her eyes wide as an owl's, staring up into his face.

"I just explained to him that he should be nicer to his employees." Sam's words interrupted Sara's attempts to form any sort of question. "Come on, we need to get to gate six."

The rest of the trip through the airport was quiet, with Sara stealing glances at her father every chance she got. *It's not her fault.* Sam tried not to look back, to return the stares. *You'd be curious, too. You'd be staring.*

"Ummm...Sam?" Sara's voice was meek, quiet. "What the fuck was that?"

"Can it wait until we get on the plane?" Sam did not turn as he spoke. "I really don't want to miss it."

"I guess." Sam spared his daughter a look; she had retreated into the classic posture of self-defense, her arms crossed across her chest as her eyes held to the ground. The stone walls he had erected to keep out judgment and whispers crumbled, and he stopped, putting a hand on her shoulder.

"Hey." Sara stopped, still not looking up. "Look at me for a second, okay?"

Sara did so, her brown eyes meeting Sam's. They were wide, shaking, searching his face.

"I promise, I'm not crazy. There was just something that I had to take care of, and I did."

Sara licked her lips. "Then what the hell was that?"

"Sara, do you remember that show we watched together, 'Mind Control'?"

She looked up at Sam from the corners of her eyes. "With that Darren Brown guy? Where he made people do all sorts of weird shit."

"Exactly. He was using psychology, tricks of how the mind works." Sam felt the bite of the lie in his chest, but he forged ahead. "When you need to get someone in a suggestible state, you do something that throws their mind off track. Something unexpected."

"...Like throwing a napkin on their head?" Some of the tension had left Sara's muscles, and her posture was loosening.

Sam smiled. "Exactly." *God help me, now I feel like Caitlin, grinning in front of a fawning crowd.* "It shook him up, let me talk to him for a second, give him a suggestion."

Sara's eyes had become saucers, all fear and confusion gone in the wake of this new revelation. "You can hypnotize people? Why the hell didn't you tell me about that before?" Then her eyes narrowed. "Wait a minute. Have you ever hypnotized me?"

Sam laughed, and this time it was genuine, a rich, warm sound from the happy places in his heart. "No." He waved one hand as he spoke in an attempt to calm her down. "Now, can we keep moving? I don't want the security people coming by and telling me that we shouldn't be blocking the walkways or something."

"Okay, okay." They resumed their walk. They had been moving for about thirty seconds when her voice came again. "So...can you?"

"Hypnotize people?"

Sara nodded.

"In a fashion, but I prefer not to." Sam stood up and he and his daughter began walking again toward their terminal. "The skill does come in handy during therapy, though."

"I bet. Must be nice." As she walked, Sara grasped hold of an imaginary clipboard. "Yes, all this deep-seated abuse from your childhood is gone. You'll walk out of here as sunshine and roses. Congratulations."

Sam shook his head. "No, Sara. That's not quite the way it works in psychology. I'd be wasting my time and theirs if I tried that kind of treatment for most of them."

The two arrived at the boarding area for their flight and sat down. "What do you mean, 'wasting your time'? Why would that be wasting it?"

Sam laid his bags on the floor in front of him. "Solving people's problems for them doesn't help them get any stronger. He pursed his lips. "I try to...to remove the obstacles that are getting in their way and then let them figure it out. Not to take the easy road, you know?"

Sara cocked her head. "Whatever. Just seems like you'd be able to help more people that way."

"Yeah." Sam laughed, shaking his head. "It does seem like that, doesn't it?"

THE AWAKENED

Jamila Al-Nour stepped out of her tent in the Egyptian desert. The stars twinkled above and she shivered as a cool wind cut through the light jacket she wore. She hitched up her garments and turned to look at the unearthed structure. It was long, but low to the ground, a silhouette of solid black against the diamond sky on the horizon.

"We did it." She pulled out a small cedar box from an inner pocket, running her fingers over the smooth lid before opening it. From amongst the metal compass and a roll of ancient

Arabic writing, she drew out a small photograph of a middle-aged man of Middle-Eastern descent with a little girl perched on his shoulders.

"We're here, Dad. You were right."

Replacing the box, Jamila looked around the sleeping campsite. Most of the lights were off and the workers down for the evening, but she could hear a few night owls still up, murmuring about the day's work, or the last hand of their card game. She pulled on her shoes, zipped up the tent flap, and headed toward the building, doing her best to keep hidden.

Too easy. She suppressed a giggle as she moved into a full run, her feet sinking into the sand with each step. The structure grew larger as she approached, until she stood at one of the three doors leading in. She traced a finger across the hieroglyphs that guarded the entrance.

"Enter and your name shall be forfeit, food for the Gods in Duat, and your soul shall fall into the vaults of Ammit the Devourer." She stepped away, moving toward the walls again. "Powerful threats, whoever you are."

It's so well preserved. Jamila reached out, her hand brushing off some of the remaining earth to reveal the marble underneath. It was pitted in several places, worn by moving sand, but still whole, still recognizable. *And why marble? No one ever used that for a mastaba, not that I remember.* Excitement coursed through her spine like an electric shock. *This must have really been someone special.*

She took her first steps in, reaching into her pocket and pulling out her flashlight, the beam cutting through the darkness like a spear. The workers had broken through earlier that day, clearing the dirt and rubble that had overlain the tomb.

Jamila smiled at the memory of the crowd of workmen making way for her and her team to investigate the ornate doorway, to take rubbings and photos before breaking the long-held seal.

Never heard of a curse like that one, either. She glanced back at the dark shapes behind her that led into the chamber, then refocused on moving forward.

Can't touch anything or they'll know I was in here. Step by step she advanced, the beam lingering whenever she found an artifact or inscription. *But I had to see it first, before everyone else got in.*

She stopped in front of an ornate vase, decorated in hieroglyphics and drawings.

What is this? The pottery depicted two men, throwing fire from their hands at what seemed to be...

What are *those?* She knelt closer. The other figures were also humanoid, but with great wings stretching from their backs. One held two flaming swords, while the other carried a mighty horn, curved into a circle, at his waist. Her fingers stretched out, reaching for the vase, caressing the contrast between pottery and paint.

A small fragment flaked off.

Oh, shit! She scurried backward, running the flashlight over her fingers. Her flight sent her into the arms of an imposing statue, its ibis-beak curving over her head. She turned and wrapped her arms around it just in time to keep it from tipping over and crashing to the ground.

"God, that was close." This time she backed away slowly until she reached the wall, then let out a great exhalation. "I wonder what they'd say if they walked in here with that thing falling over." She laughed, shaking her head. "All right, get it together. And don't touch anything!"

She moved her flashlight beam around the rest of the room. The whole chamber was filled with artifacts, but there didn't seem to be an exit other than the one she had come from."

There's no way this is the only room. It's not big enough. There must be...a hidden door or something. She examined the wall opposite the entrance, peering into the cracks between bricks, searching for a fissure.

She found it.

Her fingers sank into a groove in the wall, and, with a *hiss*, the wall rumbled, a weight deep inside the stone rolling and grinding as it pulled the six-inch-thick slab aside. She turned her light inward.

Her eyes turned into saucers.

"Wow."

THE FALLEN

The takeoff was uneventful, but Sam had to fight to keep from nodding off as the ground shrank from view, obscured by occasional cloud cover.

"At least you got us good seats." Sara stretched her feet out and her arms up. "I've never flown first class before."

Sam leaned back in his chair. "Well, we have a lot of ground to cover, you know. It'll be a while before we get there." He pulled out a paperback copy of *The Dark Tower* by Stephen

King. "I should finally get a chance to finish this."

Sara rolled her eyes. "Why do you even bother with paper books any more, Sam? They're so heavy and boring. I mean, how many of those can you carry at once? Compared to a tablet? Not to mention all the other things you can do with it."

Sam shook his head as he thumbed through the pages to find his place. "You might be right, but I still remember a time before you could read books on-line, and I'm not ready to give that up just yet."

"Whatever." Sara looked out the window again. "Jerusalem, huh?"

"Yep. Huge factor in several different faiths. Lots of cultural mixing, a strange balance of tolerance and anger." He glanced out of the window. "Supposedly, the Angels have been there, too."

There was a moment of sober silence. "Thanks for bringing me."

Sam put his right thumb between the pages and his left hand on his adopted daughter's shoulder. "You're welcome."

Sara put her hand atop his for a moment, then her laconic grin returned. "So, anyway—"

She stopped in mid-sentence; Sam's face had gone blank, distant, as if he were listening to something far away.

"Sam?"

I was wondering if I would see them. The rich timbre of the music, of angelic speech, was penetrating the walls of the aircraft and reaching his ear. A smile began to stretch across his face, and he pushed past Sara to look out of the window.

They're here.

Outside of the airplane, luminous forms of angels were streaking through the sky, their voices resounding over the landscape. They were singing of simple things—the wind moving through the clouds, the wonder of flight, the joy of God's love. Their music weaved its way underneath the wings of the ocean birds, lifting them up with the breeze.

Sam sat back and closed his eyes, his spirit buoyed up by the notes of angelic song, the music rejuvenating his soul.

"Sam?" Sara glanced out of the window. "What's going on?"

Sam shook his head, eyes still closed. "Just thought I saw an eagle out there."

"Oh." Sara took another look, then sat back herself. "Next time you can just ask me to move out of the way, all right?"

"Yeah, no problem." The music stopped, and Sam opened his eyes. "I guess I just—"

Then the angels started to scream.

Sam's hands flew to his ears to cover them against the assault. Again he pushed his way to the window, and he felt the blood rush from his face.

"Oh my God."

In streams of fire streaking from the sky, the angels plummeted toward the Earth. Their wings burned as they fell, screaming, shrieking, red smoke trailing after them. The air turned black in their wake, like cracks in the very sky, spiraling downward, and those gaps seemed to scream themselves in protest at the violation.

Sara beat her fists on Sam's shoulder as he leaned over her. "What the hell, Sam? What are you *doing?*"

Sam could not take his eyes off of what he was seeing. *How can this...this is impossible. They're...they're all Falling.* He looked up toward the heavens. *Why?*

The firmament was boiling, the blue wavering with tendrils of darkness, blackness bubbling in the sky. Sam's breath caught in his chest as he stared down toward the ground.

"No." He stood and stepped into the aisle; several of the nearby passengers glanced up before returning to their conversations or books. He brought out a Sharpie from his pocket and began to draw on the aisle floor.

"Sam?" Sara scooted over to the aisle seat, her eyes darting as more and more passengers began to murmur about the strange man inscribing symbols on the carpet. The Sharpie stuttered and skipped over the fabric.

"Damn it!" Sam stood up and looked around for a clearer writing space, glancing out of the window again as he did so. An attendant walked up to him as his head swiveled back and forth.

"Sir?" He did not answer. "I'm sorry, sir, but I need you to..."

Sam made a gesture in the air, and a small sylph spirit, feminine in form but visible only to him, giggled and flew into the attendant's ear. The man blinked several times.

"Wh...what was I saying?"

"Nothing." Sam waved him off. "You were leaving me alone."

"...Right." The man turned away. "I was leaving you alone. Have a good day."

Sara jumped out of her seat and grabbed Sam's hand. "What is going on? You're freaking me the hell out here, Sam!"

The young man turned to his daughter, and she gasped, pulling back from him as she looked into his eyes. "Sara." He licked his lips. "I didn't want this to affect you yet. You aren't ready. But I don't have a choice right now." He extended a hand. "Do you trust me?"

She trembled, took a step back. "I don't know, Sam, I..."

"Please."

Sara hesitated, and Sam could feel his heart pounding in his ears. "Is it about those tattoos?"

Sam nodded.

"And you're going to tell me? What it's all about?"

Sam's brow twitched, his impatience growing. "I'll tell you what I think I need to, what you need to know. All right?"

"Yeah." She took his hand. "All right."

Sam stood, walking toward the emergency exit. He gestured for Sara to stay put, then waved his hand again; the sylphs dashed around the cabin, ensuring that everyone was buckled down. Passengers yelped in surprise and confusion as they were pushed into their seats and their belts pulled over them and locked into place.

Sam turned to the door, then brought his marker out again, inscribing a multi-layered pentagram and runic script on the hatch.

Then he knocked.

"Open Sesame."

The door opened, and air rushed out of the airplane, pulling the two out of the craft and into the sky.

The giggling sylphs shut the door, laughing at the remaining passengers' faces.

~~~

"SAM!!" Sara was panicked, her hands scrabbling over him, trying to find purchase.

"Don't scream in my ear!" Sam shouted to make himself heard over the rushing wind as the two of them hurtled toward the ground. Already the aircraft was tiny above them, and the landscape below was getting closer. "If I can't concentrate, we're going to have a very bad landing. All right?"

Sara began to hyperventilate, the blood rushing from her face and leaving it a pasty grey color.

Sam shook his head. "Okay, okay." His left hand came up. "Djinn, spirit of the north winds, protect us!"

A dark cloud formed below them, thunder and lightning roiling within. As the two landed
~~~

on it, they felt a gentle, cottony surface that gave way until their fall had slowed to a stop, leaving them atop the small cumulonimbus. Sara fell to her knees, her hands moving from one place to another, looking for solid ground but finding only mist.

"Sam!? What the hell is going on?" Her hyperventilation kicked up a notch, her words coming out in sputters between breaths. She grabbed at Sam's pant legs. "We're on a fucking CLOUD!"

I could just put her to sleep. It would probably be easier for her. Sam shook his head, then resumed scanning over the ocean. "You need to breathe, Sara."

Sara stopped, blinked several times, then pointed over the edge of the cloud. "We just jumped out of an airplane, we're floating in mid-air, and the best you can do to calm me down is to tell me to *breathe*?"

"Not really." Sam narrowed his gaze. *There they are.* "But I don't have time to walk you through it right now." He pointed outward, over the sea. The smoking contrails left by the hundreds of fallen Angels were still evident, the ripples in the sea below, where they had landed, clear to his vision.

"Damn it!" Bringing his hands up, Sam began an incantation. "Sea giants, genies of the waves, I call on you to obey your ancient oaths. Rise up and obey!"

Sara stood, her legs shaky as she tested the stability of the cloud. "Who are you..." Her eyes moved down, following her father's, and her words trailed off.

The waters below began to shake and churn, bubbles erupting like an undersea volcanic eruption. Huge founts and geysers stretched up into the sky, plumes stretching hundreds of feet high.

Sara's voice was very low. "...Did you do that?"

Sam's smile was tight across his face. "No." He pointed with his left hand, and, with his right, traced a sigil on Sara's forehead. "They did."

Standing upright out of the water were gigantic blue humanoids. Waterfalls cascaded down their flesh as they straightened, golden rings dangling from ears, noses, and lips. There were both males and females, each wrapped in dark blue cloth—the men topless, the women not—and tattoos in Arabic script covered their exposed flesh. They stretched all the way up to the cloud, and one, a female with one eye covered by scarred flesh, stepped up to where the two humans stood.

Sara's eyes followed the creature's head as it rose up and moved toward her. One hand reached up, trembling, as if the figure were a dangerous animal that she was being told to pet. She glanced from the enormous head to Sam and back again.

Sam stepped forward, bowing his head. "Hail, Marid. Forgive my urgency, but time is short. Many have fallen into your waters below, and I ask that you save them from drowning, bringing them back to the land."

The marid scowled, then looked down toward the ocean. "Very well, Keeper, but we shall speak of this later." She nodded at her brethren, and each of the genies knelt down and began scooping up the tiny, limp figures. Each marid held dozens of them by the time the work was done, and they strode off into the distance, back toward land.

Sam waved again, fingers curled, and sylphs spun out of the surrounding winds and began pushing the cloud, keeping pace with the scarred genie. Sara's hands, unable to find a solid hold, were wrapped around one another, fingers moving like a nest of snakes, rubbing against each other.

"...Sam?" Sara's voice was weak, small. Afraid. "What...what are these things?"

Sam pointed to the small spirits surrounding the cloud. "These are sylphs. They're small air spirits, very useful for confusing people or erasing memories. Making suggestions." Then he opened his hand and extended it toward the giant beside them. "And these are the Marid, genies of the oceans and seas. Very powerful, but proud."

"As if man is not?" The scarred genie curled her lip as she walked. "You claim dominion over the world, yet your rule is that of a child who still soils himself when the sharks come."

Sam nodded. "To be fair, great Marid, if a shark came for me I might be tempted to do just that." He reached out his hand and helped Sara back to her feet.

"So...what?" Sara rubbed her eyes, looked around again. "Are you some kind of..." She shook her head. "I can't believe I'm saying this."

"Am I some kind of wizard? Sorcerer? Magic-man?" Sara looked up and saw Sam's grim eyes, set and focused. "Yes. I am the Keeper of the Keys, Heir to King Solomon."

Sara's mouth moved, then she licked her lips and looked past her father to the marid walking beside them, to the spirits giggling and poking each other as they ferried their cumulus raft. "Am I dreaming, Sam?"

Sam's smile reappeared, sad and nostalgic. "No, Sara." He glanced over at her, and his eyebrows lifted slightly. "But you'll wish you were by the time this is through."

"No." She shook her head, backing away until she was a step from the edge. "This...this isn't real. This kind of thing doesn't happen. I...No."

Sam took a step toward her. "Sara, stop moving. You're going to fall."

She glanced behind her, her gaze almost vacant, her eyes dancing on the cloudtop. "So? It's not real. If I fall, I'll...I'll just wake up." She edged toward the side of the cloud.

Sam whipped his hand in a circular gesture. Diaphanous sylphs wrapped around Sara's face, tittering and giggling. She brought one hand up to her face, but by the time her fingers reached her lips, her eyes had closed and she began tipping forward. Sam lunged and caught her, laying her down some distance from the drop.

I'm sorry, but it's probably better this way.

"The girl is weak." The marid's voice cut into his thoughts.

Sam scowled. "No, the world has changed. Magic is gone. No one believes in it anymore."

"Then they are fools." Her scarred face turned, ponderous, toward Sam. "Infants who think themselves grown, ready to leave their parents, unaware of their own ignorance."

Sam felt his hackles rise. "It's not fair to judge us based on our ignorance of an invisible force, invisible agents. If I didn't have—"

"Is the force invisible, or are you simply blinded?" She cut him off, her breath washing over him like a sea breeze, thick with salt and the smell of fish. "Are the agents hiding, or are you ignoring them and their actions? Perhaps, *Keeper*, your race would not have made the mistakes they've made if they were less intent on themselves and more on what surrounds them."

"We don't have time for this." Sam pointed to the coastline. "Just put them down there."

"Impatience is another of your flaws, human, that we can add to the list." The group of genies forged through the water toward the shore. "And so is disrespect for your betters."

Sam ignored the marid, keeping his focus on guiding the sylphs to a gentle landing. The cloud dispersed as they coasted to the ground, depositing Sara's unconscious form with a small *thump*. The marid were less careful, dropping the fallen angels into heaps and piles before turning back toward the sea and sinking into the water.

"Keeper." Sara stirred at the sheer volume of the giant's voice. "I have pressing matters to attend to in my domain." Sam watched as the marid closed her right hand into a fist before continuing. "Do I have permission to depart?"

Sam extended his hand, and the sigils swirled and reordered themselves. "Yes. Go with God."

Without another word, the genie turned and began walking, following her fellows. The lapping waves parted as she moved, welcoming her back into the salty depths of the ocean. When the top of her head disappeared under the water, there was a final rush of bubbles...and she was gone.

Sam stood a moment longer, watching the giant woman vanish beneath the surf, before turning and running to the stacked bodies of the fallen Angels.

Glad there wasn't anyone here. Be awkward explaining this. Sam knelt beside the nearest one. The Angel was vaguely male, with long, flowing brown hair and sharp features, but his robe was decimated, burned black in his meteoric fall, and there were scorched stumps where his wings had been.

They don't even have *wings unless they want to.* Sam laid his hand on the Angel's shoulder, feeling the irregular breath moving in and out. *And he's breathing. What the hell?*

"Hey." Sam shook the Angel, who stirred, his brow creasing and a low moan escaping his lips. "Hey, wake up. Wake up."

Sara moaned, shifting on the grass. Sam glanced over before readdressing the Angel.

"...Sam?" She put her hands under her, picked herself up off the ground. "What happened? How did we—"

"Sara, I'm sorry, but I really don't have time to explain right now." Sam moved to another Angel, performing the same cursory examination. "But I would appreciate it if you'd stop asking questions for a few minutes and get me the water bottle from your bag."

Sara opened her mouth to reply.

"Now!"

"Fine, fine!" She reached into her bag and came up with a bottle of Dasani. "Here. Happy?"

"Ecstatic." Sam spun the top off and upended the bottle over the Angel's head. His eyes snapped open as he coughed and sputtered. "Sara, go check on the others. Make sure they're all breathing, but you don't need to try waking any of them up, okay?"

Sara scowled, then nodded and moved off, dropping her bag into the dirt. The Angel rolled over on his side, his cough transforming into a low moan. His eyes were shocking blue, but wide, looking toward the sky.

Sam took a breath before speaking. *He doesn't smell like anything. No flowers.* "Are you all right?"

The Angel's eyes turned to Sam. "No. Not all right." His hands came up to his ears, fingertips walking over the lobe. "Where is he? What do you want from me?"

"What are you talking about?" Sam rested his hand on the Angel's forehead. *He's warm.* "Where is who?"

The Angel shook his head, eyes tearing as he curled into a small, defensive ball. "He's not talking to me. I can't hear him anymore. I can't hear the Voice." His hands shot out, gripping the other man's shirt. "Where is he?"

"The Voice?" Sam gripped the Angel's hands. "You mean the voice of God?"

"Yes." The Angel began to sob. "He turned from us. Abandoned us. All of us. Why?" He scrambled to his knees and held up his hands. "Without the Word and the Voice, we are lost." His fingers stretched out, reaching to the sun. "Why, Father? What have we done? Why have you banished us here?" His sobs intensified as he folded down so that his forehead touched the ground, his laments and exhortations to the Almighty obscured both by the dirt and his wails.

Shit. Cast them out? All of them? Does that mean... Sam glanced heavenward once more, at the dark, purple mess that was the celestial dome, then set his jaw. Rooting through his own bag, he pulled out a fountain pen.

"They're all still breathing, but they look really bad. Sam?" Sara took a knee, her breath coming hard after jogging back from the last group. "Who are all these people?"

Sam dug the pen into the dirt and began tracing a large circle. "Angels."

"What?" Sara took a second look at the fallen man, noticed the burnt-off wings protruding from his back, oozing scorched blood, and recoiled. "What the hell?"

"I told you. Later." Sam motioned toward the heavens with his free hand. "I'm going to see if I can summon one of the Archangels."

"A...Archangels? You mean...like Gabriel?"

Sam stopped drawing, taking a deep breath. He glanced over at Sara, and a sad smile played on his face.

"Yes." He turned back and resumed working. "Like Gabriel."

THE ACCUSER

Sara watched as Sam traced his lines and symbols in the ground. Her eyes tracked every movement, every gesture.

This doesn't make sense. He can't be...this can't be magic. Can it? Her mind was consumed by the recent revelation. *There's got to be another explanation, right?* She wiped sweat from her forehead. *Maybe...maybe I'm drugged or something.* Her gaze danced from her father to the strange people, moaning and praying. *Or maybe he's crazy. Or both.*

"Okay, Sara." Sam stood and paced around his circle. Stretching twenty feet across, it bounded a ten-pointed star, each point containing an ornate symbol. After two trips around, he nodded and looked toward his daughter. "Looks about right."

"What's...what's going to happen?" Part of her mind mocked her own words as they came out of her mouth...but another part did not.

Sam shrugged. "Maybe nothing. The Archangels don't usually come to Earth, you know." He pointed to the angry firmament above. "So, if that's become some sort of barrier, then they won't be here."

"Sam...even if the Archangels were real, you couldn't just summon one. If people could do that, we'd know about it...wouldn't we?" Sara looked around once more, gaze lingering on the moaning, wailing forms.

Sam sighed, rubbing his eyes with the heels of his hands. "God, now I understand. I'm sorry for being so obstinate." He removed his hands and refocused on his daughter. "Sara, you need to trust me. Everything I've been saying is true. God exists. Angels exist. These—" He waved his hand toward the piles of Fallen; more of them were waking, adding their groans of pain and anguish to the chorus. "These Angels were cast out of Heaven for some reason. I'm going to try to bring the Archangel Gabriel here, to ask her what happened."

"But—"

"Now be quiet. I need to concentrate." He turned back toward the circle, mumbling to himself. "If Gabriel's here, she'll know. She knows everything He does."

Sara took a step toward the diagram, her eyes flicking between the Angels, Sam, and the inscriptions.

"All right." Sam nodded, stepping into the circle. Opening up the golden locket around his neck, he extracted a tiny bottle filled with liq-uid.

What's in there? Sara almost spoke the words aloud, but Sam's admonishment from earlier kept her quiet.

Sam spun the top off the bottle, glanced heavenward once more, then dripped several beads onto his hand, onto the crescent moon-shaped scar which decorated it. Sara's nostrils opened as an errant breeze brought the aroma to her nose.

Honeysuckle. She scrunched her face. *Why is he pouring honeysuckle on his hand?*

Sam raised that hand up, then flicked his wrist downward. Droplets spattered onto the symbol in the middle of the diagram as he intoned his spell, chanting two sentences over and over.

"Servants of the Almighty, the Keeper calls for your aid. Holiest of the Holy, Solomon's Heir summons you in God's name."

Sara watched, waiting for something to appear, yet terrified that it might. She noticed she was holding her breath and let it out in a rush.

This is insane. He's lost it. Sara's eye wandered off, looking at the angry sky, the surf pounding the shore. *I wonder if...*

She was suddenly overcome by the smell of cherry blossoms. The odor was so powerful that she choked, gasping for breath. Sam coughed, waving his hand in front of his face to clear the air. The wind picked up, stirring dust and swirling fallen leaves, but the smell only got stronger.

"Sam?" The wind intensified, transitioning from a breeze to a gale, and Sara's eyes closed in response. *God, I can barely breathe!* "Sam?!"

She could hear Sam saying something, but couldn't make it out over the howling wind. Forcing her eyes open, Sara stumbled forward. "WHAT?" The wind tried to pick her up off her feet, billowing her jacket and shirt like a sail. "WHAT DID YOU –"

All at once, the tempest changed direction, ceasing its counterclockwise swirl and moving as a unit toward where Sam stood, the center of the magic diagram. Sara tumbled onto the ground, catching herself just before her face hit the dirt.

A *boom* of thunder detonated and Sara threw her hands up to protect her ears from the sudden shock. Blinking her eyes clear of the grit that threatened to crust over them, she looked to the source of the detonation.

Sam was still on his feet, although his hair and clothes were windswept and disheveled. Beside him knelt a form, hazy at first until the dust settled, wrapped in torn rags the color of used hospital linens.

A young woman, with dark eyes and brown hair, was revealed as the cloth fell from her head. There were numerous cuts and bruises on her face, skin-deep but open. She stood, her eyes uncertain, skipping from one place to the next. Her knees wobbled, and Sam reached out to catch her before she fell.

Sara ran forward, tennis shoes skidding through the lines of the diagram. "What's going on? Who is she? Is she all right?"

Sam waved her off and adjusted his grip. The woman's head lolled, her muscles loose and weak, before her eyes landed on Sam's.

Her lips moved, cracked and leaking blood. "Keeper."

~~~

Sam recoiled, almost dropping the woman. "How do you know me?"

Her dry, parched tongue dabbed at her lips. A scraping croak emerged, but no words.

"Sara!" His daughter scurried up. "Water."
~~~

She reached into her bag, rooted around for a second, then turned it upside down and dumped it out. "You used up the last bottle, Sam!"

"Damn it." He reached out his hand and drew a quick circle; at once, a naiad bubbled out of the earth, blurbling its greeting. He cupped his palm and the spirit poured itself into his grasp, flowing through his fingers and leaving behind water that he brought to the young woman's mouth. She slurped it out of his hand, wetting her lips and tongue.

"Thank you." She sat down, picking herself out of Sam's grasp and settling on the ground, then refocusing on his face. "It is good to see you again, Samuel Buckland. I am sorry that I had to appear to you this way."

She's talking like an Angel. Sam's eyes went wide. *But it couldn't be Gabriel. Who...*

The woman laughed, but it devolved into a cough. "You're trying to remember. I didn't look like this when we first met." Another cough. "I was younger, and –"

"...had red hair." Sam shook his head. "...Satan? Really?" The young lady nodded, the corners of her mouth twitching. "But I wasn't looking for you; I expected –"

Satan's next coughing fit cut Sam off, and he patted her on the back as she choked and sputtered. After several seconds, the hacking subsided.

"Look, never mind." Sam stepped up to the edge of the cliff and spread his hands. "Marid! Answer my call! Come forth from your waters once more!" The sigils on his hands moved and shimmered, forming great chains and circles. "Rise!"

As before, the waters surged below and the massive form of the water genie appeared. Her one good eye glared at Sam from above as the waterfalls cascaded over her shoulders, arms, and chest.

"What is it now, Keeper?" The creature's voice rumbled like the surf as the tide came in. "This is twice you have called me away from my affairs, with no regard as to the burdens of my office and my people."

Sam growled. "You forget yourself, genie. My authority over you is granted by God Himself and is not for you to question."

"My name is Savanth Lal, Queen of the 12th Great Current." She crossed her arms, her one good eye lancing into him. "You would do well to remember that."

"I shall. Bring us all back home, to Acton, California."

The Queen hissed. "You command that I enter a *desert*?"

Sam nodded. "Yes."

She stared at him, a tempest roiling grey in her eye, the skin near her scar twitching.

What is her problem? Sam searched her face. *I've never met one who fought me before.*

Her lips moved and she raised her hands into the air. "Very well, Keeper. We shall obey."

The Queen's followers joined her, shaking off the sea in great sprays and scooping up the fallen angels once more. She turned away from Sam, allowing one of the others to come forth, laying his hand down as a platform for the

Keeper and Sara, supporting Satan's battered body between them.

"Sam?" Sara's fingers tightened on Satan's arm. "Do you...I mean, do you...?"

The two moved up into the air, supported by the marid's giant hand. "Do I what, Sara?"

She smiled, tremulous, afraid. "This is real, isn't it? I'm not dreaming, am I?"

He shook his head. "I wish."

"How are they going to bring us home?" Sara looked down, then up at the creature's face. "I mean, we can't exactly walk all over California, can we?"

Sam nodded. "Don't worry. If we did, nobody would see us anyway, but no." Sam adjusted his grip on Satan's shoulder. "Water has other ways to get where it needs to go."

"What do you mean?"

Sam didn't have time to answer. Once the three of them were at the marid's chest level, all of the genies looked upward. Their forms began to dissolve into mist, sweeping into the air on the wind like fog.

It feels like that time I was in London, caught in that mess. Sam could feel the water droplets that his body became. He could see the same thing happening to his daughter and the Angel with him, could see them dispersing into mist, separating and swirling until they joined the clouds in the sky, surfing on the wind. Their mist-bodies held together, staying close to one another despite the turbulence and the speed of travel.

The ground below them rushed past, faster than a jet airliner. They followed the coast for several minutes, then their path turned inland. Greenery gave way to chaparral, then to Joshua-tree filled deserts before crossing the highway and stopping at Sam's cookie-cutter neighborhood.

How are we going to get –

At once, Sam felt himself tumble toward the ground, his body turning solid just in time to hit the grass in his yard, his skin and clothes soaked by the sudden downpour. Sara and Satan followed afterward, and the mist that formed the bodies of the fallen Angels streamed into the house through the windows.

"Your will is done." The Queen's voice echoed in the thunder. "Goodbye, Keeper." A gust of wind kicked up, sending the mist and clouds away and leaving, once again, a clear blue sky.

"Holy shit." Sara stood and brushed off the grass that was sticking to her outfit. "That was—"

"Sara!" Sam slipped his arm underneath Satan's unconscious body. "Can you get the door? Please?"

"Oh, damn!" She ran over and pulled out her key, wrestling it into the front door lock.

"Sam?"

Sam turned; the voice was his neighbor's, Sharla. She looked up at the sky, then back to the trio. "I...did you..."

Sam sighed, then reached out his right hand and made a twisting gesture. "Don't worry about it."

A pair of sylphs spun out of the desert breeze and began whispering in Sharla's ears, one on each side of her head. The tension and confusion disappeared from her face, her brow smoothing and the wrinkles around her eyes vanishing.

"Oh." She smiled, her eyes vacant and wide. "I'm happy to see you again, Sam. Have a good day." She turned and walked back to her own door, repeating the same thing over and over.

Sam shook his head and Sara raised an eyebrow, then they resumed moving to the door.

"Trust me, I'd rather not have to do that." Sam reached out his hand and turned the doorknob. "But I don't have time to dick around right now."

Sara snickered. "I don't think she'd appreciate tha..." Her words trailed off and her smile evaporated as they entered the building.

"Oh my God."

The house was much warmer than outside, the heater doing a good job of keeping out the winter chill. The Angels were scattered through the house, holding each other or rocking back and forth. The low sound of moaning and weeping filled the air.

Even their sadness is beautiful. Sam almost buckled under the weight of their grief and fear, their songs raw, tearing at his soul. The sofa was open, so he led Sara and Satan toward it, depositing his unconscious burden onto the soft cushions.

"Sara, go get a glass of water and a warm washcloth. And alcohol. She looks pretty bad."

"Yeah, all right." Sara ran off to the bathroom. Sam listened for a moment, hearing her rooting around in the cabinets, then turned his attention back to the Angel on his couch.

She groaned, her brow tightening, then opened her eyes. Unfocused at first, they found his, and the tension left them.

"Thank you, Samuel."

THE LION

"So, wait, you're the devil?"

Satan sighed, curling her fingers around the steaming mug of tea, and Sam allowed himself a small smile.

She must be so tired of hearing that by now.

"No, Sara. They're two different people." Sam's smile dropped and his eyes looked off into the distance. "Two very very different people."

Satan sipped her drink. "It's not important right now." She looked back at the horde of fallen Angels, some of whom had fallen asleep, propped on walls and wrapped in blankets, others who were still moaning, staring out the windows at the heavens. "What is important is what has happened to the Host, and to Heaven."

Sam nodded, shaking off his reverie. "So, let's go over it, then. What do you know?"

Satan shook her head. "Not much, which is intensely frustrating." She put down her mug. "As the Tempter of Humanity, I spend much of my time on Earth, devising small tests designed to help people overcome their own weaknesses, to gain confidence." A breath, and she locked eyes with Sam. "As I was traveling over Egypt, I heard my name."

Sara sat down next to the Angel. "Your name? So what?"

"Sara, just let her finish. I need to hear what's going on."

"But it's—"

Satan turned toward Sara. "My name is, like that of my elder brothers and sisters, immeasurably complex. It describes the core of my being, the sum total of my existence...and, somehow, someone else knew it."

Sam leaned forward. "You mean someone *besides* the Host? Besides God?"

"Yes." Another sip. "This voice was human, but strong. Immeasurably strong." She shuddered, rubbing her hands across her arms under the blanket. "It was *spoken*, Sam, and when it was done, I was no longer myself." She stretched her arms out. "I was trapped in this body, unable to ascend." Her lower lip began to quiver and tears boiled up at the corners of her eyes. "Unable to hear anything anymore."

Cries and singing caught Sam's attention. Several of the stricken Angels had formed a circle and were raising their hands high, begging God for forgiveness. Blood from their severed wings stained the blankets and wrappings Sara had given them.

That must hurt so bad. They're still bleeding. Sam shook his head and turned back to Satan. "How did you....how were you able to respond to my summons?"

A thin-lipped smile. "I may be trapped in human flesh, but I am still an Angel. I heard you beckon Gabriel, heard the power of the Keys thrumming across the ocean, and I threw myself into the current." She shuddered. "It was a near thing, I think. I had no control, no sense of myself while I traveled."

Sam flexed his fingers. "There's still so much about this that I don't know yet." He closed his eyes, collecting his thoughts, then re-opened them. "So let's back up a second. You awoke in Egypt?" Sam scooted closer on his couch. "That's where your body was when you were trapped in it?"

Satan nodded, squirming in her seat. "I think so. I was in some sort of archaeological dig site, surrounded by workers and scholars. They were speaking to me, but...I didn't under-stand what they were saying."

Sam pursed his lips. "That's not great. Not great at all."

Sara interjected, shouting. "You say that like *any* of this shit is great, Sam!" The two adults looked her way, eyes wide. "The two of you go ahead and have your goddamn mysto-magical pow-wow or whatever the fuck this is. I'm going back to the *normal* world, where people make sense and don't fall out of the sky and there aren't giants walking in the oceans and...fuck!" She jumped up from the couch, storming away, out of the house. She slammed the door on the way out, rattling the mirrors and furniture.

Sam watched her go. "Shit."

Satan cocked her head. "Your daughter is weak at present, Keeper. Her trial seems to be wearing on her."

"It's no different than I was." He rose. "If I know her, then I know where she's gone." He looked down at the Angel, tried a small smile. "Hold on a second, all right?"

"Of course." Satan took another drink, her eyes glazing as she looked away. "I have nowhere else to go."

~~~

"I figured you'd be here."

Sam slipped under the trellis, laden with roses, that formed a small alcove at the side of the house. Sara didn't glance up, her face alight with the glow of her iPhone.

"Go away."

"No." Sam sat down next to her.
~~~

"Fine." Her fingers worked the screen, a blur as she texted and posted, browsing her Facebook timeline and Twitter feed.

Sam waited.

"*God,* it's so fucking annoying when you do that!" She tapped the button on top of the phone, shutting the screen off, then stowed it beside her and folded her arms around her knees.

"Do what?"

"Just sit there and don't say anything!" She spiked her fingers outward, glaring at him from the corner of her eye. "It drives me fucking crazy."

"Hey." Sam leaned a little closer. "I know you're stressed. Things are changing really fast, and—"

"And a little bit of a heads-up would have been *awesome!*" She turned her head away. "Instead, I get all this weird shit happening before I get a fucking chance to wrap myself around it, and you keep telling me to shut up, that there's no time to explain." Her body began to quiver as tears leaked down her face and her voice cracked. "Well, *Keeper*, I'm fucking sorry that I don't already know all this shit. Maybe you should've just left me with the fosters if you didn't want me slowing you down."

Sam closed his eyes. *Ouch.*

"So, go on. Go talk to the Angel or whatever the hell you say she is. I'll just wait out here until you're done, since I'm so obviously in the fucking way." She dug out her phone again, the screen shining blue and white.

Sam waited another few seconds while Sara took her frustration out on the electronic device, using much more force than necessary to input her commands, before he reached out and put his hand over the phone.

"Sara."

She didn't respond.

"I'm sorry. You're right. I fucked up."

A sidelong, cautious glance.

"You have to understand. *No one* knows about this." Sam's lips pressed into a thin line. "Well, almost no one. And it isn't fun, Sara. It isn't like I go out every day and have lunch with

Angels and go flying through the sky. Most of it is...well, most of it sucks, that's what."

She looked away again, but put the phone down.

"But I do it because I'm the only one who can." A small laugh. "I know it sounds corny and ridiculous, but I got picked to do this job and I'm going to do it the best I know how. But this...Sara, this is crazy, what's going on right now." He put a hand on her shoulder. "And I guess I got so focused on trying to figure it out, trying to solve it, to fight the good fight, that I forgot you were being dragged along."

"Damn right."

Sam smirked at Sara's low comment. "So, I'm not going to ask you to come back in right now if you don't want to. And I can't promise that I'm going to be perfect at making sure that you know everything that's going on while I work on figuring out exactly how bad this is and what I need to do. But..." He dragged out the pause, waiting for Sara to turn and look fully into his face.

"But what, Sam?"

"But if you'll be patient with me, and you decide you want me to, I'll tell you everything I know. One way or another. No more secrets."

Sara's eyes flared, just a bit. "...Red pill or blue pill?"

Another small smile. "Exactly right. That's the best I can offer you, Sara." He pressed his lips into hard lines. "And...and if you decide that it's too much for you, then I'll...I'll take you wherever you want to go, make sure you're set. I'll use my magic if I have to, to get everything set up the way you want it."

Before he had finished, Sara was shaking her head. "No, no. That's not what I want. I just..." Her eyes welled up with tears. "I got scared, I guess."

"I'd think you were fucking insane if you hadn't." Their eyes met, and smiles were exchanged. Sam put his arms out, and, after a moment, Sara leaned in to his hug.

"Come in when you're ready, all right?"

She nodded against his shoulder, and he gave her a small squeeze before they separated.

Sam put a hand on her shoulder, then backed out of the little alcove.

That's why you chose her. Not a mouse but a lion. He looked toward the angry skies. *And that's what Heaven needs right now.*

~~~

"Is everything all right, Samuel?"

Sam nodded as he closed the front door behind him. "As well as can be expected." He shook his head. "You know, I wonder how God manages it. It's hard enough to be father to one kid, let alone everyone ever."

"I imagine that He feels much of the same stress you do." Satan took another sip of tea, draining her cup. A look of discomfort crossed her face.

"So where were we?" Sam resumed his seat. "What were we talking about?"

The *creak* caught his attention as Sara peeked into the room. "Um...can I come in?"

"Sure."

Sara stepped into the room, the anger and defiance of a few minutes ago gone. She addressed the seated Angel first, head bowed, eyes
~~~

on the floor. "I'm sorry that I ran out and yelled and all that shi...stuff. I know that I'm not like Sam, but if I can help, I want to. If you're really an Angel, you...you shouldn't be trapped like this." She glanced up into Satan's face.

The Angel beamed.

"You have triumphed over tribulation, young one. Feel proud of yourself. Most would have failed, when put into the same position."

Sara shifted, an uncomfortable smile uncertain of its place dancing on her lips. "Um...yeah. Thanks." She scratched the back of her head. "Can I sit down? I'd...I'd like to hear what's going on."

"Please." Sam motioned to the free area of the couch. "Now...back to it. I think that we were talking about how you were summoned in Egypt, right?"

"Yes." Satan crossed her legs, then uncrossed them. "I...I couldn't understand their speech. It was foreign to my ears, sounds that made no sense."

"So what?" Sara's brow wrinkled as she leaned in.

"Think about it for a second, Sara." Sam opened his palm upward, indicating the sky. "Do you think Angels normally have a hard time with languages?"

Sara tapped her finger on the coffee table. "No, I guess not. I mean, if they're really from Heaven, I guess they should be able to understand just about anything."

Satan nodded. "That's correct. An embodied Angel knows all tongues, even those of beasts and plants, should we choose to speak them."

Sam held out one open hand. "Now, she woke up and couldn't understand these people. Right?"

"Right."

"What does that mean? What are the implications?"

"Well..." Sara bowed her head, her hands in her lap and her fingers restless. Satan shifted her weight from one side of her couch cushion to the other.

Come on. Sam resisted the urge to push his daughter to answer. *You can get this.*

Sara's eyes went wide. "Is it...does that mean that she's human? I mean, not in her mind, but in her body? Her senses? Her...her brain?" She looked over at Satan, scanning her up and down. "So she's lost her angel powers, or whatever?"

"I think so. And if that's the case, then this is even more time-critical and important than I thought." Sam turned back toward the celestial. "So now...are you okay?" He raised an eyebrow. "Is something wrong?"

"I...I'm not sure." Satan was now in a constant state of motion, bobbing up and down. "I feel...something..." Her hands came up to her waist, making a semicircle around her stomach.

"Oh my God!" Sara jumped out of her seat. "You've been drinking all that tea—you need to take a piss!"

"A what?"

She took a deep breath. "You need a bathroom break." Sara took two steps backward, then beckoned Satan. "Come on, before you pee yourself."

Satan stood, her legs still shaky, and followed Sara out of the room. Sam watched them go.

Food. Drink. Biology. He shook his head. *That's going to be tough for her. She—*

"Damn it!" He stood as well, then started moving from Angel to Angel, drawing the veil of Sight across his eyes and examining each one.

They're still Angels...just Fallen. He breathed a sigh and leaned against a wall. *At least that's one thing I don't have to worry about.*

Sam turned to the hallway his daughter and Satan had taken. *Hope she'll be okay.*

~~~

"That feels much better." Satan finished washing her hands, drying them on the green towel next to the sink. "Thank you, Sara."

"No worries." Sara turned back toward the Angel. "Must be weird for you, huh? Needing to use the bathroom and all. You've never had to do that before? Really?"

Satan shook her head, the corner of her mouth lifting. "Never. Even when an Angel takes human form we are not mortals. We re-
~~~

semble you, greatly, but we have no organs unless we choose, undergo no biological functions unless we think we must." She turned to the mirror, her fingers exploring the reflected face.

"So..." Sara fidgeted, her feet shuffling on the floor. "How did you and Sam meet? He's never told me about you or..."

"Your father is a rather unique individual, Sara." Satan ran water over her hands, lathering them with soap as she spoke. "He is the chosen emissary of God on Earth, the descendent of King Solomon."

Sara nodded. "I gathered that. I dunno...it just seems...he's just so *normal*."

Satan laughed, the sound erupting from her mouth as water splashed in the sink. "I had the same conversation with the Lord, or near enough." She reached over, grabbed the hanging green hand-towel, and started cleaning up the scattered drops. "Sam was...not exactly a shining example of what the Keeper of the Keys should be."

Sara's eyes expanded and her words rose in pitch. "Why not? What was he like? Was he..."

She looked back and forth, her eyes checking the door. "...Did he get in some kind of trouble?"

"...We should probably get back." Satan replaced the green towel on its ring. "He'll be worrying about us, and we have things to do."

"...Okay." Sara followed after her as she opened the door and left the room. "But after we get this figured out, I want to hear about it, yeah?"

"Hear about what?" Sam walked in from the kitchen, a plate of salami and cheese in his hand. "What were you two talking about, anyway?"

"None of your business." Sara thrust her nose up into the air. "Girl stuff."

Sam chuckled. "You *do* realize that she's an Angel, right? Not an actual woman?"

Sara waved off his comment. "Hey, Sam? Don't you think she needs something different to wear?"

Sam blinked, then turned. His eyes ran up and down the celestial's tattered robes. "You're probably right. Here." He reached into his pocket, dug out his beaten leather wallet, and started counting out twenties. "Why don't you take the bus to the mall and pick out a few things?"

Sara stared at the growing mound of cash in her father's hand, eyes wide by the time he had reached five hundred. He held out the bills.

"...Really? I can go pick out whatever?" She took the cash and riffled the stack. "Anything I want?"

"Try and keep it tasteful, Sara. That's all." Sam smiled. "Have a good time, but don't be too long, okay?"

"Yeah. No problem." She turned to Satan and moved her hands to the Angel's shoulders, her waist, her hips. Sara pursed her lips and scrunched up her eyes.

"This should be fun." Without another word, she turned and dashed off, slamming the front door behind her, leaving the two adults blinking at the space she had vacated.

A small laugh escaped Sam's throat. "She's like a whirlwind sometimes, I swear."

Satan smiled. "She is turning into a fine young woman. Not just anyone could overcome such trials. I feel the weight of them on her still, but she pays them no mind."

"Yeah." Sam sighed, then drew himself back up, his face sharpening again. "But we have work to do. If you woke up in this body in Egypt, then maybe there's a clue at that dig site." He rubbed his hand across his lips, took a gulp of water. "I think we should start there, see if there's anything to be seen."

Satan leaned back, her eyes darkening. "I awoke in front of a very old *mastaba*, a tomb for ancient Egyptian nobility."

"How do you know that?" He cocked his head. "That's an obscure term for an English-speaker."

"Perhaps..." She pursed her lips. "Perhaps the body that holds me still has memories, residual, left in the brain. Perhaps I speak English because this woman spoke English."

"That's possible. All right. We'll go with that." Sam rubbed his hands together as he contemplated. "Did you notice anything about the spell that summoned you? The person who did it?"

Satan tipped her head. "I don't know. No mortal except the Keeper should have the power to affect the Divine, the Host. This was not your power, Sam. It felt different."

"Well..." Sam massaged his temples with his fingers. "Could it have been Caitlin? Could he still know the Keys, be trying something else?"

She considered, then shook her head. "Gregory Caitlin has been watched for some time now. He did not do this. Even if he had, I would have recognized the power as coming from the Keys." Satan put a hand over Sam's. "Do you still worry about him?"

"A little. But it's not that important right now, I guess. We'll deal with that if we come to it."

Satan nodded. "I agree. I think that—" Without warning, she wavered in her seat, putting one arm on the couch and the other on Sam's shoulder to steady herself. He turned.

"Are you all right?"

"I...I think so." She shook her head. "I'm sorry. I just felt so weak suddenly. I suppose it's probably a side effect of being trapped in this body."

Sam looked at her face, his eyes scanning her skin. "Maybe. Or..." He pulled back a little and frowned. "I should have realized. You're hungry, aren't you?"

She stared back.

"Yeah, that's what I thought." Sam withdrew his phone from his pocket and brought up his contacts. "Yes, Domino's? I'd like to place a delivery order, please..."

THE EARTHBOUND

Satan came out of the bedroom, dressed in a pair of loose jeans and a light green wrap-front blouse. "Will you use the marid again to transport us?"

Sam shook his head. "We live in the desert, and calling them here would be more trouble than it's worth." He grimaced, his lips tightening. "Not to mention that the Queen didn't seem to like me very much, if you noticed."

"Yeah, she looked like she wanted to drag you down and feed you to the sharks." Sara grabbed another slice of pepperoni and mushroom. "Then are we going on another flight?" She took a bite, chewed, swallowed.

"No, I wasn't planning to have us fly again. I just don't want to mess with the marid. They're unpredictable and, as you saw, easy to anger."

"So what method will we be using?" Satan nibbled at the remaining pizza crust, then put it back into the box. Sam crossed one foot over the opposite knee, his head dipping in thought.

"We need to be outside." He stood, striding out the door, waving the two women along. Once they arrived in the middle of the yard, he drew a series of concentric circles in the air; they hung in front of him like faint golden sparkles, dust in the sunlight. After completing six circles, he stretched forward one hand through the center ring. At once, the ephemeral drawing became material, a diagram of brass, silver, steel, iron, copper, and tin attached to his arm.

Sam turned his head to his audience. "I hate this part. Brace yourselves."

They nodded, and Sara took a step closer to Satan.

Sam turned back to the ground, then nodded to himself.

"Let's go."

He raised his arm high, then brought it down into the ground. The earth beneath his hand seemed to clamp onto his fist, sending tendrils of crystal and rock into his veins. Blood poured out of his hand, rivulets dripping into the soil.

"Noble jann, spirits of the earth. Bend your knee to the Keeper of the Keys in the name of Almighty God, and take us from this place."

As if Heaven itself were replicating the patterns of the diagram on Sam's arm, the ground fell away in sections, piece by piece, until only the concentric circles and stars remained.

Sara closed her eyes and struggled to control her breathing.

From within the hollows of the Earth, thousands of deep, rumbling voices echoed in unison, the sound crashing down upon the three who stood above.

"IN THE SERVICE OF HEAVEN, WE OBEY."

The remaining ground, the pillars that held them aloft, vanished from under the trio's feet, sending them tumbling into a tunnel of rock. They flew through, bumping against the sides, against rough edges of quartz and anthracite and granite, three children on a waterslide without the water, the movement in the dark disorienting, disconcerting.

And then it was over. Sam reopened his eyes, wincing against the bumps and lacerations from the trip. The hole in the ground was closing, shrinking, but he forced himself up from the ground and touched the receding edge.

"Your service is appreciated, noble jann. Go with God."

A subsonic vibration shook his hand, and then the opening was gone.

"Ow." Sam rubbed one of the many sore spots, then turned toward where the two women were lying. They were tumbled together, Sara on top of the Angel. "Are you two all right?"

"You couldn't have warned us?" Sara shifted, moving off of the other, trying not to plant the heels of her hands or feet in any sensitive areas as she untangled herself. "Just saying 'brace yourselves' is kind of like saying 'wear your seatbelt' before driving a car off the fucking cliff."

The corner of Sam's mouth twitched. "Suffering brings character." He leaned in to help his daughter with her predicament. "Doesn't it, Satan?"

She didn't answer. Her shoulders trembled, and she inhaled a ragged breath.

"Hey." Sam put out a hand. "Are you okay?"

She raised her head. Tears streamed down her reddened face; tiny cuts decorated her flesh.

Sam tried to suppress his shock, but she saw his flinch and managed a small smile.

"I will be fine." Her voice was thick, clotted. "I am unaccustomed...to pain. But it is already fading." Satan put her hands underneath her body and pushed her way up. "In a few moments, I should be well again."

Sam nodded. "Okay." He brushed a loose hair from her face. "No worries."

"Hey, Sam?" Sara had taken a few steps away from the two of them. Sam turned his head to look at her, and found her pointing at a gathering of shapes off in the distance.

"What's that?"

THE PRIDEFUL

The three turned to survey the scene. Scattered in the desert were the remains of a campsite—some tents still stood, a few isolated pieces of equipment stuck out of the sand, and, half-buried near Sam's foot, a full bag of beef jerky held its ground in defiance of the elements.

"What the hell happened here?" Sam knelt down next to one of the broken tents. "It's like everyone just ran away as fast as they could, like..."

"Like the fear of God had been driven into them." Satan's voice was slow, deliberate. "Like the shepherds before Gabriel."

"Damn." Sara shook her head.

They kept searching. Sara moved from one piece of debris to the next, peeking inside torn tents, examining electronics. "Sam, some of this stuff looks *expensive.* Like, I don't even know what half of these words *mean.*"

"Hopefully we won't have to decrypt them, then."

Sara laughed assent as she headed off a little farther out.

Sam turned back to Satan. "Okay, so exactly what happened? Lay it out for me."

Satan nodded and took a deep breath. "Of course. I had been tempting several men and women in Giza, seeking to help them overcome certain prejudices. As I observed the test, I heard a call."

Sam paced in the sand. "Okay. But you didn't recognize the voice?"

"No." Satan's hand drifted to the cord at her belt and started to fidget and twist. "It beckoned me, called my name. My true name, Sam, as I explained."

"That's like what I used to find Gabriel, before."

"Yes." Satan brushed her hair back from her eyes. "I could not resist the summons, and it pulled me here."

Sara jogged back up. "Nope, nobody here. At least not that I could see, but it's getting dark." She glanced back and forth between the two of them. "What'd I miss?"

"We're just trying to figure out what's going on." Sam glanced around, then whipped both of his hands around in a double circular motion. Dozens of small flame spirits appeared, floating until they lit up the whole site with flickering golden illumination. "Go ahead."

"Yes." She pointed toward the marble structure, now dark and silhouetted against the night sky. "I was pulled toward there, on the top of the building. This woman was standing there, naked, her arms raised up, and she was singing my name." Tears welled up in the Angel's eyes. "And then...then I was *her*, I was in her body, and I couldn't stand upright, and I couldn't hear anything anymore. I tried to leave, tried to ascend, but I fell down and tumbled off."

She sank down, weeping now, and Sara came running up next to her, reaching out. Satan embraced the young woman as she sobbed.

I can't even imagine what that must have been like. Sam turned to the mastaba, the tomb. *So she was up there. Guess that's where I should go first.*

"Okay." Sam looked back. "You two stay here. I'm going to go check out the top of that thing, see what's going on. Maybe I'll be able to find something up there."

Sara nodded.

"Right then." Sam stretched out his hands. "Lift me, sylphs. Carry me on the wings of the wind."

Tiny, translucent air-spirits swarmed Sam, each one grabbing on to a piece of clothing, and pulled up. Hair formed from mist swirled around his arms and legs as the sylphs brought him through the air to the mastaba's roof. One of the ifrit followed, a torch in the darkness, floating.

Glad it's a bright moon tonight. Sam released the spirits and touched down on the marble building. *Let's see what's going on.*

Once more, Sam drew the Sight over his eyes. He could see the elemental spirits playing in the sand and the moonlight, could feel the jann, nearly omnipresent beneath the surface of the ground.

Then he looked down at the mastaba.

The building coruscated with bolts of white lightning, arcs trailing from one side to the roof and back. The air was filled with them, sizzling and crackling, and Sam closed his eyes in reflex and pain.

"Sam?" Satan stood, her voice carrying over the desert. "Are you okay?"

Sam waved her off, cracking open his eyes to allow them to adjust to the magical brightness. The whole structure was glowing with more power than he had ever seen, and he could feel a knot of fear rising in his belly.

Okay. Wow. He glanced up at the firmament. To his Sight, dark clouds blanketed the sky, allowing starlight through even as they blocked Heaven. *Okay, still locked. What am I...*

No. I can't do that.

I don't have a choice. Sam ran his hand through his hair. *I need to find out what's going on here.*

"Goddamn it." Sam rolled up his sleeves and pulled a stick of chalk out of his pocket. He set to work, inscribing the top of the mastaba with summoning sigils, binding circles, and wards.

"Incarnate, Pride, deadliest of the sins. Come forth, Vassago, and show what Was and what Will Be. Come now and match yourself against the Keeper, that I might use you for my own ends and that you might fall once more." The air inside the circle shimmered, becoming a mirage, reflecting Sam's image. "Prove your worth to the Heavens, or forever be alone."

The wavering picture of Sam solidified, leaving an exact copy within the diagram. The duplicate Sam grinned, its teeth perfect, its face unmarked by the concerns and worries of the last two years.

"Greetings, Keeper. I am glad to finally meet you. Lord Lucifer speaks often of the encounter you shared." The demon prince bowed low; in his wake, the aroma of spoiled cherries hung thick, drawing a grimace from Sam. "How can I assist you?"

"Don't think you can deceive me, demon." He kept his guard up, hands ready to move in the gestures of the exorcism. "I called you because I have no choice."

"Of course." Vassago stood and spread its hands. On its wrist was a gleaming gold watch that Sam did not possess. "What do you need me to do, Keeper?"

Sam gestured to the mastaba. "There is some form of magic here that I don't understand. I need to know what happened here, how the user of this power was able to summon and trap an Angel in a human body."

"I see." The demon clasped its hands, looked up toward the sky. "And you can't call on

God because He's been severed from the world, from His Host? Is that right?"

Sam narrowed his eyes. "How do you know this?"

"Please." Vassago polished his fingernails on his sleeve. "Don't insult my intelligence."

"...Yes. You're right." Sam frowned. "That's the main reason I called you."

"Then...no. I'm sorry, Keeper, but it really isn't in my interest to help you." Vassago smiled again. "So you can just send me back to Hell, if you don't mind. I have pressing appointments and things to do."

Sam flinched, then drew himself up. "No. I have summoned you, and, by the authority of God, you *will* obey."

The demon laughed. "Bad news, Keeper, but God *isn't here*." He pointed up at the mystical barricade in the heavens. "He can't reach you just now, if you hadn't noticed. All of His operators are busy, please leave a message after the tone." He shook his head. "Nothing doing. Send me back."

Sam could feel his gut roiling, anger churning in his stomach and chest. "How dare you? You think that He's actually *absent?* That He can't reach through whatever that magic is?" Sam balled up his fists. "That's ridiculous!"

"Is it, Keeper?" The demon walked to the edge of the diagram, facing off with Sam. "It seems to me that, if you have the earthbound Angels falling, His chief advocate trapped in human form, and a resounding busy signal coming from Heaven, that you might need to consider the idea that either He can't reach you...or that He can't be bothered." It crossed its arms and laughed. "Sucks either way, doesn't it?"

Is he right? Sam stepped back from the circle and took another look at the sky. *What if...what if we're alone? What if God is somehow trapped, or what if He just won't do anything to help? How can I...*

In his uncertainty, Sam's eyes had fallen, looking at the diagram and the demon's shoe.

The shoe that was still behind the line.

Sam raised his head, eyes burning. "If you weren't still subject to God's power, you would have left on your own, you lying fuck." Sam turned his hands so that the backs, where the tattoos were inscribed, faced the demon. "So let's try this again. You are going to help me find out what happened here and who is responsible, and in return, I *don't* dissolve you into a heaping mass of mirror shards. How's that?"

The smile vanished from the doppelganger's face, and he nodded, swallowing hard. "All right, Keeper. You got me. I do this for you, and you let me go. Agreed?"

Sam nodded. "Yes. But you do nothing else. Understood?"

"Of course." The demon stepped out of the circle, but Sam could see the chains of their agreement hanging from its arms. "Now, close your eyes, Keeper."

Sam looked sidelong at the demon, then nodded and did as he was bid.

"All right." Vassago touched Sam's forehead, and the Keeper felt himself being *pulled*, pulled out of his body until he stood beside it. He watched as his flesh fell to the ground in a heap, smacking its head against the marble.

"Oops." The demon shrugged in response to Sam's glare. "Sorry, but mortal flesh can't survive what we're about to do."

"Which is what, exactly?"

Sam's double waggled his eyebrows. "Time travel."

"Bullshit."

"Just watch." Vassago waved his hand, and Sam's eyes transitioned from disbelieving to awestruck. He watched as the day moved backward, the sun rising in the west and setting in the east, watched as the wind picked up the sand and moved it away from the dunes that had formed, watched as people arrived, undid their campsite, and left again, all the while moving backward.

"It's like a movie on rewind."

"Something like that." The demon laughed. "This isn't real, you understand. I can't go in there and start messing with things that have already happened, change the present. These are just impressions, energy left on the fabric of the world."

"Fine. So when did it happen? When was Satan trapped here?"

Vassago nodded. "About three days ago. Here." And the rewinding stopped. Sam could see the form that Satan now wore, naked except for a gold and ruby amulet around her neck and her arms stretched out to the sky. The woman was singing, and Sam could, as before, understand every word that swept from her lips, every sound she made. The music was pure, was real, was more powerful this time, emerging as it was from an actual human throat and not a speaker system, and Sam had to fight to keep his feet, to not fall to his knees before the sound's glory.

The demon prince reached into his jacket and pulled out a set of noise-cancellation headphones. "Fucking obnoxious, isn't it?"

Sam wiped his eyes and watched as the celestial form of the Angel, an androgynous figure with rainbow colors scintillating in the skin, was drawn to her, pulled towards her, struggling and screaming in the Angelic song.

The ephemeral drew closer and closer to the material, fighting a losing battle, until, with a golden flash, the deed was done and the Angel was trapped within the body, weeping, praying for forgiveness. The necklace was gone.

Wait a minute... Sam waved one hand at the demon. "Can you go back, to right before Satan touched the body?"

"Huh?'

Sam knocked the set of headphones off his head. "I said, go back to when the Angel was about to enter the body."

"Oh." The demon shrugged. "Sure."

The scene stepped backward, the wailing body stepping back from the edge, rising from prostration, then standing again as the silvery-white rainbow peeled away from her.

"Forward, now."

Again, Satan's celestial form was pulled into the body she now occupied, and Sam could see the facial expression change from exultation to fear, see the tears spring to life.

"One more time. Step by step."

The demon crossed its arms. "This isn't a fucking DVD, Keeper. Real life doesn't work in frames."

Sam glared at his doppelganger, and it sighed.

"Fine."

Sam turned back as the images moved backward again, this time in the tiniest of increments. He focused closely on the space that Satan's form would cross, watched as the ephemera spindled away, as the horrified face emerged from the flesh.

"Stop!"

I knew it! I fucking knew it!

In the gap between the two, another shape reached toward Satan. This one was thinner than the other, dewdrops in mid-air and invisible but for the slight distortion that it made in its wake. The ruby in the amulet glowed a bright red.

"There was someone else in that woman, possessing her." He leaned in. "I...I don't think it was a demon. It doesn't look like any demon I've seen."

"And, of course, you've seen them all." Vassago coughed, then wiped its hand on its sleeve. "So you're an expert."

"Did I ask you?" Sam didn't turn, but waved one hand in the space with the new creature. "It looks almost human, but it's really blurry. Can we focus in, clear this up?"

The demon rubbed its temples. "Keeper, this is not TV. Seriously. We can't just 'Zoom-and-enhance.'"

"Fine." Sam turned, looked down. "Can we go into the tomb?"

"Of course we can." Vassago spread his hands. "In we go."

The two sank into the marble, passing through the iridescent magical aura until they came out the ceiling and floated to the floor.

"Voila!" The demon spun in a circle. The interior of the room was laden with treasures, artifacts from a distant age. Bronze sickle-swords hung from the walls alongside shields decorated with strange symbols. The center was dominated by a golden sarcophagus, and in each of the four corners stood a statue formed from the same metal.

It's all so bright. Sam's eyes were half-closed against the radiance that poured from each of the statues and the tomb between them. Sparks of power lanced from each humanoid form into the sarcophagus, miniature lightning bolts of magic.

"Go ahead, Keeper, take your time." The demon checked its massive gold watch, stretched, and yawned. "Not like I have anything else going on."

God, he's annoying. Sam shook his head and approached one of the statues. It rose up about eight feet tall, a man with a pointed, Egyptian beard, a large, two-pronged hat, his chest bare and his hands holding an ankh and a staff across it.

"Is this one of the Egyptian gods?" Sam stepped closer as he spoke. The magical energies thrummed through the statue. *Almost like it's alive and moving.*

"Amun, the god of hidden knowledge." The demon's voice sounded distant, almost inaudible. "And the one over there with the jackal head is Anubis, the bird-headed one is Thoth, and the last one is Osiris. In case you were wondering."

"Mm-hmm." Sam looked up into the statue's eyes. *What are these made of, anyway? Maybe ivory or something? They look almost real.* He reached out a hand toward the face, and a spark leapt from the nose to his finger.

"Ow!" He brought his wounded finger up; the ephemera was singed black, but the normal shimmering blue color crept over it until the injury vanished. "What the hell was that?"

No answer.

Sam turned. The demon prince was sitting against the wall, eyes closed, a light snore rumbling from its lips. Despite himself, he laughed, moving over to the creature to shake it awake.

Vassago's eyes fluttered open. "What? What? Are we done?"

"Not yet." Sam put out a hand to help the demon up. "I need you to do like you did up above—take me back to when all this went down so I can see it."

Vassago yawned again, stretched, popping and cracking sounds erupting from its back. "Okay. No problem. Exactly how far do we want to go?"

Sam considered, his eyes dipping for a moment before responding. "I want you to bring me to when the woman that we saw first shows up here. I don't know how long that is, but if I'm right, then whatever it was that went into Satan's angelic form must have gotten into her, possessed her at that point."

The demon nodded and waved his hand one more time. The scene blacked out for several seconds, leaving Sam in an empty darkness, before reappearing and resolving once again. This time, however, the young woman who served as Satan's host was pushing open the main door to the chamber.

Sam could see the woman's eyes widen and a smile creep over her face as she moved from object to object, artifact to artifact. Several times, her hand reached out, but she would always bring it back without touching. She spoke to no one in particular.

"My God. What is all this?" She stopped in front of the statue of Amun. "So intricate, so ornate...obviously New Kingdom in design, but where is the Ra influence?" She stepped up close, leaning in toward the face like Sam earlier. "The eyes...what are they made of?"

Again, her hand came up toward Amun's cheek, but she held it back. "I wish you could see this, Dad. It's incredible." The woman turned back and crossed her arms as she looked at the sarcophagus. "And you did all this, didn't you?"

To Sam's mystical Sight, the tomb pulsed, an almost invisible vibration humming through the air.

Dark eyes scrunched together. "I wonder who you were, Mr. Mysterio." Her fingertips hovered over the golden surface. "No name, but a sarcophagus worthy of a Pharaoh. A tomb made of marble, not clay. Why?" She arrived at the inscribed face, staring into the eyes.

The pulse came again, stronger this time, a subsonic rumble.

"Oh, wait." The woman's gaze dipped down to the neck. "This is a strange-looking amulet…"

Fingertips brushed over the ruby surrounded by ornate symbols and hieroglyphs.

The gem flashed a bright crimson, and Sam saw the same creature from the rooftop rise up out of the sarcophagus.

It was a man. A man with runic tattoos on his face, running from his left forehead and across the bridge of his nose to his right cheekbone. He resembled the statue of Amun, but his features were sharper and his smile wicked.

Then he was gone, and the woman's smile mirrored the spirit's as she reached out and took hold of the amulet. The jewelry liquefied, flowing up the woman's arm and around her neck, reforming.

"Hold it there."

The scene froze. Sam brought his face closer to the amulet. The inscriptions remained hidden from his understanding, refusing to unravel themselves into English as his own spells and incantations had done.

"What is this?" He shook his head. *I should be able to understand it.* "Why can't I read it?"

"It's Egyptian, obviously. Various blessings from the Egyptian deities. Prayers." He shook his head and laughed. "I thought that you were supposed to be intelligent, Keeper."

Sam bit back his retort. "It's magic, isn't it? I mean, normal rubies don't glow and liquefy. I could read the Sephirot. I can read the Keys. Why can't I read this?"

"I would think that's obvious." Vassago polished his fingernails on his shirt and examined them. "This magic doesn't come from God, that's all. The Egyptian gods granted this man his power."

Sam blinked. "Wait...what?"

The return smile was blinding. "What? You didn't know? Don't you remember all the sorcerers in the Bible, the ones that God struck down or humiliated?"

Sam shook his head. "I...I thought..." A small laugh. "I guess I never really thought about it at all."

"Of course not." The demon checked his watch again. "Well, that's it. I've got to go."

Sam recoiled. "Go? You can't just 'go.'"

He crossed his arms. "Yes, I can. Our agreement is fulfilled, I've done as you asked, and you can't bind me again without something to write or draw with." Vassago stepped forward and its face *melted*. Sam's own features dissolved and dropped off of the underlying structure, revealing a scarred and tortured monster, spikes impaled through its nose and gouges in its forehead revealing bone beneath. It had holes in its cheeks that showed its pointed teeth and scabrous tongue, and no ears at all. Its voice morphed into a hissing spittle, water drops on a burning iron pan.

"I would kill you for this affront if I could, Buckland. You called me here like a mewling, groveling servant, using my knowledge without so much as a by-your-leave. I would see you boiled alive, flayed by the whips of Hell, your skin peeled off while you scream your apologies, but that is beyond my power...for now."

Its tongue lashed out like a snake, and its next words shook Sam to his core. "You should guard yourself, Keeper of the Keys, for even such as you can fall." Its eyes glittered in its head. "I look forward to seeing you again...if those whom you have crossed don't see you first."

The creature waved its hand and Sam flew away, through the ceiling and back into his body. His flesh was stinging like he had been immersed in jellyfish and he curled up on himself, hissing and rolling on the stone roof. He felt like someone had punched him in the gut, knocking the wind out of his chest, and he couldn't speak, couldn't whimper or wail, for several moments.

"God *damn* it!" As air began to creep back into his lungs, Sam put his hands and knees under him and coughed, scattering the light layer of dust and sand that overlaid the mastaba roof. "What a fucking *asshole*."

He glanced to the right. A ways in the distance, standing in a circle of magical firelight, were two women, one larger than the other. Despite the lingering pain, Sam felt tension lift from his heart.

He put up a hand and waved. The two ladies began moving toward him, Sara jogging and Satan at a brisk walk. Sam forced himself to his feet, rubbing the tingling out of his muscles and skin and brushing the sand off his clothes. When he felt he could move without his legs folding underneath him, he crawled down the side of the tomb, dropping onto a small dune below.

Sara was first. "What happened, Sam?" She looked up at the top of the mastaba, where Sam had just been. "We just saw you fall down on the ground. Are you all right?"

"Yeah." The Keeper rubbed the back of his neck and winced, then looked toward Satan. "Demon princes are real assholes, you know that? At least Vassago is, anyway."

The Angel's eyes widened, then narrowed. "You conversed with Vassago? Be—"

Sam nodded. "Be careful, I know. I didn't think I had any choice." He pointed up at the sky. "Heaven isn't answering me right now."

Satan followed his gesture, then sighed. "I'm sorry, Sam. It's difficult to trust humans, knowing all the mistakes that they make, but you are the Keeper, and I found you worthy before. I apologize for second-guessing you."

Sara's face turned back and forth, tracking the adults as they spoke, but she leapt in at the pause. "Right. Talking with demons. That's not a bad idea at all."

"No, it's a terrible idea." Sam knelt and drew a quick circle in the dirt. The misty form of sylphs danced among the stolid shapes of jann within the diagram. "But I think that not knowing what we're up against is a much worse one, don't you?"

Sara's snarky grin fell away. "I...I didn't mean..."

Sam rolled his neck. "I know." He addressed the gathered genii. "Keep a look out, will you? I don't want to be surprised." He waved his hand and the spirits scattered, dispersing in all directions out of his sight. Sam stood again. "All right. We need to go in."

Sara gasped, looking from her father to the tomb and back. "In *there?*"

"No choice. That's where the magic is, and I need to see it for myself."

"You know what?" Sara backed away. "I think I'm good, not going in. You...you go right ahead. I'm sure you'll be fine, won't you?"

"Is something wrong?" Satan put a hand on her shoulder, but Sara turned out of her grip.

"No, no...I just..." She shook her head, then ran off toward their gear.

Sam watched her go. "Wiser than I am."

Satan's eyes were narrowed, concerned. "Should...should I stay?"

"No." Sam turned back toward the mastaba and started his march toward it. "If she comes, fine. If not, fine. It's not our place to force her or coddle her right now." He spared his daughter another glance; Sara was digging through her pockets, pulling out her phone and plugging in to her music.

"I understand." The two of them reached the entrance. Satan pointed at the hieroglyphs surrounding and guarding the doorway.

"Sam, look at this!" Satan touched one of the symbols, several squiggles and drawings enclosed by an oval. "This says 'Enter and your name shall be forfeit, food for the Gods in Duat, and your soul shall fall into the vaults of Ammit the Devourer.'"

"How do you know that?"

"I...I'm not sure. I think maybe she...this body...knows it." Satan shivered and rubbed her arms with her hands. "I don't like it here. It feels like death is watching, Sam." She shook her head. "Like something is waiting for us."

Sam reached out and took one of Satan's hands between both of his, holding it at chest level. "Don't worry. I was just in here, and there's no crazy monsters or demons. Just some sort of weird magic."

Satan looked from Sam's hands to his face and back again. Her eyes narrowed.

"Sorry." Sam let go, then turned toward the door. "Shall we?"

~~~

"So the magical energy was centralized here." Sam waved his hand to encompass the
~~~

central chamber. "These statues are charged with it, and so is the tomb in the center. I saw…" He hesitated, glanced over, continued. "I saw the woman who came in here, the body you're in."

Satan nodded.

"She was looking around and remarking on how strange everything was, how it was weird that this guy was entombed in a place like this. She didn't touch anything in this room, not until she got to the sarcophagus…and then the possessing spirit kind of leapt out at her."

Satan nodded again and turned toward the tomb. "It doesn't look like anyone has tampered with it, or opened it. It is likely the body is still inside."

Sam shook his head. "I don't think that matters. See, right here?" He pointed to a groove in the neck of the golden figure on the top of the sarcophagus. "There was a medallion here. Golden, with a huge ruby on it and all sorts of magical writings that I couldn't understand. The necklace went with the spirit—it melted and attached itself to her neck."

Satan frowned. "That sounds familiar, Sam. Something I should know…"

Sam stepped toward her. "Really? You've seen it before?"

The woman nodded, looking away and down at the ground as she thought. Several times, her mouth opened and closed.

Then she made a fist and punched the marble wall.

Sam jumped back. Satan's face quivered and her arm shook as she withdrew.

"…Why did you do that?" Sam's eyes flicked to the wall.

Satan's skin was red and tears blossomed in her eyes. "I can't…I can't…"

Sam leaned closer. "Can't what?"

Satan's dark eyes stared into his for another few seconds, then she crumbled, falling onto the ground and cradling her hand. She began to weep. "It *hurts*!" She rolled around on the floor, rubbing her injured hand, hissing whenever she touched a sensitive spot. "It hurts so much, Sam, I…"

Sam blinked, then knelt beside her and took the Angel's wrist. He prodded at the injury, where purplish bruises were beginning to appear. Satan winced several times, but did not cry out again.

"I don't think it's broken." Sam released her hand and wiped his brow. "But that must have...why the hell did you hit the wall, anyway?" Sam looked up at the wall again and shook his head. "Was there like the world's nastiest spider on there or something?"

Satan wiped her eyes with her good hand. "I'm sorry if I upset or scared you. I was just...I felt this swelling in my mind, some sort of pressure, and I just..."

"Oh." Sam felt a weight lift from his shoulder. "You got mad. Angry."

"Mad?" Satan's eyes skittered like a frightened animal. "Is it...is it always like that? That terrible force, overriding your thoughts?"

Sam rested a hand on her on the shoulder. "Yeah. You can learn to deal with it, channel it, rationalize it...but, yes, it's always a little like that."

Satan reached across her body and gave Sam's hand a squeeze before dropping her own. "Um...thank you. I was saying, though, or what made me mad, was that I was trying to remember where I had seen that amulet."

Sam nodded. "Yeah, I know what you mean. Forgetting things gets to me, too."

"No, it's not that." Satan rubbed her temples with her good hand. "I'm not used to forgetting. Angels don't forget anything, not from the beginning of time. I can remember when I awoke, the first word of God, everything...or, at least, I *could*. Now..."

Sam held up his hand. "Now you're stuck with a human brain, and it's having a hard time processing the equivalent of eons of memories. Is that about right?"

"I think so."

He pointed at the impact point on the marble. "And so you got frustrated, and then you got mad, and then you tried to break your hand against the wall."

The corner of Satan's mouth twitched. "I...Yes."

"Okay then." He stepped up to the sarcophagus, then turned back toward her. "Next time, make sure you warn me before you go ballistic on the architecture. I want to be out of here before the ceiling comes down, okay?"

This time the smile was too strong to suppress. "As you wish, Keeper." She joined him in looking down at the gold carving, and her levity faded away. "What do you think it is?"

"Hell if I know." Sam shrugged. "Problem is, I didn't even know that there was other magic. I should have, I guess. Done more research."

"Other magic?"

"I don't know." His brow furrowed as he thought back. "When I had to save Gabriel, there were these markings on the door. She called them the Sephirot, symbols of the concepts of the universe or something."

Satan's head turned.

"I could read them at the time. I knew what they were. But still, I had never seen them before. They weren't part of the Keys and nothing I could do was budging them."

"Sam." Satan pointed. "The statue over there. It...I think it blinked."

Sam followed her finger to the statue of Amun. *That's the one with the weird eyes.* "Are you sure?" He kept a respectful distance from the figurine. "It's definitely magical in some way, so I wouldn't be surprised if it did something weird like that, but..."

"No, I'm not sure." Satan sighed. "It just looked like it, out of the corner of my eye."

"Okay. Well, let's see what I can do." Sam brought his hands in front of him. The tattoos began to shift, in small increments at first but then blurring.

"Which one do you plan to use?"

Sam knelt down and began tracing another diagram in the sand. The lines were thin over the marble floor, but clear. "It's called the Immersion, or near enough. Do you know that one?" He looked up again. "Has anyone ever used it before?"

"There have been many Keepers, Sam, and I don't keep track of the ins and outs of their lives." Sam looked askance in her direction. "But to answer your question, no, I've never heard of the spell."

"Yeah." Sam tossed a small handful of dirt into the middle of the concentric pentagram, then extracted his pocket knife and flipped the blade open.

"Why...why are you cutting yourself?"

Sam paused with the blade pressed against the pad of his thumb. "After Gabriel...after you all left, I had to figure out what to do to make sure we never had another Caitlin. The book is too important, but I didn't know what to do with it at first." The knife slid across his flesh, bringing forth a small trickle of crimson flowing over the metal. "Couldn't keep it at home. Too easy to steal. Couldn't even trust it with a bank or anything, because what if I needed it? So I came up with a...a sort of homemade security system. Best I could think of."

As the first drops ran over the handle and fell to the earth, a small, snarling mouth emerged from the dirt, followed by a round body the size of Sam's fist. Its skin was wrinkled and grey, the color of dead flesh, and the creature had no eyes or ears or legs—an overgrown, fleshy leech with teeth that snapped and a tongue that slavered over the spilled blood.

Satan took several steps back. "Sam?" The Angel pointed a trembling finger at the creature. "Do you know what that is?"

"It's a minor demon of gluttony." Sam glanced up with a shrug. "They eat anything, but they're especially fond of blood." Its prize gone, the demon started its version of looking around, snapping at the air and licking its chops. Sam intoned a few syllables and the demon froze.

"You might want to take a step back." Sam pointed two fingers at the frozen monster. "From what I read, this part isn't going to be pretty."

The demon screamed, its leech-mouth stretching open wider and wider. Blood and viscera gushed from the creature's open orifice, pouring onto the sand and marble, covering the floor around it in a thick blanket of red chunks soaked in fluid. Its body stretched, contorting and expanding in strange places as if something were pressing on it from the inside, thrusting hands or elbows or feet against its stomach walls.

Then it exploded in a huge fountain of gore and guts, spattering pieces of itself all over the inside of the tomb. Several chunks landed on top of the sarcophagus, with many others reaching the heads and noses of the various divinities in the room.

Satan's hand quavered as she reached up to her face and pulled a gobbet of flesh off of her cheek. Her chest hitched as she tried to breathe in. Her eyes bulged, and her head twitched and pivoted in small jerks.

"Holy hell." Sam brushed strands of intestine and stomach off of his chest and shoulders, his face pale. "I...I didn't think it was going to be *that* bad." He grimaced, swallowing down the acid taste in his mouth, then knelt down and reached into the thickest mass of clotted flesh and blood that lay on the floor. From within he pulled out a rectangular solid dripping with putrid, runny ooze.

Satan's eyebrows pinched together. "You left the Keys...*inside* of a demon?"

"Yeah." Sam whipped his hand in a circle and several undines swirled out of the air, washing the demon filth and leaving the book clean. The silver cover gleamed in the light from the ifrit and the water droplets were stars upon its surface. "Best place I could think of."

Palms slammed into Sam's chest, sending him stumbling backwards and the book *clanging* to the floor.

"Ow!"

Satan advanced on the Keeper, gripping his shirt, teeth bared. "Are you *insane?* You delivered your greatest weapon, the arts of God, into the hands of your enemy? What if Lucifer had gone looking for that demon? What if—" She pulled back a fist for another attack.

Sam straight-armed her, planting his cut palm in her chest and knocking her back as his other hand came up, ready to conjure. "Touch me like that again and I'll throw you into the same pocket dimension I had that demon." His eyebrows came together, his teeth bared in anger.

"But..." The Angel's eyes fluttered, unable to settle. "If—"

"If what? It's not like there's a fucking instruction manual on how to do this...this job, is there?" Sam's voice overtopped hers, and he advanced on her position. "I got left here to handle this by myself, remember? You're the one who said I measured up. If you don't like how I work, then lodge a complaint with the fucking Big Guy and see if he'll take this off my hands!" He loomed over her, staring down at her. "Or maybe you should get control of yourself."

Their eyes locked for several moments before Satan nodded.

"Yes." Satan's nostrils flared as she inhaled, closing her eyes. "You're right. I'm sorry, Sam."

Sam rubbed the front of his shirt where she had hit him and took his own deep breath. "Yeah. Yeah, me too."

Satan didn't respond, instead bending down to pick up the book.

Sam shook his head and took the tome from Satan's hands; their fingers brushed and he felt a small shock.

Satan jumped. "Ow!" She stared at her finger. "Why did you –"

"It was static electricity, that's all." Sam opened the book and paged through until he reached a portion in the middle of the text. "Here we go. The Immersion."

"Are there any dangers, Sam?" Satan was also behind him, looking over his shoulder. "As I said, I've never seen this spell performed before."

"Sure." Sam pointed to a passage. "It says here that it's possible to lose oneself in the Divine thought, to lose the sense of being and never return from the Immersion. It also says that care should be taken to guard the body against possession or invaders."

"Such as demonic influences?"

Sam nodded. "Yes. Like demons. Or spiritual projections. Even after one returns, they may be more vulnerable to such for some time." He looked around the room, noting particular points with his finger and nodding. "Yeah, this room is actually pretty set up for it, which is nice. It's got the right shape and there's nothing in the places I need to draw the diagrams."

Satan nodded, then covered her mouth as she yawned. "All right. I suppose Sara and I should wait outside..." Another yawn. "I'm sorry. I think that I'm feeling tired now."

Sam smiled. "Don't worry. We should be done soon, and then you can get some rest."

Satan turned and left the burial chamber, leaving Sam alone. The outside door closed, and then there was silence.

Sam looked down at the book again. He had left out the parts where the text had described the risk of permanent insanity or paralysis, becoming insensate or a vegetable, memory loss...all possibilities when attempting to comprehend the Divine with only a human's brain.

His eyes strayed upward. There was only marble ceiling, but he knew what he would see if the stone did not block his vision: Heaven, closed, sealed off by some unknown power.

He set to work.

THE IMMERSION

"What's he doing in there, anyway?"

Satan sighed, wrapping herself up more tightly in the jacket Sam had loaned her. The night sky twinkled with stars, and the temperature was falling fast—the two girls had bundled up to ward off the chill. She cast a glance back toward the tomb, but the door was still closed, as it had been for the last half-hour. "He is attempting to merge with the divine will, the holy consciousness." Her eyes dropped.

"Is that what...what Gabriel does? Isn't that what the two of you said?"

"Yes."

Sara tilted her head. "But you seem nervous. Is it dangerous?"

"It could be. He warned me of some of the possible effects...but I think that he was concealing the full extent of the threat."

"What?" Sara climbed to her feet. "So why are you letting him do it?"

Satan laughed, but the sound was harsh, angry. "As he reminded me, he is the Keeper of the Keys. Not me. I am just the hollow shell of an Angel, trapped in decaying, rotting flesh."

Sara's eyes narrowed. "That sounds like..." She sat again, but her voice was tight, wary. "Like you don't like people very much."

The Angel raised her eyebrows. "You misunderstand." She lifted a hand, palm out. "I don't dislike your kind. You are the chosen of the Creator. His favored children. I simply..." She exhaled through her nose. "I dislike being hungry. And angry. And..."

"And using the bathroom."

"And being cold." Satan nodded. "Exactly. But please don't take my frustration at my current state as my attitude toward your species." She turned away, so that her profile faced Sara. "Those that felt that way towards humanity still suffer for it."

Realization washed over Sara's mien. "You mean...the Devil? Lucifer?"

Another nod.

"He was an Angel like you?"

Satan shook her head. "He was not like me. He was an Archangel, like Michael and Gabriel. The Lightbringer. There were none more respected save the Voice of God himself."

"What was he like?" Sara leaned in and took a sip from her own mug.

"Why do you wish to know?" Satan's eyebrow rose. "What good can it do you?"

"I just wanna know." Sara didn't move. "Besides, you brought it up."

Satan closed her eyes and leaned back against the marble. "All right. I just hope I can remember everything." A few seconds passed; Sara fidgeted, opening her mouth to speak several times before closing it again.

"He was...he was glorious." Satan's voice was filled with awe, a low tone that colored every word. "His every gesture radiated light, and his speech sang to our souls. He stood in judgment of our work on God's creation, and we competed, as much as Angels do, for his favor." She shook her head. "Only the Archangels saw the Voice. For the rest of us, Lucifer was the Word of God."

"Wow." Sara looked out into the night. "They never tell you that kind of thing in church."

Satan laughed, and, after a few seconds, Sara joined in. The sound rolled over the sand dunes and bounced off the walls of the mastaba, echoing and bubbling with the ins and outs of their breath.

"When Lucifer Fell, he stood before the Gates of Heaven with his forces. He was so beautiful, still, and his words so compelling. He cried out for justice, said that the Father had forsaken us, his first creations." Tears welled up in Satan's eyes. "So many went over to him then, so many turned their backs on their brothers and sisters to challenge the Throne."

Sara was rapt, her eyes huge. "What happened then?"

Satan glanced toward the girl and a small smile touched her face. "Michael."

"So it's true? Michael beat Lucifer, threw him out?"

A nod. "Yes. Michael is and has always been the leader of Heaven's army."

"Hey, that's another good question." Sara's eyes narrowed. "Why did Heaven need an army? I mean, before the Fall?"

Satan opened her mouth, then closed it again. Considered for a moment. "I...I don't know." She shook her head. "I must have forgotten."

"Oh." A few heartbeats passed. "So...?"

Satan started in surprise. "What?"

"So what happened? Was there a huge battle? Did Michael kick Lucifer's ass out of Heaven? What?"

Satan's lips drew tight. "No. These memories are too clear, and I don't want to relive them. What happened then echoed throughout history, and it should, *must*, never happen again."

"Can't you—"

From the sky, a massive lightning bolt, blue and white against the darkness, lanced downward into the mastaba. The marble shuddered and small pebbles rolled off the ceiling onto their heads, and the thunder blew them backwards into the sand covering their ears.

"What the hell was that?" Sara shouted.

"I don't know!" Defying all laws of physics, the lightning stroke held, dancing in place even after the thunder subsided. The mastaba swelled with light, taking on the same colors as the bolt, until a great *crack* rent the air and shattered the stone.

Satan threw herself on Sara as the building exploded.

Sizzling chunks of white and grey rock broke into smaller pieces as they flew. The two women braced themselves for the impact.

A light pitter-pattering on their coats opened their eyes.

~~~

Sam dusted off his hands and admired his handiwork. Concentric circles mixed with pentagrams and Stars of David and coupled with Angelic script. A warding diagram, designed to keep foreign energies out, lay at each corner of the room, and, at the feet of the sarcophagus, lay the seven-pointed heptagram. Each point held one of the symbols of the Archangels, connections to the Divine.

Now for the fun part. Sam slipped off his jacket, unbuttoned his shirt, took down his pants and drawers, and stepped into the middle of the heptagram.

"Don't know why this spell has to be done naked, but..." He sat, flinching at the chill of the stone, then closed his eyes.

"I surrender my hope, that I might be given grace."

A gust of wind kicked up, biting into Sam's naked flesh.

"I surrender my sight, that I might be shown the truth."
~~~

A subsonic rumble shook the stone underneath him.

"I surrender my flesh, that my soul might bear witness."

Sam felt a tingle creeping over him, starting at his feet and moving upward. His nose filled with the scent of honeysuckle.

"I surrender myself, that I might be like God."

~~~

There was nothing.

For several moments/minutes/years/eons, nothing existed. Not matter, not energy, not the puny construct of flesh and spirit that would become Samuel Buckland.

Then there was the chorus of voices, sound from the soundless void, calling for the universe to awaken, to open its eyes and take its first breath.

And it did.

In a riotous explosion of light and joy, $e=mc^2$ was given form, and Newton's laws found momentum and inertia to utilize. Matter and anti-matter collided, and their explosions radi-
~~~

ated throughout the nascent universe, casting shadows on its wall. Still the voices rumbled through, some louder than others, commenting on the birth of the first stars.

Then it was gone, and two men wept in the desert, in a large crater in the sand. One lay broken, bleeding—his breath came in tattered gasps, and his raiment was charred, both cloth and skin flaking off under the fingers of the other, undamaged man. Dark of skin, his eyes ran with tears that fell on the flesh of the wounded creature in his arms. A tattoo, Egyptian hieroglyphics and other, more esoteric, symbols, wound its way from his forehead, over the right eye, and across the bridge of his nose. He wore a gold chain with a red gem, and he was sobbing.

"Jambres!" He shook the other man, whose eyes fluttered and struggled to focus. "Jambres, you have to wake up!" He ran his hands over Jambres again, chanting, focusing; his red gem burned with an inner fire, but nothing happened.

A large figure, a muscular man in Egyptian garb, stepped forward from the shadows. He reached forward to take the burned man's hand, but the other slapped him away.

"No! You can't take him!" He held the amulet in his free hand, pointing it toward the newcomer while clutching Jambres close to him. "Begone, Anubis. This is my brother. You cannot have him."

The man knelt, his eyes and smile blurring until those of a jackal replaced them. "He is dead, Jannes. I must take him to Duat and weigh his heart in the Scales of Ma'at."

"He served you!" Jannes shook his head, scooting away from the god. "We both did, dedicated our lives to you and to the rest, and what? You turned your backs on us, let him die?"

Anubis stood. "Jambres is dead because he stood naked before his enemy. You are alive because you did not make that same mistake."

"Liar!" Jannes stood, staring up at the deity. "You could have helped us before, helped us defeat Moses. Where were you then? Why did he defeat us?"

Anubis sighed. "The Compact forbade us. There was nothing we could do."

Jannes seethed, his eyes narrowing and his teeth grinding in his mouth. "You make excuses. You, a god, make excuses for yourself."

Anubis bristled, drawing himself up to over ten feet in height and looming over the sorcerer. "Silence, little man. Do not presume to understand the affairs of your betters."

Jannes held forth his amulet, but Anubis caught the red blast which erupted from it, holding it in his fist until it dissipated.

"The spells you worked to protect yourself from the Angels will not work against me, Jannes. In respect for your brother's service and your own, I give you one more chance to walk away." The god's eyes locked onto his. "I will not say it again."

For a moment, the sorcerer stood his ground, defiant in the face of annihilation. Then, with a nod and a defeated sigh, he stepped away from Jambres. Anubis touched the dead man on the forehead and his flesh dried, shriveled, receding from his gums and hair.

The god turned back toward Jannes. "Your grief will pass soon. You have my word that, when your time comes, I will bring you to your brother and you shall be reunited."

"And you have mine," Jannes spat, "that I will never forget what has transpired this day." He looked once more into Anubis's face, and this time the jackal's head recoiled from the fire in the man's eyes. "Any of it."

The scene faded into light and shadow, a poorly remastered black-and-white movie that blurred into nothing and left only the sand. The night sky shifted, stars wobbling in the celestial vault, and the paths of the wind carved new dunes in the desert.

The world began to withdraw, the scene receding from view until Egypt, Africa, the Earth became visible. The sun peeked its crown over the horizon, bringing new light to the darkness.

And then came the screams.

They erupted from everywhere, all corners of the world. Men, women, and children in torment, begging their gods to save them. In the Middle East, hordes of helpless were impaled on great stakes of green wood, blood running from their stomachs down the smooth spears onto the desert sands, pooling below each one. Mothers reached for their children on adjacent spikes while onlookers snapped cell phone pictures and uploaded them to their friends.

In New York City. Beneath the shadow of a synagogue, a rabbi's hat fell from his head as he was tied to the back of a Ferrari. He clasped his hands in prayer, fervent words and tears begging for salvation, but it did not come—the engine started, and, within seconds, his words were but echoes in the spattered brain matter on the road. His daughters cried after him as they were being bound to their own cars, but his wife watched his death with a smile teasing her lips, surrounded by the cheering crowd.

Sunset Boulevard, Los Angeles. The Church of Scientology burned, flames licking the sky and smoke billowing out into a dark column that reached up for miles. The last few surviving members of the congregation begged their tormentors to release them, to save them, to help them...but an old man stuck his cane on a crawling woman's forehead and shoved her back into the fire, raising the stick and receiving a shout of triumph from his fellows.

All over the world, it happened. The faithful of all stripes—monotheists and polytheists, Christians, Ba'hai, Wiccans, and Buddhists, all found themselves trapped in torment and death, bleeding, burning, suffocating, weeping...

And, watching it all, God laughed.

~~~

Sam's muscles spasmed back to life, his fingers and feet twitching, his hands reaching for nothing. His chest heaved in quick bursts as if he could draw in enough air to drown out what he had seen. Between gasps, he cried out, his heart unable to bear the pain.

"No!" Sweat and tears spattered together on his hands as he tried to brace himself, tried to keep his face from smashing into the ground. "God, no! Why?" His eyes danced over unseen dangers, blind to the world.

He could hear scrabbling over stone nearby, rocks being shoved out of position by tennis shoe treads, but it was a moment before he real-
~~~

ized that he couldn't see, that his vision was gone.

"Sam!" Sara crested the rubble. "What happened?" He could feel the warmth of the fire spirits around her, and a soft glow began to fill the dark void of his sight. She took another two steps toward him, then stopped as she examined him.

"Wh...why are you naked?" She looked back and forth, confused. "Where are your...?"

Satan tumbled down the small rubble hill, stripping off her coat as she slid and wrapping it around Sam. She took him into her arms and he folded, reaching out for her like a life raft.

"It was...it was...oh, God, they were all..." Sam's words strung together, incoherent and rambling. "So much death, so much pain." He curled up as the emotions washed over his consciousness again. "No! Please, don't!"

Satan brought his head to her shoulder, stroking his hair. "Shhh. Calm down, Sam. It's okay. No one is dead."

Sara stood watching, her face and eyes wide with horror. She began to speak, but Satan waved her silent, mouthing *get him some water* before returning to her comforts.

They sat like that for over an hour, the bottle of water lying untouched, before Sam was able to speak or see again. He wiped his eyes, blinking several times, and sat back, covering himself as best he could with the jacket.

"God, I must look like fucking hell, don't I?" He ran one hand through his hair. "Holy shit."

"Sam?"

"What is it, Sara?"

"You're cursing."

Sam sighed, unable to laugh. "Yeah."

Satan reached out and put a hand on his shoulder. "Are you ready to tell us what you saw?"

Sam licked his lips, his eyes falling on the water bottle nearby. He stretched out a hand, then pulled it back to keep the coat from falling. "Tell you what. How about I get dressed first, and then we go home and talk about it?"

Sara pointed at the rubble around them. "I don't know if you're going to be able to find anything in there—you tore it apart pretty well."

Sam looked around for the first time. The heptagram was clear of debris, but the rest of the tomb had collapsed, shattered into small chunks of marble and basalt.

"Damn." Sam extended a hand, paused as his eyes touched the tattoo sigils on it, then pulled it back. *No. I can't do that unless I have to.* "Can you two help me look?"

"Of course." Satan stood and surveyed the disaster. "Do you know about where you put them down?"

"Um..." Sam put a knuckle to his brow. "They were outside the circle so they didn't interfere with the magic. I think I had them in that corner over there."

Satan and Sara followed his pointing finger, taking care not to fall as they moved over the rough landscape. No longer flush with adrenaline and panic, Sam shivered as the nighttime chill brushed against his body.

"I think I found 'em!" Sara's voice brought the older woman to her location. "See, his shirt is caught underneath that weird jackal-god's head."

Another tremor passed through him at those words. *Anubis.*

Satan nodded and knelt down, pushing with one hand against the blank-eyed god. "It's heavy. I'll push it, you can grab the clothes, all right?"

"Yeah." Sara dug around for a moment until she found the rest of Sam's garments, all folded in a neat pile before the rock trapped them. "Okay, got it!"

Satan dug her feet in for leverage, lifting with all the strength she could muster. Up, up, up came the golden jackal-head, metal flaking off as it rubbed against the sand and rock debris. Satan rolled the head away from Sam's clothes and Sara snatched the garments out of the hole before the appendage rocked back into its resting place.

"Thanks." Sam took his clothes and began shuffling himself into them. "So let's get home, all right? I..." He drifted off, shook his head, and regained his composure. "I think we've got a lot to talk about."

Sam hobbled through the desert, leaning on Satan's shoulder, until the group reached the place they had emerged from. Sam waved his left hand, reversing the incantation he had used, and they were swallowed up by the earth once more, tossed and battered.

I don't understand. Sam's thoughts turned inward as they traveled under the ocean toward California. *What the hell is going on?*

THE THIEF

"They were all dying." Despite having a blanket wrapped around him, Sam struggled to fight back chills. "And then...and then God was laughing about it, like He was enjoying it, like it was what He wanted."

There was silence, broken only by the continued mantras of the Fallen Angels as they prayed to the Father to forgive them, to welcome them back into Heaven.

The refrigerator door slammed and Satan emerged from the kitchen holding three cans of A & W Root Beer, picking her way around her brethren. "That makes no sense, Sam. Forgive me, but I think you must be mistaken about who was doing the laughing." She sat down on the couch next to the Keeper and passed over one of the cans. "God has nothing but love for all of His creations."

The sound of the shower began, distracting Sam for a second before he replied. "This was the Immersion, remember? It couldn't lie, or, at least, that's what the book said. It's supposed to be a perfect divination, designed to show me what it was I needed to see."

Satan shook her head, a sharp *hiss* heralding the escape of carbon dioxide from her soda. "It doesn't matter. Seeing is not the same as understanding. There could be factors at work that you were not privy to."

Sam ran a hand through his hair, scattering grains of sand over the blanket and coffee table. *Can't wait for my turn in the shower. Feel like I've walked three miles through a fucking sewer line.* "Maybe. That's not what it felt like, though."

There were several moments of silence; Satan adjusted her position on the couch, and Sam leaned back, allowing his head to loll on his neck.

"Who was the other man?" Satan tapped Sam on the knee, bringing him back to the moment. "The one that Anubis spoke to? What was his name again?"

"Jannes. And his brother was Jambres." Sam drew out his phone and laid it on the table. "I did a little bit of research. Those were the sorcerers that battled Moses in Exodus."

Satan's brow furrowed. "And he...he was wearing the amulet? The one with the red gem?"

Sam nodded. "Anubis said that it had spells on it to fight the angels." He turned his head to face his companion. "Were you...I mean, did he...?"

"Did he fight me?" Satan shook her head. "No, but I remember it now. All of Michael's hosts couldn't stop them as they tore through the first three Heavens."

"There's more than one Heaven?"

"Yes, just as there are several levels of Hell." She shuddered, took a sip of her drink, then laughed. "This is actually rather nice, you know. It tickles my tongue and my nose."

"Good old CO_2." Sam brought his can up in a mock toast. "So, you were saying?"

"Yes. You see, the Angels are not permitted above the third Heaven. Higher than that is the realm of the Archangels and the Voice. I never saw what happened there, but one of the sorcerers was thrown out in a fireball, and the other chased after him."

Sam's eyes were wide. "Thrown all the way back down to Earth?" Satan nodded. "Wow. That must be what I was seeing, the aftermath. The dead brother looked like he had been burned up pretty badly."

The water shut off, and Sam's gaze flicked over to the bathroom door. *About time, girl.*

"I imagine that it would have been—"

A very loud *crash* interrupted Satan's sentence, bringing both her and Sam to their feet. Sam leapt over the back of the couch toward the bathroom as Satan followed, and, without slowing down, Sam put his shoulder to the wood, splintering the hinges and sending the wreckage into the room.

"Sam!" Sara stood with a fluffy green towel wrapped around her body, staring at her adoptive father like he had just been revealed as a mass murderer. The shower curtain rod was lying halfway in the tub, and Sam's face transformed from concern to abject panic and embarrassment.

"Oh, God, I'm sorry, Sara!" He fumbled with the door-handle that he still held in his right hand. "I...I didn't mean..."

"Just get out!" Sara reached out and threw a washcloth into Sam's face. This shocked him back into action and he retreated, still mumbling apologies. Satan put her hands on his shoulders to guide him out.

"Oh my God." Sam had his face in his hands, and the rush of blood was hot against them. "I didn't mean, I didn't..."

Satan held her hands over her mouth, suppressing the laughter which was boiling up, struggling to escape. Several of the fallen Angels roused from their meditation to stare at the two in the hallway, tilting their heads as their wide eyes tried to make sense of the scene.

"You...you are so red right now!" The strangled gasps transitioned into guffaws and chuckles. "You look like...sweet merciful Heaven...you look like—"

Sam crossed his arms and turned his head. "Yeah, I get it. It's a human reaction. It's called being embarrassed by something."

Satan nodded, tears still running out of her eyes and her lips stretching over her teeth as she struggled to stop laughing. "But...but it's just...just..."

Sam felt a different burning in his face, now. *She doesn't understand.* He repeated the words to himself to fight the anger that was welling up inside. *It's not her fault. She doesn't get it.*

"...Sam?" Sara peeked around the doorframe. She wore one of her nicer outfits, foregoing a bit of comfort in favor of elegance. "Is everything okay?"

Satan stood up, taking huge gulps of air, before dissolving back into uncontrollable giggles and titters and howls.

"She's just learning a bit about human shame and embarrassment." Sam still didn't look at the Angel. "But in a few minutes, I think I'll need to have a discussion with her about empathy."

Sara glanced between the two of them. "Don't be too hard on her." Then she looked up toward her father. "Besides, it *was* kind of funny."

Sam threw his hands up in the air. "There was a huge crash! Someone could have broken through a window, or come up through the water pipes, or..."

Sara had already walked away, bringing her clothes and towel to the hamper outside the laundry room. Satan's laughter subsided, first into a steady stream of chuckles, then an occasional suppressed giggle, until Sam turned and looked her in the face.

"Are you done?"

Satan nodded. Her eyes were still teary and the corners of her lips quivered a bit, but she did not laugh again.

"Okay. Just for future reference, you shouldn't laugh at people when they're feeling embarrassed." Sam took a deep breath, releasing some of the angry tension before he continued. "It tends to make them feel bad, gets them upset."

Satan's eyes snapped to Sam's, flicking, looking at the lines on his face and the emotions he carried. "Oh, no." In an instant, her visage metamorphosed, transforming from suppressed mirth to horror and sadness. "I'm sorry, Sam. I'm..." She stretched out a hand toward him, then dropped it. "I didn't realize."

Sam reached out for her and rested his hand on her shoulder. "Don't' worry about it. I know it wasn't on purpose." When she didn't respond, he continued. "I'm not mad at you, you know. I was just...it's hard when you feel like a fool and someone laughs at you."

Satan exhaled. "I should have, though. That occurs, even in Heaven."

Sam blinked. "Wait...people tease each other in Heaven?"

Satan shook her head, her dark hair spreading in a semicircle. "Not exactly, but there are levels of status even there. Everyone is kind, but a mistake is chided by ones' superiors." She turned and went back into the main area of the living room. "While unavoidable, there is still the sting of Pride that bites when one is reprimanded."

"Exactly." Sam sat down, tossing one more glance toward Sara's closed door as he did. "I'm surprised she wasn't more freaked out afterwards, though. Teenagers are supposed to be."

Satan moved to the front window, looking outside. "I think they're also supposed to be unpredictable, aren't they?"

Sam leaned back in his seat, finished off his root beer. "You know, I can't quite figure you out. Sometimes it seems like you have no idea what it's like to be human, and then you come up with some ridiculously insightful thing like that to say."

The sinking sun silhouetted the Angel as she turned her head toward Sam. "I've watched humans for millennia, remember? Despite the best efforts of this meat brain to dumb me down, I still haven't forgotten everything yet."

Sam smirked. "Fair enough." He rubbed the back of his neck, took another deep breath, and reoriented himself. "So I think that the key must be Jannes, the sorcerer. Is it possible that he's still alive?"

"They were powerful magicians." Satan's eyes drifted downward, her lips pressing against one another. "They were able to fight through Angels without being harmed. They penetrated the vault of Heaven in their material bodies."

Sam looked toward the great silver tome lying on the dining room table. "I haven't seen anything in the Keys that would let me do any of that, but I haven't gotten through everything yet."

Satan sighed. "I wish I could remember more of the details, but I believe it was the Voice who finally drove them out." She waved one of her hands in the air as if brushing off lint from her sleeve. "I don't imagine it was very difficult for him."

"Him?"

Satan shrugged. "Generic pronoun of choice. 'It' just doesn't sound right in English."

"Right."

"So. You say you saw Jannes's ephemeral form as it...exchanged...with mine?" Satan glanced up and Sam nodded.

"More like merged with you, almost like a demonic possession."

"Then what? How do we track him down?" When Sam did not immediately answer, she crossed her arms and scowled. "No offense, Sam, but I don't want to stay in human flesh forever. I have work to do."

"I know that it must be terribly inconvenient." Sam's eyebrow rose. "All those fleshy sensations gumming up the Angel senses."

"It is!" Satan leaned against the wall. "I mean, first off, there's..." She trailed off, then shook her head. "You were teasing me."

"No!" Sam put a hand on his chest and made puppy-dog eyes. "Well...maybe a little."

She looked away, then back. "I suppose I deserve that."

Sam smiled as well. "Okay. Enough joking around." He strode over to the table, stepping between groups of outcast Angels, and flipped open the book. The heavy silver cover thumped against the table and samite pages riffled across his fingertips.

Satan approached, stopping about three feet from him.

"I don't see anything." He turned the pages faster. "It's not showing me anything."

Satan reached over and put a hand over his. The sudden contact brought Sam up short. He felt the heat from her body through his clothes. *When did she get so close?*

"Maybe you're asking the wrong question, Keeper." Her fingers moved, skin trailing over skin before landing on the cloth of the book. "Maybe..."

Sam glanced up toward the woman. Her skin was flushed, darker than usual, and her eyes were half-closed and staring at her own hand.

"Are you all right?"

Her neck swiveled, an inch at a time, eyes flicking over him as she brought her gaze to meet his. She licked her lips. The heat passing between them took on a familiar flavor, the carnal desire in her eyes reaching out for him, drawing him in.

Oh, crap. Sam took a step back, suppressing the reciprocal urge, drowning it in logic and fear. "No. No way."

"What? What's the matter?" Her words were slow, languid, someone just roused from sleep.

"You're..." Now Sam's face filled with blood. "You're being distracted by your body."

Satan's arms wrapped around her abdomen, but her eyes never left his. "I feel warm. Heavy." She breathed in through her nose. "And you smell good."

Satan scooted toward the young man, who moved back, trying to stay out of her reach. "What? I just...I just want..."

"I know exactly what you want, believe me." Sam took a deep breath. *Got to snap her out of it. Maybe...*

"And the Sons of God saw the daughters of Men that they were fair; and they took them wives of all which they chose."

Satan blinked, and some clarity returned to her eyes. "No, we didn't."

Sam shook his head, startled. "Wh...didn't what?"

"We never took men—or women—as mates. We can't." Satan withdrew a step. "We don't have those feelings."

Sam felt his heart drop in his chest. "Wait...you mean you don't...Angels don't..." He swallowed. "They don't feel love?"

"Of course we do!" Satan drew herself up, the cloudiness gone now, replaced by indignation. "We love, and we burn with love, but we do not *lust*, we do not *desire* another." Her eyes widened and she stumbled back toward the wall.

"That...that was lust, wasn't it? Oh, Father, forgive me..." She fell to her knees, clasping her hands in prayer, whispering supplications to the heavens.

Sam wasn't listening.

Why am I so upset? His mouth was dry, and his pulse pounded in his ears. *Of course she wouldn't care.* His hands clenched. *It's not even her fault. God made them this way.* Enamel ground against enamel.

Drip.

The sound was weak, muffled, from the other end of the house, and yet it caught Sam's ear as if he were listening for it down a long metal amplifier. He turned his head toward it.

It was coming from Sara's room.

There's no water in there. He moved, each step rippling up his body, each pace longer as he flowed into a run. *How long has it been since she went in there?*

Reaching the door, Sam resisted the urge to slam his shoulder into it and break it open. Instead, he knocked.

"Sara? Are you in there?"

There was no reply. Sam turned the knob, and it moved under his fingers.

"Sam?" Satan's voice drifted down the hallway. "Is everything all right?"

No. Sam felt his chest hitch. He couldn't breathe.

The entire room was soaked in briny water. Seaweed hung from the overhead fan, and sardines flopped on his daughter's bed. Starfish dotted the walls, unaware of how far they were from their home.

Satan came up behind him, and Sam heard her breath catch. "Oh, God...what happened?"

Sam caught the smell—the smell of the open sea, still trapped in the room—and felt the hot air from the open window.

"Marid." He stepped to the window and looked out. The yard was untouched save for one large, sodden imprint in the grass, as if a giant knee had pressed into the dirt. Sam's voice dropped an octave. "Marid."

He stormed out, shouldering past Satan on his way to his own room.

"But why?" Satan followed after, her head still turned toward the scene of Sara's disappearance. "Why would they take her?"

He tore off his shirt and threw it onto the bed before clearing a space on the floor. "I'll make sure to ask them when I get there."

"Get there?'" Satan brought her attention to bear on Sam. "What do you mean? Can't you just summon them and command them to give her back?"

"No." Sam knelt down and began inscribing his spell on the floor. "That's not good enough. Not this time." Once the inscription was complete, he pulled a notepad from his bookshelf, drawing new and different diagrams on each.

"Sam." Satan crouched outside of the nascent circle. "Don't act because of wrath. Wrath goes against—"

"This isn't wrath." Sam threw the marker across the room. It clattered against the wall, then rolled onto the floor in slow spirals. He shoved the papers into his pocket, then spun his hands in the air. Contrails of blue and green light floated off of him. "My home is supposed to be protected. My daughter should be safe in my home."

The light brightened, throwing stark shadows onto the walls. Sam's every movement shed more power, and his voice deepened until it echoed in the room. "Never again."

A huge thunderclap sounded, and, amidst a torrent of green-blue light, Sam opened up the passageway to the ocean, the passage left by the marid that had stolen Sara. The intangible sound of currents drifted through the opening, and filtered sunlight cascaded in waves onto Sam's floor. A school of sardines shot away from the portal, afraid of this new development.

Sam stepped through, disappearing into the dark ocean water. Naiads responded to his call, covering his skin and bringing oxygen to his lungs so that he could breathe. He glanced back, saw Satan's large eyes examining the portal, unsure and confused, and motioned for her to go back.

She hesitated, then nodded.

Where are you, you crazy bitch? Sam's eyes turned toward the open ocean, seeking traces of the marid that had come through here with

Sara. Remnants of magic, of genie, trailed throughout the sea, obscuring any path.

Fine. Sam dug through the papers in his pocket until he felt one sing under his fingers. Pulling it out, he held the multi-layered star out toward the water and bellowed.

"Queen of the Marid!" Instead of forming bubbles, as one might expect underwater, Sam's words pulsed out like sonar, making almost-discernible disturbances in the ocean. "Attend the Keeper of the Keys! God wills it!"

A small voice echoed in Sam's mind

(*deus vult*)

but vanished amidst the growing flames of rage licking at his brain. Three heartbeats passed with only the currents and the fish near-by to witness.

Then they came.

One by one, out of the darkness of the ocean, the giants strode forward. Here, in their native environs, they were almost impossible to see, and the sea life moved through them as if they were water themselves. Ten, twenty, thirty and more there were, dwarfing the man in their midst, watching him with their sea-blue eyes.

"Where is your queen?" Sam held one hand in his pocket, ready to draw forth another spell. "Does she not answer?"

"I am here."

The crowd of marid parted to reveal Savanth Lal, clad in battle armor that reflected the sunlight in pearlescent colors. In one hand she held a trident, and in the other a sword forged from liquid metal, changing shapes as she adjusted it.

"Why are you in my realm? No mortal has ever come here before."

Sam felt the naiads holding him up tremble. "You, or one of your subjects, have taken my daughter from my home."

The marid murmured before being cut off by their queen. "Perhaps we did. Perhaps we did not. Perhaps you have other enemies. You are not our master, Keeper, no matter how much you pretend to be so. Our business is our own." She waved him away. "You intrude."

For a moment, Sam could not speak. He watched as the smirk appeared on Savanth Lal's face, watched as it stretched her cheek and scar.

"You dare?" He moved forward through the water, and his hands began to glow a deep ruddy red. "You take my daughter from me, and you *dare* to say that?"

The assembled genies moved back, glancing between themselves and then back at their queen, who stood firm, her weapons at her sides, smug look remaining.

"Yes, I dare, Buckland." She pointed her sword toward him; its point was wider than he was, and the metal rippled in the currents. "What are you going to do about it? You are nothing to us, to the sea."

Sam could feel the power he commanded boiling in him, rising to his fingertips to be commanded. "I...nothing?" The water around him began to bubble and the naiads surrounding him screamed, unable to flee. "We will see which one of us is nothing when this is over, genie."

Savanth Lal laughed, her head rocking back and her hands moving to her hips. "Yes we shall."

Sam stretched forth one of his hands and drew out a spell with his other hand. "Submit to my power before it destroys you."

The marid's smile only widened.

The Keeper raised the paper high, his tongue moving to invoke the magic.

You should guard yourself, Keeper of the Keys, for even such as you can fall.

Sam's head snapped around, searching for the source of that voice. He saw no one. *Just my imag-*

Sam felt a numbing tingle spreading over his body, starting with his fingers and sweeping up his arm, enveloping his chest, and expanding to the rest of him. Wherever the tingle passed, all feeling was lost; as it approached his neck, his breathing became ragged and harsh and fear clawed at his mind.

Oh, God. The cold numbness tickled his cheeks, and he could hear the Queen's laughter, tinny in his ears. *Help me, God. Please help me.*

He felt his lips move.

"God isn't here, remember?"

THE DECEIVER

Satan watched the portal, her mind warring with itself. *Is he all right?* She squeezed the fingers of one hand with the other. *How long has it been?* Her eyes flicked to the alarm clock on Sam's dresser. Ten minutes.

Calm down. It's going to take a little bit of time for him to get her back. For the third time, Satan sat down on Sam's bed, only to spring back up a few seconds later and resume pacing.

I wish I could see what was going on in there. The sea behind the portal was featureless, with only the occasional fish or sunbeam breaking the landscape. *Why am I worried? He's the Keeper of the Keys. He's going to be fine.*

Still nothing. She licked her lips, tasting the salt from her nervous sweat. *Maybe I should go in there.* The laugh which burst out was bitter, almost angry. *Like I could do anything anyway. I can't even muster enough energy to see him. I'd just slow him down.*

The portal undulated, pulsing, a sullen grey hole in the brightly-lit room. *I don't know what I'm thinking.* She sighed. *I'd have to breathe water, after all. Unless the portal is in an enchanted water palace that lets in human beings.* She shook her head. *Not likely.*

The urge grew, and Satan approached the entrance, stretching her fingers out to within inches of its surface. Ripples crossed from one end of the doorway to the other. *I wonder what would happen if I put my head in, looked around.* An irrational giggle rose up, but she stifled it. *Wonder if some sort of shark or something would bite it off.*

Another half-step forward. She peered into the darkness, her nose a hair's breadth from it.

This close, she could see the sediment carried by the ocean currents, could catch glimpses of tiny striped fish darting in and out of view.

I can't see my reflection. Her eyes traced the outline of the door before returning to the area in front of her. *I wonder if –*

At that moment, a large white shape surged into view, breaking through the water and entering the bedroom. The sudden movement knocked Satan down, and she landed on the floor in the middle of a new puddle of water.

What... Sam stood above her, holding an unconscious Sara in his arms. His wet jeans clung to him like a second skin, water raining down from him onto the hardwood. The portal behind him was closing, and he turned and dropped Sara onto the bed, where she bounced and flopped to the creak of bedsprings.

"What happened?" Satan braced herself on the bedframe and pushed up to stand. "I was worried, so—"

Her words were cut off as Sam covered her mouth with his own, a combination of seawater and sweet fruit overwhelming her. Her eyes widened and, despite herself, she responded, moving against him before regaining her senses. She recoiled, covering her lips with one hand and holding the other out in a warding gesture. Sam's grin stretched across his face, and he raised his eyebrows.

"What's wrong?" He tilted his head and smiled, water running down his chest and his abdomen, highlighting the results of many hard hours in the gym. Satan gasped and stepped back.

Not this again. She could feel the emotion from before, the lust, bubbling up in her body. As she inhaled, she was conscious of Sam's smell floating off him in the now-humid air and warmth began to spread though her lower belly. *No! I won't. I can't.*

"Cat got your tongue?" Sam shrugged, then sat at the foot of the bed and removed one of his shoes, pouring the water out onto the floor. "Anyway, they gave her back once I threatened them a bit, knocked a few of them around." The other shoe and two socks joined the shirt in a pile on the floor. "Was pretty easy, actually, but I'm not really surprised."

Satan's eyes were confused. "Did...did they tell you why they took her?" Her hand was still up in a defensive position, but her stance changed, opening. "I mean, it didn't make much sense to me."

Sam sighed and stood again. "Didn't ask." His fingers moved to the button of his jeans. "Didn't matter."

Satan's eyes locked onto his actions, even as her mouth spoke. "But...don't we need to know that? What if it has something to do with—"

A loud *zip* sound broke through her sentence. "I know I'm something to look at, but I need to change out of these wet clothes."

Satan's cheeks filled with blood, and she pressed her hands against them in a futile attempt to hide it. "Oh, God, I'm sorry, I just –"

"...So, unless you're staying to watch, you should probably go get changed yourself." Sam's hands were still on his zipper, and one corner of his mouth was turned up in a smile. "Not that I mind, you understand. I am quite stunning."

Satan shook her head, backpedaling out of the door. "No, no, that's...that's..."

The door shut in her face, and she could hear Sam laughing through the wooden paneling. She moved to the side, closing her eyes as she leaned against the wall and tried to marshal her thoughts and will.

Damn flesh. Her fists clenched until nails dug into the palms. *Always makes it so hard to think.* One arm stretched across her stomach as if to hold in the emotions roiling within. It felt as if electricity were running through a circuit within her.

She kept picturing Sam's muscles moving under the thin patina of water.

Stop it.

The half-grin he gave her as he suggested that she stay.

No! You're an Angel. You desire no one!

The feeling of his lips against hers in that brief moment before she broke away.

Tears welled up in her eyes and she slid down the wall, weeping, unable to control the feelings of helplessness and confusion.

Why, Lord? Why are you testing me like this? Have I grown too prideful?

Sam's bedroom door opened and Satan's head snapped up. Sara, her eyes a little bleary but moving well, stepped out of the door.

"Make sure you close that!" Sam's voice drifted through the opening. "I've got to finish getting cleaned up."

Sara nodded and shut the door. She turned to see Satan wiping the tears away, trying to hide the emotional turmoil within her.

"Are you all right?" The girl knelt down beside the weeping Angel, who laughed and shook her head.

"No. No, I'm not. But you shouldn't be worrying about me." She stood up and wrapped Sara in a hug. "You were kidnapped! Sam and I were worried about you."

Sara shrugged. "I don't remember any of it. I went into my room, and then suddenly I was waking up in Sam's bed while he was brushing his hair." She shook her head. "I've never seen him that worried about it before. He was leaning in to the mirror, making sure that each strand was perfect."

A flash of Sam's face, that half-smile, the hair falling over his eyes. Satan closed her own and rubbed her upper arms. "He was so angry. I was...I don't know. When he went in there I thought that he was going to get into a fight of some kind, maybe get hurt trying to rescue you."

"Are you all right?" Sara leaned in, just a bit, examining the Angel. "You look..."

Satan averted her eyes. "Yes. Yes, I'm fine."

"...Okay." Sara backed off. "Are you hungry? I am. Let's go grab something in the kitchen."

~~~

Goddamn you! Sam screamed as his eyes watched Sara walk out of his room. *Release me! Let me go!*

"Oh, I don't think so, Keeper." The demon wearing his skin laughed as he turned back to the mirror, adjusting the fall of one strand of hair. "I think I'll just keep you in there where you can't do any harm."
~~~

Sam pushed against the restraints on him; it felt like he was trapped in a strait-jacket, unable to move his will out of the small pocket of his mind he occupied. *What do you want? Why are you doing this?*

"You affronted me." Sam's lips moved back from his teeth and the demon picked a small fragment of lettuce from between them. "You know, you really should take better care of yourself. You're a very good-looking man, after all."

So this is just because you're pissed off?

The demon shrugged. "Mostly. Why? Do you think you're so important that it took some sort of conspiracy, that this is some long-term, laid out plan?" He laughed Sam's laugh, but with more cruelty and anger than Sam had heard in his own voice before. "Sorry, buddy, but you're just not all that. I'm glad you thought you were, though, to be honest. Made things a lot easier."

Sam stopped struggling. *If you hurt them, I'll destroy you. I'll send you back to Hell where you will burn forever.*

Satisfied with what he was seeing in the mirror, the demon walked over to Sam's closet. "You need to spend some more money on your wardrobe, my friend. You're missing, like, everything that would look good on you." He reached out and brought down an aqua button-up shirt, shook his head, replaced it. "And, no, you won't destroy me. You're about the only one who could really get me out of here, and you're trapped." He turned back to the mirror, and the look in his eyes made Sam recoil.

"I think I'm going to have a lot of fun with this." He licked the pad of his thumb and ran it along his eyebrows. "After all, how many of us have ever gotten to play with a Keeper of the Keys? Or make it with an Angel?" He waggled his eyebrows at his reflection. "Did you see the way she was checking you out? If you put a little effort into it, you'd be banging Cherub all day long."

Sam set to fighting the internal bonds again, but they yielded like firm rubber, giving but never breaking, rebounding back to their original position, holding him tight within his mind.

"Oh!" The demon's smile grew as he slid an arm into a red silk sleeve. "And you don't even have an heir, do you, Sammy? What a shame. Her name isn't in the book yet." The other arm followed suit and the hands went to buttoning. "Wonder how long it's going to be before you take a swan dive onto the I-5 or something. French-kiss a woodchipper, maybe. "

His face hardened. "I win, Buckland. In Lucifer's name, I win." He turned about and headed for the door.

Sam had no reply.

~~~

"Hey, Sam!" Sara called out as the *creak* of her father's door reached their ears. "We made you a BLT!"

Satan put the finishing touches on the sandwich, adding a dollop of mustard and placing the slice of bread on top. Her eyes came up as Sam exited the hallway.

"Oh my God."
~~~

Sam was a vision. He was dressed in a fitted red silk button-up shirt that showcased the powerful musculature he usually kept hidden, and black jeans that clung to him. His hair was loosely combed and his smile lit up his entire face.

"Was that for me?" He put a hand on his chest. "Because it'd better not have been for anyone else."

Satan felt the ever-present blush threatening again, so she looked down and pushed the sandwich plate to the other side of the table.

Sara cocked an eyebrow. "So what's our next move, Sam?" She pulled out her chair, sat down, and bit into her own BLT, speaking around the mouthful of lettuce and bacon. "I mean, we've got to figure out what that vision meant, don't we?"

Sam waved his hand. "Don't worry about it. I'll get to it soon enough." He took a bite, then leaned back and rolled his eyes as he hummed. "This is sooooo good!"

Satan pulled out her chair, breathing in as she tried to calm herself. *This is ridiculous. If humans can get along all day without throwing themselves at each other, then I should be able to! I –*

A smell cut her thought short. Cherries. A sudden, very strong aroma of overripe cherries.

"Sara, were there any cherries in the refrigerator?" Satan started looking around for the source. "It smells like we left some out."

Sara shook her head. "No, we ran out of cherries a couple of weeks ago and Sam never got any more at the store." She took a breath. "I don't smell anything, anyway. Maybe it's drifting in from somewhere else."

Sam laughed. "Or maybe you're craving them. Tell you what—I'll run out and grab a pound or two." He tore a paper towel from the roll on the table and dabbed at the mayonnaise on his mouth, then stood. He spent a few moments adjusting his shirt and brushing off the breadcrumbs before speaking again.

"And when I get back, the two of us can...pop a few of those cherries, mmm?" His eyes caught Satan's, and her breath hitched.

Sara looked back and forth between the two of them. "Wow. Okay, I think I'm gonna just..." She edged away from the table, then, as soon as her chair was clear, bolted out of the room, leaving the seat to topple over onto the floor. Sam watched her go, chuckling.

"At least she knows to get out of the way when her father has things to take care of."

Satan's mind was careening. *What is going on? He's never acted like this before.*

His face drew down as he glanced over the still-wailing fallen Angels. "This is gonna cramp my style, though. All these whining bitches." He rolled his eyes. "But where there's a will there's a way, I suppose. Nice, romantic music, the right wine, cheese."

"I..." Her face was a study in confusion and indecision. Her eyes danced back and forth, fighting the duel between desires—one to accept, to drink deeply of the man before her and let the hormones wash through her body, and one to question, to fight, to wonder. "That sounds...really nice, Sam."

"Oh, it will be, I promise." He leaned up against the bar, caught a glimpse of himself in a picture frame, and reached up to adjust his hair. "What do you think? Should I keep it like this, or maybe grow it long? I think I could pull off long, don't you?"

Focus. Now that his eyes were off her, Satan was able to recover a measure of herself. She took another breath, and again the thick, cloying aroma of overripe cherries hit her.

Did the marid do something to him? Something's *wrong.*

"Well, I suppose I'll let it grow out. I can always cut it if I don't like it." Several more seconds passed as Sam examined his face from every angle, waggling his eyebrows and winking at his reflection.

Then he turned around, and there was no mistaking his expression. He leered at Satan, his eyes lingering on her chest, her hips, her legs. He licked his lips as he advanced toward her.

She bumped into the wall in her retreat.

"Uh-oh." His grin grew as he swooped in, wrapping one arm about her waist and lifting her toward his face. "Another Angel in danger. I'd better make sure I take care of her." He brushed his lips against her ear and slipped a hand around the curve of her ass, squeezing and pulling Satan tight against him. "In the Biblical sense, of course."

The involuntary inhalation that followed his caress led to a coughing fit; the cherry smell overpowered her, drove the oxygen out of her lungs.

"Are you all right?" He hadn't changed position, but both his hands were moving, sending thrills through her skin.

As the coughing subsided, she tried to respond. "Yes, I'll be—"

Her words cut off as she felt the length of him against her thigh, pressing against her through several layers of clothing, but unmistakable.

Please Lord, grant me strength and forgive me my trespasses. Almost of its own accord, her left hand began its journey, moving along her own body toward his. *Lead me not into temptation, but—*

"Heavenly Creator, deliver us from evil!"

The sudden outburst drew several more from the crowd of fallen Angels; Sam's lustful gaze flickered, then fell, and he exhaled through his nose, nostrils flaring like a bull as he turned a scowl on the transgressor.

"Damn it. Fine." He stepped back, out of easy contact. "I'll go pick up those cherries and we can have a...proper evening."

Satan was dazed; her mind fogged with desire and lust, but something in what he said tickled her awareness. "W...what? What was that?"

Sam raised an eyebrow. "I promised you a pound or two of cherries, didn't I? I'm sure you've never had them before."

Oh, God. Her eyes widened. *The cherries. Vassago. Of course.*

Sam turned back, and Satan rearranged her expression. *I hope he didn't notice...*

"So? Can we...finish this when I get back?"

Oh, God. Now what? Angels don't know how to lie.

Satan shuffled her feet, looked down at the floor. Twisted her hands. Stammered. "I...I don't..."

"Don't worry." The smell of cherries strengthened, and she looked up to see Sam's face inches from her own. "It'll be like nothing you've ever felt before, I promise...Angel mine."

The aroma in her nostrils seemed to drain all of the physical craving from her body like a plug pulled from a drain. She forced a smile. "I...I believe it."

Sam straightened, laughed again, ran a hand through his hair. "See you soon." Whistling, he strolled out of the house, grabbing the keys from their perch on his way out.

Satan ran to the door, peering through the peephole, watching him leave. He pressed buttons on his phone and slipped a headset into his ear.

"Can you direct me to the Chief's desk, please? This is Sam Buckland. Yes, I'll hold." His voice faded as the car door slammed.

When he was out of sight, she pressed her ear against the wood, waiting to hear the car take off, to hear the tires thump on their way out of the driveway and into the road.

She slid the lock shut, fixed the chain.

Then she was off, running to Sara's room and trying the doorknob. It was locked.

"Sara!" Satan kept looking back toward the front door. *He could break through that like it was nothing.* "Sara, I need to talk to you!"

Sara's door *clicked,* then came open. The young girl's brow was wrinkled.

"What do you want?"

Satan moved in, pushing Sara into the room and closing the door behind her. "I don't know how much time we have. How close is the nearest grocery store?"

Sara fumbled for her words. "What? I...I don't –"

Satan rubbed her face, her hands jittery, trying to get control of the chaos in her mind. "Sara—I think that Sam's been possessed. That cherry smell was the smell of a pride demon, one of Lucifer's lieutenants."

Sara shook her head. "Wait, what? But how? When? And I didn't smell anything."

"You wouldn't. I'm actually surprised that I did—I guess there's still some of the Angel in this flesh-sack after all." Satan grimaced, grasping Sara by the shoulders. "Look, if I'm right, then we're in danger, and so is Sam. If a demon has hold of the Keeper, then, as soon as it's done having fun with him, it's going to kill him."

"What?!" Sara began to pace around the room, mumbling to herself. "Okay, the nearest store is about fifteen minutes away. You figure shopping time, that there'll be a line...we probably have just over an hour." She looked back up toward the older woman. "Is there a way we can free him, get the demon out of him, whatever?"

"I don't know." Satan sighed. "Very few mortals know how to conduct an exorcism today, and since we seem to be cut off from Heaven I can't request aid there."

Sirens sounded outside. Sara peeked out of her window. "What the hell? There's like thirty police cars and ambulances all out front."

Satan moved the blinds aside as well. "Oh, no."

Emergency responders were moving, taking traumatized Angels into the back of ambulances and shuttling them off, wrapping them in blankets as they shuffled, unresisting. Police officers were locked in conversation, pointing toward the house and doors. Several began to move around the house, heading for the back door.

"Damn it." Satan stepped away from the window. "This is bad."

"Yeah." Sara ducked her head back behind the curtains. So now what?"

"I don't know." Satan rubbed her eyes with her hands.

"Hey, what about that book? The Seals or whatever? Did the demon take that?"

Satan shook her head. "That's not helpful. It would take us months at least to figure out how to—"

She stopped. *Wait. That should work.*

"What? What is it?"

"There is someone who might be able to help us, but we need to get out of here first." Satan tensed as she heard the knock at the front door.

"Open up! Police!" The Angels in the front began to shuffle and renewed wails broke out. "Open the door! We hear you in there!"

Sara moved to the side window. "Hey, the fence is only a little bit out. Can you get over it?"

Satan gritted her teeth. "If the alternative is being locked in prison while the Devil's lackey kills the Keeper of the Keys, I can do pretty much anything I need to."

Sara slid the window open. "Okay. Let's go."

THE QUEEN

Sam bit back his joy as he watched Satan's face transform from lustful and confused to wary and watchful. *And he didn't even notice. What an arrogant son of a bitch.*

He closed his mental eyes once more, listening to her sad attempts to hide her realization from the demon, laughing to himself when the bastard missed the whole thing. Then he flexed his mind like a hand, preparing it for exercise.

All right. I just have to have faith that she'll be able to figure something out. Sam visualized his physical body, imagining that he had breath, a pulse, hands and feet. The sensations prickled through his mind, grounding him, giving him something to hold on to.

He felt himself relax, running his fingers through the grass which appeared as he reached for it. Soon he could feel the sunlight playing on his face and hear wind in the trees.

And, of course, he could smell honeysuckle.

He opened his eyes. *All right, it worked. Thank God.* The meadow looked just like it did every time he dreamt of it, down to the stereotypical red-and-white checkered cloth with the picnic basket. *The only thing missing is...* He shook his head. *Doesn't matter anyway. I have more important things to worry about than that.*

Sam stretched out his hands, watching the sigils playing on his skin. He grinned as memories bubbled up in his mind. *I never thought that I'd be* happy *that I was almost killed by a sloth demon.*

"Okay." He tried the word, feeling it vibrate through his imaginary throat, hearing it echo through the imaginary air. "Okay. I can't wake up because the bastard has my body, but no one said I had to stay in it."

He shook his head. "I sure as hell hope that they figure something out before I end up on the 6 o'clock." He squared his shoulders. "Egyptian sorcerers. Egyptian magic. I saw Anubis, which means that there must be other Egyptian...things." The crescent-moon mark on his right hand tingled, and his left scratched at it while he mused. "But there isn't any magic in the Seals for finding other...well, anything. It's all about angels and demons and genies." He laughed at himself. "Nothing about other gods."

But dreams are connected to the dead, Samuel.

Sam's head snapped around and his surroundings wavered for a moment. "Who...?"

No sounds came, no answer to his question.

"All right, whoever-you-are. I'm game." Sam closed his eyes again, bringing to his mind an image of the Great Pyramid. He dredged up every image of it he could remember, from high school textbooks to history documentaries and news reports. He breathed his will into it, bending his dream, feeling the ground shiver under the new weight.

When he relaxed, the full, marble-covered glory of Khufu's pyramid rose up into the air before him. The top cleared the clouds, causing an effect reminiscent of the classical Mount Olympus, complete with circular-swirling stormclouds. The sky was dark, with thunder and lightning erupting in sharp staccato bursts, shaking the trees and the grass around him.

"I didn't imagine *that*." Sam smiled. "I guess that's a good sign, then, huh?" He lifted his hands and rose through the air. The atmosphere sparked and sizzled as he cut through it toward the roiling clouds, but he pressed forward, covering his eyes with one arm.

Entering the cloud bank was like diving into a deep, slow-moving river. Sam choked on the thickness of the vapor, and his sight was blocked by the sheer density. He moved his hands through the gauzy cotton.

It even feels like water, it's so heavy. He coughed, sputtering a little before he could regain control. *Got to get past it.*

Sam could see flashes of light flickering within the cloud, indistinct but for their intensity. The water on his skin was chilling, and he had to repress involuntary shivering. Upward and upward he pushed. *Am I even going up anymore? I can't see anything.*

His head broke the surface, sending water droplets scattering in a thousand directions. He brought his hands up to wipe the liquid from his eyes, sputtering and treading water.

"Where the hell am I?" Sam looked around. He had surfaced in the midst of a vast river, stretching farther than he could see in three directions. In the fourth, the shoreline rose up about one hundred feet distant.

What's making that light? Sam paddled his way over to the shore and waded through the reeds to get out of the water. He took a few steps up the bank and looked over the landscape.

"Now what?" A huge ship, hundreds of feet long and almost as wide, wrought from a deep brown wood, was drifting down the river. The water glistened on the sides of the boat. At the prow of the ship, he could make out the form of a woman, standing with spear drawn, leveled downstream.

And it was glowing with a glorious golden radiance, casting off the darkness as it moved.

Sam started running down the shore after the ship, trying to keep within the radius of its light. He stumbled and tripped over unseen obstacles as he hurried, pushing aside reeds and squelching through the warm mud clinging to his toes.

The barge went over a small dip in the river, splashing the dark water as it came back to rest. In the brightening gloom ahead, Sam could make out an archway stretching over the length of the river. It was pitted stone with green and black growths spidering over its surface, obscuring the carvings that once bedecked its surface. The river itself was blocked by a great wooden gate that severed the waterway.

Sam caught his breath. *Funny how you can get tired in a dream.* He took the moment to watch the ship cast sunlight sparkles over the river. The beams pushed back the darkness almost like it was a living thing, and the grasses and reeds near the edge of the river unfolded as the light touched them, stretching toward the barge.

A massive snake stretched upward from the gate, its grey scales glistening with river-water and its fangs distended and primed for attack. "Ssspeak my name before you can pass, goddess, or ssspend the rest of eternity on the river, trapped." Fire erupted from its mouth as it menaced the ship, but the woman at the fore did not flinch.

"Samuel Buckland."

"Yeah?" The word broke out of Sam's lips unbidden. The goddess turned toward him, and, despite the distance, Sam could make out the chair-shaped headdress and the ankh that she clutched in her right hand. She raised her left and beckoned for him, her voice carrying over the intervening distance with ease.

"Please, come. My husband is waiting for you."

Sam began to walk before he fully decided that he was going to. The woman was beautiful;

mature, with wisdom etched in the gentle lines over her eyes and her mouth. To Sam's magical Sight, she thrummed with suppressed power, yet there was a hollowness within her, an echo in the depths of her being.

The snake turned, hovering over Sam as he approached the barge. Burning spittle fell from its mouth around him, but it made no move to harm him.

One of those fangs would go right through me and pin me to the ground. Sam did his best not to look up as he walked under the cavernous opening, avoiding singe marks in the ground. He waded through the river until he was within reach of the barge. A small rope ladder stretched from the deck to the water's surface, and he took hold of the wooden crossbars, hauling himself up to the ship.

The goddess held out her hand to help him on the deck. Her skin was warm and just a bit rough, and her eyes twinkled down at Sam.

"Who...who are you?"

She smiled at him, then turned to address the gate guardian. "You are the Guardian of the

Desert. Let the barque pass, in accordance with Ma'at."

The serpent let out one last hiss before the wood of the gate began to creak and the river water rushed through the expanding opening. The barge rolled in the swell, then began to nudge forward again.

The goddess sighed, her shoulders slumping for a moment before she straightened herself once more. "We have an hour before the next Gate, Keeper, and the same to the one after, where my husband awaits you. That should be enough time for us to talk."

Sam shook his head. "I don't know how much time I have. My body...a demon has my body right now, and it's only a matter of time before he decides to get rid of it."

She nodded, still looking out over the water. "Unfortunately, the barque cannot be rushed. It moves as it has moved since the beginning, and will until the end, as long as there are those of us willing to guard it." A small frown touched her lips. "Though there are fewer now than there once were."

"Why?" Sam stepped up beside her and watched the landscape unfold in the light of the ship. The river was more narrow here, and he could see people moving on its banks in an imitation of ancient villages in Egypt. They waved as the barge passed, and the goddess raised her ankh to cheers from the crowd.

"They have no idea what the world outside has become. Osiris has not the will to tell them, and I have no wish to defy my husband in his own realm."

"Are you Isis, then?" Sam glanced at her sidelong. "I'm not up on my Egyptian legends, but I didn't think you lived in the underworld."

Isis sighed again. "I did not, until our people lost their faith. Osiris commanded that we withdraw into the Duat, and, in the absence of Ra's commandments, we did so."

"What happened to Ra?"

Isis turned and looked fully into Sam's face. "He is dead."

Sam tried not to show his shock. "How did he die?"

She turned away again. "He gave up his own existence. My son Horus followed him, and Sobek. Some others. They chose not to struggle against Yahweh anymore." She took a shuddering breath. "I do not pretend there are not days I think of joining them."

"I don't understand." Sam came closer; the goddess was taller by a few inches, and he could feel her strength baking off of her. "Why are you struggling against G...Yahweh? I didn't even—"

"Didn't know that we existed? Unsurprising." Isis laughed, a sound filled with broken glass and blood. "Yahweh prefers not to admit such to his followers."

"You mean God is lying to people?"

"Not lying, except by omission. He came into existence as we did, but he has proven victorious, spreading across the globe and stamping out the worshippers we all held dear." She spread her hands. "Few come to the Duat now, and our power dims. Only here, in the presence of the faithful, can we still act with some semblance of what we were once capable of."

"No." Sam shook his head. "God created the Heavens and the Earth. He created the Angels. He's the only true deity that there is."

Isis smiled down at Sam. "I am not here to argue theology with you, Keeper of the Keys. We have more important things to discuss. Perhaps, one day, when this is over, you will return to me and we can speak further."

Sam bit back his burning urge to question the Egyptian goddess. "...All right. So what are you here to discuss with me? Why is the Queen of the Gods on a boat with a mortal man who doesn't even follow her religion?"

"All good questions." A few moments passed; waves brushed against the cedar planks of the barge. "A mutual enemy of ours threatens the Earth."

Sam's attention narrowed, a stiletto in the dark. "The sorcerer?"

"His name is Jannes. He was once one of our greatest followers. When we knew Yahweh had sent his messenger to see Pharaoh, we ensured that Jannes and his brother Jambres were members of the royal court so that they could challenge Moses." She chuckled. "As you know, they failed. Yahweh's power overcame theirs."

Sam waited, listening, as the ship began to take a wide turn in the river, bending around huts and cookfires.

"They did not take this well. After the Exodus, they traveled the world, seeking out new magics, learning new sorceries. They discovered the secret paths to Yahweh's realm and they attacked it."

Sam's grip tightened on the railing. In his mind's eye, he could see the two men, Jannes and Jambres, fighting with the Angelic host on their way through Heaven.

"They failed again. I do not know why." Isis slumped her shoulders, and Sam felt her presence flicker. "After Anubis took Jambres, we lost Jannes. He no longer prayed or made sacrifices to us."

Sam couldn't hold back. "You didn't think to keep track of him? Wasn't he important to you?"

Isis turned toward Sam once more. "You must understand the time, Samuel. We were engaged in a war for our survival. The Exodus and the events brought on by Azrael had taken a great toll on us. The Duat was filled with the souls of those in judgment, and those of us above were trying to hold our people together." She held out a hand, and, upon it, a small globe appeared, a perfect model of the Earth. Blue and green lights sparkled on the surface, concentrated in Africa but scattered throughout other nearby landmasses.

"When Yahweh's people fled, your Angels went with them, helping them spread throughout the land of Jerusalem." The green lights multiplied and moved outward, occupying more and more space, while the blue lights flickered and stayed in one place. "They grew in number and strength, then began converting our citizens, as well as the citizens of other faiths. My people fell to Ptolemy, then to Cleopatra."

"I get it." Sam looked out over the nearby shores, at the people gathered there. "You were too busy to keep track of one man."

"Time is different to us, Keeper of the Keys, but even we knew that he had not entered the

Duat. We did not have the luxury of considering this further until the completion of our retreat, almost two thousand years ago."

"So what do you know?"

Get to the point, already!

Isis gave him a sidelong glance.

"I'm sorry, but my friend is in trouble, there's a whole bunch of Angels that have had their wings cut off, and if this guy is responsible, I need to get back out there and find him."

Isis reached out a hand and laid it on Sam's; warmth flooded his body, unknotting his muscles, relaxing his thoughts. "Patience. Your enemy has waited for millennia for this opportunity. At least take the time necessary to learn what you need to know to face him."

"You're right, you're right." Sam took a deep breath. "So what else can you tell me?"

"When we realized that he had found a way to extend his life, it was already too late to search for him. We had to wait until he revealed himself in some way."

Sam exhaled through his teeth. "Yeah. He made a real big entrance. What do you know about his plans?"

Isis' lip curled up at the corner. "Nothing. My husband knows the rest, I believe, and he has not told me."

Sam stared for a moment, incredulous. "Seriously?"

Her smile spread. "Yes." She turned fully towards Sam and put her hands on his shoulders. "Remember that he is the Lord of the Dead here in the Duat. He expects your respect, and, although he is waiting for you, he may...he may have forgotten."

What, is he senile or something? Sam swallowed his immediate response to form a kinder one. "How would he have forgotten?"

Isis shook her head. "Many things preoccupy his time. Survival, mostly. When one sees all the world as your enemies, it becomes difficult to remember that you may have allies as well."

"Oh. Okay." Sam looked back out over the river, watching the ripples from the barque's passage glimmer in the ship's radiance. "So, nothing to do but wait, I guess."

"That is what we have said for centuries, Keeper. But now, the waiting is over."

THE REPENTANT

Satan pushed open the door of the Los Angeles Mission, then turned and watched as Sara untangled herself from the bus and ran to join her. A pair of small children playing on the stairs looked up as they passed, pressing themselves against the door.

"So he's here?" Sara put her hand over her mouth as if to quiet her own voice.

"You're the one who did the research. I just hope you were right." Satan stepped fully into the building, running her eyes over the crowd. The place was filled with supplicants needing assistance, seated at tables and standing with hot bowls in their hands. A young woman in a pink T-shirt held an elderly man in coat and slacks as he cried. A pair of old ladies sang hymns to each other, and several men and women ladled food into their mouths like robots, devoid of independence.

"After what happened, why didn't he go to jail?" Sara's voice was low, and she huddled close to her companion. The smell of human flesh mingled with savory spices and herbs in a disconcerting waltz of aroma.

"You'll need to ask him that." Satan pointed toward the soup line, where the volunteers were serving the meals to the residents. Sandwiched between a portly old man with thin grey hair and a beaming smile and a college-age woman with glasses and a slight sneer was a tall, mid-thirties gentleman. His eyes were bright and cheerful as he worked. He nodded as each person came up to his station and asked for something.

"How are you today, Freida?" He pushed his wire-frames up his nose before dishing the fruit.

"Things will start looking up for you soon. God bless."

"I hope you're right." Frieda sighed as she looked down at her son. "I'm hoping that we'll be back on our feet by Christmas."

The man smiled. "I'll pray for you."

"Thank you, Mr. Caitlin."

Satan slid into the line and motioned for Sara to join her. The two shuffled forward, refusing the offered comestibles until they arrived at his station.

"Are you two new?" He adjusted his glasses again, then smiled. "I'd shake your hand, but I need to keep them on this side of the line. Sanitary reasons, you know." He glanced from Satan to Sara, then back. "Excuse me for asking, but is she yours? We get a lot of separated—"

Satan raised a hand. "Gregory Caitlin?"

Gregory's eyes narrowed, skipping from one to the other of them, then searching the crowd over their shoulders before returning. "Is this...are you more interviewers?" His body tensed and his brow furrowed. "I'm just trying to do good here. I don't need to be bothered or reminded of anything." His hand clenched around the tongs. "Now move on or I'll have you removed. You don't have the right to—"

Sara leaned closer, her voice low. "Mr. Caitlin, my father is Sam Buckland. He's in trouble and he needs your help."

Gregory's eyes scanned her face, then Satan's. The anger gave way to cautious acceptance, and he nodded. "I can give you five minutes." He straightened up and turned to the older gentleman. "Hey, Jorge, I'm taking my break now, okay?"

~~~

"I don't believe this." Gregory ran his hand through his hair and paced up and down the alleyway. "I didn't know him very well, but to get caught by a demon like that?" He stopped his walking. "How did it happen?"

"He was confronting a marid over the abduction of his daughter." Satan put a hand on Sara's shoulder. "When he returned, he was..." The Angel rolled her shoulders, looking at the ground. "He was different. I didn't notice why at first."
~~~

Gregory nodded, his lips pursed as he considered. "Then we don't have a lot of time, do we? I mean, if he's under the control of a demon, then—"

"Exactly." Satan began to power-walk toward the end of the alley, then turned back to the rest. "Are you coming?"

Gregory nodded, and Sara rolled her eyes. "Geez, for an Angel you sure are pushy, you know."

"What?" Gregory's hands sprung up and he assumed a defensive position. "An Angel?" He stared Satan down, his lower lip quivering until he straightened his spine.

"You?" He retreated a step. "Why? Why are you here for me?" He put his back against a nearby Dumpster. "I've tried to do better, dammit. I know that I did horrible things, but—"

Satan raised her hand. "I am not here because of your past sins. I swear, by the Host, that I am not here to punish you or harm you. I simply need your help to save the Keeper of the Keys."

Gregory hesitated before lowering his hands. "I...I'm sorry." He sighed. "I've just been...I just..."

"Mr. Caitlin?" Sara reached out as if to tug on his sleeve, but pulled back before she touched him. "Maybe you can go into that later? Sam could be dead if we don't hurry and find him."

"Yes, yes." He rubbed his arm across his eyes, then squared his shoulders. "Okay, let's go."

"Right." Satan paused, licked her lips. "Do...do you have a car? Otherwise we'll have to catch the bus again."

~~~

"Wow." Sam paused on the threshold of the judgment chamber. "This is incredible."

The room stretched for over a hundred yards. The walls were covered with hieroglyphics and carving and lined with statues of Egyptian gods forged from gold and bronze. The light from dozens of torches illuminated the room and cast shadows from the myriad of servants and runners that populated the place.
~~~

The ceilings were high, and birds flew in their upper reaches, swooping from one rafter to another in slow, lazy arcs. As he took a step into the room, however, the musty odor of mildew and decay almost overcame him.

God, the air is so foul in here. Sam shook his head. *It's like there hasn't been a breeze in centuries.*

At the end of the walkway, atop the steps leading to a massive set of bronze scales lit from beneath by flames, was a tall, otherworldly figure. He wore the headdress and robes of a Pharaoh, but he did not move to acknowledge Sam's entrance.

"Okay." Sam turned to look out the door, and could just make out the barque easing around the next bend in the river. He began to walk toward the scales, and, as if signaled, men, women, and children swarmed him.

"Sir, do you have news?"

"What of our children? Are they well?"

"What has become of the world?"

The questions bombarded his ears and hands grasped at his clothing. Every step felt like it was through a kelp forest, tangled up with tendrils of long-forgotten hope.

"Enough."

The god's voice reverberated through the hall; it was not loud, but it shook the wood and metal like an earthquake. The Egyptians backed down at once, moving to the walls of the chamber and prostrating themselves as Osiris approached.

I don't know what to do. Should I walk up to him? Should I just wait? After a second, Sam moved toward Osiris, extending his hand as he walked. The god's face came into sharper focus as Sam got closer.

Oh, God. He's dead. It was one thing to know the legend, but another to see the result of it in person. Sam looked into a visage that was rotten and decayed; only the eyes seemed completely alive, trapped in beetle-infested flesh. Pieces of jaw were visible underneath loose-hanging flaps of skin.

Sam tried not to stare.

"Keeper of the Keys." Osiris reached out and took Sam's offered hand; his grip was powerful, and Sam ground his teeth to keep from wincing. "I was wondering if you would arrive."

Sam flexed his fingers once Osiris released them. "Well, this was the only lead I had. I would have been here sooner, but the barge was slow."

Osiris turned back toward the scales and the throne beyond them, his skin moving against itself, paper on paper whispering. "Time is short, now. Jannes has set his plan into motion, and we must act quickly."

That sounds like every stereotypical advisor line in a movie. Sam tried to keep a straight face. "Do you know what his plan is?"

"No." He strode toward the dais, his steps so long that Sam had to jog to keep up. "But I think you do. The knowledge lies on your brow, heavy but unseen, a crown of lead."

Sam followed after him. "You mean from the vision? Where I saw..." He shuddered. "There were so many terrible things, people hurting and killing their own."

Osiris stopped. "If he has sealed himself within Yahweh's realm, I do not know how he can be reached." He clenched his left hand; flakes of skin and desiccated muscle floated to the ground. "Yahweh's power outstrips my own significantly. I can no longer penetrate his domain."

Sam shook his head. "I'm sorry, but I still can't accept that you ever could. I mean, let's be honest, but...you're not a god." Osiris froze, but Sam kept on. "Not really. You're some kind of really powerful spirit, sure, but there's only one God. The Creator of the Heavens and the Earth." Sam raised his hand toward the ceiling.

"I mean, come on! Have you *seen* the Angels? The genies? Hell, even the demons! They all acknowledge that God is God. Where do you fit in? Why haven't I even heard of you until now? If you were so important, then why haven't I heard about you?" He took a breath. "Just because somebody worshipped you sometime doesn't make you a God."

Silence enveloped the room. The supplicants stood as statues, holding their breath at Sam's words, and the torches on the walls subsided, their bright flickers dimming to an expectant orange glow.

"You dare." It was a statement, not a question. "You come into my house, my sanctuary, and you spit on my hospitality." Osiris clenched his fist and his teeth, and the muscles in his neck tightened under his papery skin.

"I have watched as thousands of generations of your ancestors have spread over the Earth, watched as my empire rose and fell and others took its place." Like a cobra, his greenish-grey finger struck Sam in the middle of his chest, forcing the man to stumble backwards to keep his footing. "And yet you question me?"

Sam rubbed at the now-sore spot on his sternum. "Just because you're old doesn't make you right, you know." He drew himself up. "I've seen God's power, felt it touch my heart. I know what a God can do. Can you do that?"

Osiris's eyes burned into Sam's, but the Keeper held his ground. "You wish to feel my power, Samuel Buckland? You wish to know what I know, to touch my divinity?"

Oh, shit. What am I doing? "If you are will-ing, then yes." Sam took a deep breath. "I would know the truth, if you could show it to me. I have spent too much of my life in blindness to refuse sight when it is offered."

"Ha!" The sound of Osiris's laugh boomed through the chamber, and the torches flared to life once more before fading again. "Spoken with the wisdom of the Pharaohs, and a true heir to the strength of your ancestors." He mo-tioned for Sam to follow him and the two of them soon came face-to-face with the massive scales which stood in front of the throne.

So it is over a pit of fire. Sam looked down into the flames, raging about fifty feet down, an inferno that could melt steel. Beads of sweat formed on his face, and he backed away, blink-ing the sting from his eyes.

"These are the scales of Ma'at." Osiris opened a hand, and a feather appeared within. "This is one of her feathers, given to us that we may judge the worthy and the wicked alike."

"I think I've heard this story." Sam looked up toward the ceiling as he pulled the legend from his memory. "If...if your heart is heavier than the feather, then you're condemned, but if it isn't, then you could go on."

"You see, our mysteries have not been entirely destroyed, even today." Osiris nodded. "Yes. Every one of our people came to us and, after passing through the gates with the Barque of Ra, they would swear that they had done no theft, no murder, no blasphemy..."

Sam frowned. "Basically, the Ten Commandments?"

Osiris sighed. "...Basically, yes."

"So, what?" Sam crossed his arms. "You want me to put my heart on this thing? Because I'm not sure if that's a good idea."

"No." Osiris held out the feather. "I want you to put this on the scale, if you would."

"Umm...okay." Sam took the feather—it was black, luminous and lustrous as if it had just been plucked, and he could feel energy, like static electricity, clinging to it. He turned and put the feather on one side of the scale, watching as it pulled the balance down.

"Okay." He turned back to Osiris. "Now wh—"

The Egyptian god's hand was buried in his own chest, the skin parting around his wrist like oil recoiling from soap. With a grunt, he removed it, drawing out his pulsating heart. Blood leaked from the now-open valves and arteries, and the whole thing radiated a blue-black light from its surface.

He held it out toward Sam.

"Now, Keeper, place my heart on the other scale, and you will see."

Sam glanced back at Osiris, then at the organ in his hands. The gaping hole in the god's chest revealed glistening viscera, pink lungs breathing in and out underneath a rib cage coated in blood.

"Warn me next time, before you do something like that." Sam shuddered, then took Osiris's heart into his grasp. "Right, then. Here we go."

He put the organ on the scale.

The balance wavered, seeking equilibrium.

I know how this works. Sam watched for any indication that something was about to happen. *As soon as I start thinking that it's all bull, something –*

~~~

Osiris heard the wailing of his people, and he felt them dying.

"Father, you must not." Horus, one eye gleaming in his handsome face, put a hand on his shoulder. "Great Ra has forbidden us to interfere. It is the Compact."

Osiris brushed off his son's grasp. "He visits plague after plague on our people. He has declared war on us, and I will not stand for it."

Clutching his scepter, he willed himself upward, away from the Duat into the land of the living. He felt the barrier between the Underworld and the Earth split around him, separating like cotton, and then he stood at the steps of Pharaoh's palace.

Osiris breathed in the strength of the living, feeling the pulse of power from the temples and shrines dedicated to him and his family. His magic flared in dark blue flames around his
~~~

staff, and he raised it high, bellowing his challenge.

"Face me, Yahweh! Murderer of the Egyptian faithful, I demand that you answer for your crimes!" The god's words flowed out over the countryside like the flood of the Nile, and, although they could not see him, the people calmed their panic, their weeping, and their fear, embracing one another and finding comfort in togetherness.

The stars overhead flickered, and there were shouts from down the street as Egyptian guards ordered Jewish slaves into their neighborhood.

"I order you to appear, by the terms of the Compact of the Gods!" The air trembled at this, a tremor radiating out from the Palace.

"Yahweh does not need to answer to you, Death God."

Osiris turned his head toward the speaker. The creature had six arms, and in five were different weapons—sword, spear, pitchfork, bow, hammer. The last was open, bearing nothing within. The figure was slight, wearing armor and sporting massive black wings from its back.

An Angel.

"Why are you here?" Osiris bristled, anger clouding his face and turning the flame of his power purplish-red. "I have commanded your master's attention, not one of his servants."

"You accuse Yahweh of murdering your people." The Angel pointed its spear out over the city. "He has not, and so your charges are invalid and without strength."

"If Yahweh has not done it, then who has?" Osiris advanced on the Angel, who did not flinch. "You are his tool, are you not? Who sent you here?"

"My Commander has sent me." The Angel spread its arms out. "I am Azrael, the Angel of Death. I have claimed the lives of this city's firstborn children." He stood. "And, if this does not suffice to change the minds of your people, then I will return for the rest."

Osiris's eyes widened, and he turned out toward the city, stretching his awareness.

As his mind reached out, he could feel Yahweh's power marking each and every oldest son and daughter in every household, from the servants to Pharaoh's heir himself.

"You lie. Your master's power has touched them." Osiris brought his scepter close. "I am not so easily deceived."

Azrael laughed, and the air filled with the deep music of his voice. "And yet he is not here. Perhaps the sand has blinded you, godling."

Osiris leveled his staff at the Angel, unleashing his power in a torrent of blinding red fire. The god could feel the strength coming from the Duat and the people around him and he focused it all on Azrael, burying the Angel within flame that tore at flesh and bone alike.

"You will not harm my people!" The ground beneath the Angel cracked and boiled, and clouds formed overhead. "It is my duty to protect them!"

The flames dissipated, swirling away like early-morning mist. The Angel still stood, but was a cracking mass of bones and scorched flesh. Its skeletal hands still held its weapons, and it gripped them tightly as burnt ashes poured down from its moving joints. It crouched down and black swirling lights erupted from the implements of death.

"Stand down, Azrael." The darkness in the sky broke and an androgynous figure clad in shimmering gold, with flaming sword and spear in hand, descended in a shaft of light from the heavens.

The skeleton turned toward the newcomer, then knelt to the ground, muscles, flesh, and skin springing from the scorched bones and wrapping around its form until Azrael was whole again.

Osiris held his weapon before him once more, prepared to fight. "Are you here to challenge me as well, Michael? I will not be defeated here."

Michael shook his head, sheathing his blade and holding the spear like a staff. "No, Osiris. I have no desire to fight you."

"Then why come? Why has Yahweh ignored my summons, decimated my people?"

Michael waved his hand out over the city. "Until now, the actions were not divine. It was our prophet against yours, and Moses proved triumphant."

Osiris scowled, but nodded. "I accept that, although I still consider this to be an act of aggression by your god against ours."

Michael did not acknowledge Osiris's statement. "Today's curse, however, has a more specific purpose. My Lord did not answer your summons because he did not command that this be done. I decided that it would be, and so it is."

Osiris staggered backward, clutching at his scepter. "But...why? You have used divine power to kill so many. How can you expect that there will be no repercussions?"

Michael's face was hard, set. "Because, with this, I will choke Duat with your dead until Anubis can no longer ferry them all. The world will know how you failed to protect your people, and they will turn to my Lord for safety and learn of His love for them."

The Archangel stepped forward. "It is past time that there was only one God in the world."

THE RESURRECTION

Sam fell backward onto the hard stone floor. The heart on the scales erupted into a burst of flame, disappearing in seconds.

"Now do you believe, Keeper of the Keys?" The Egyptian god strode forward and leveled his scepter at Sam. "The only difference between my family and your God is that he won the battle for the world."

I can't...I don't.... Sam's mind kept flashing back to Michael's face, just as he remembered it but infinitely harder. "You...what is the Compact? That agreement you tried to summon God with?"

"At the beginning of human history, we deities chose which people we would represent. In order to prevent open warfare between ourselves and the decimation of the Earth, we agreed that we would not directly interfere in each other's civilizations." He held out his hand to help Sam back onto his feet. "We invested ourselves into that Compact. It still holds today. And this is one reason I cannot help you any further than I am about to, Samuel Buckland."

"You know, I've noticed something." Sam took the god's hand and pulled himself up. "Whenever some sort of celestial being calls me by my full name, it means bad things."

Osiris stared at him for several seconds.

Yeah, okay. Sam started looking around. "So, what—"

The sudden burst of the death god's laughter interrupted him. Sam staggered, caught off guard, as Osiris's mirth poured out into the hall. The entire building brightened, the torches doubled in strength, and the stale air cleared.

He really is linked to everything here. Sam watched as the faces of the petitioners brightened and several of them broke into laughing fits of their own. *I wonder if it's like this in Heaven. If God gets angry, do the Angels go to war?*

With a final chuckle, Osiris straightened back up. "You are unique among mortals of your day, Keeper. You may be able to succeed where we have failed."

Sam hesitated, then bowed. "Thank you, great Osiris." Rising again, he glanced around. "So what was it that you were going to be able to do to help me?"

Osiris reached out his hand to his side, and, in a flare of light and dust, a thick, rolled up scroll appeared within. He brought it before him and pulled it open with a crackle and outpouring of dust. "In order to reach Heaven in its sealed state, you must have three things."

"Seriously?" Sam blinked. "Is this one of the World of Warcraft quest things or something? 'You must bring back seven wolf pelts' or something?"

Osiris frowned. "...No. It is not."

"Okay, okay." The jovial atmosphere from a few minutes ago had darkened again, and the atmosphere pressed in on Sam's senses at Osiris's displeasure. "So, what is it I need?"

The god turned back to the papyrus. "You need a mortal soul."

Sam put his hand on his chest. "Is mine good enough?"

"I expect that it is, considering that Jannes was able to ascend." Osiris moved his finger down the scroll. "You need something imbued with divine power."

Sam licked his lips. "Did Jannes do that by taking Satan's angelic body?" The god nodded. "Okay. Well, there's a whole bunch of Angels in my house, so I don't think that one will be too hard."

"And you need the proper spell incantations."

"Damn it." Sam turned away for a moment, mind turning. "Do you have those?"

Osiris inclined his head. "Even if I did, I would not be allowed to tell you. It would be against the Compact."

Sam rolled his eyes. "Okay, fine."

"…But there is someone else who knows the path that Jannes took to find the sorcery."

Sam felt a creeping sense of dread tickling the back of his mind. "Who?"

Osiris released the scroll back into the void. The space it had occupied swirled and dark purple fire erupted before taking on a man's shape. As it solidified, transforming from fire to flesh, the man stepped forward.

He was handsome, his face strong and his skin dark like his brother's. He bore a blue-jeweled amulet on his bare chest, and he was suffused with health and life.

Sam breathed his name. "Jambres."

The man blinked, then squinted, turning this way and that to examine his surroundings. His eyes fell on Osiris, widened, and he fell to his knees.

"Great Osiris, forgive me. I did not see you there."

Osiris motioned for Jambres to stand. "Your brother has betrayed us, Jambres."

Jambres shook his head. "Jannes would not do this. He is devoted to you, to Ra. He gave his entire life in your service."

"Be that as it may, he is acting to destroy everything we have remaining, and more." Osiris indicated Sam with his hand. "You must go with the Keeper of the Keys as his guide to where your brother has gone."

Jambres looked toward Sam. "I will not harm my brother. He and I are the same, and to hurt him is to kill myself."

But you're already dead. Sam bit back his comment, and nodded. "I understand, but I can't let him continue whatever it is he's doing."

Jambres curled his brow, wrinkles forming as he considered. He looked up toward his god. "Is this truly your will? The will of Ra, of Amun?"

Osiris put a hand on Jambres's shoulder. "Ra and Amun are no more. I am King now, and yes, this is my will."

Jambres's face betrayed his shock, but he recovered quickly. "Very well." He turned back to Sam. "But I will raise no hand against Jannes, not even to save your life."

Sam laughed. "I'll keep that in mind."

Osiris closed his eyes, then nodded. "I think it is time for you to awaken, Keeper. Good luck, and may your death, when it comes, be easy and your spirit move quickly into Paradise."

Before he could respond, Sam heard a familiar voice speak a single word, traveling as if it were from down a great hallway, echoing with power.

"Begone."

THE HEIR

"Did it work?"

Sam blinked his eyes open. Sunlight streamed over him, causing him to wince.

"Of course it worked." Satan leaned over his face, examining him as he tried to adjust to the light. Her own was bruised and cut, with an open wound on her cheek trickling blood down her chin. "No demon can stand against the Keys."

The Keys...what? Sam sat up, but the sudden movement caused his vision to black out and he had to put a hand out to catch himself before he fell again. "What...who?"

"Hey, Sam! Are you all right?" Sara held a washrag and a bottle of water, and her clothes were covered in dark blotches, like smoke stains. "You're not, like, brain damaged now, are you?"

Sam coughed and fought down the nausea as the vertigo began to subside. "Did you get rid of the bastard?" Dizziness again, and he put a hand over his face. "You know...now I understand exactly why Caitlin was down for a little while after that exorcism."

The familiar voice from before spoke from behind Sam. "There was also the broken arm and loss of blood to consider, if you'll remember."

Sam's eyes widened and he spun around, backpedaling on his hands and feet on the strength of his adrenaline. "What the hell are you doing here?" He looked back and forth between Satan and Sara, rephrasing for them. "What the hell is he doing here?"

Gregory held up his hands; they were covered in scratches and tiny cuts, and blood still flowed from a few. "It's okay, Sam. I'm not here to hurt you."

Sara nodded. "Yeah. We went to get him to try to get that demon thing out of you." She grabbed Sam's upper arm and helped haul him back to his feet.

"Well, thanks." Sam took a deep breath as the last of the fatigue and confusion faded from his consciousness. "I'm glad that..."

His voice trailed off as he took in his surroundings. The four of them were standing in the remnants of a burnt building. A giant hole in the roof was letting in sunlight, and the timbers looked like a huge object had busted straight through them on its way out.

"Holy shit." Sam walked over to a particularly black and burned spot, where he could make out the remnants of broken bottles of whiskey and beer. The floor he stood on was clean, however, but wood splinters around bolts on the ground caught his eye. "Did...did someone rip the bar out?"

Gregory laughed. "You did that. As soon as you saw us coming in, the demon went ballistic and started tearing the place up." He pointed behind him, toward the stage in the middle of the building. "Scared the hell out of the dancers, too."

Sara smirked. "You were sure enjoying yourself when we got here, though, Sam. You had like three strippers *all* over you."

Sam sat down again, a sudden ache filling his entire body. "How...have the police come, yet? The fire department?"

Satan shook her head. "No. Gregory has made sure that no one who was here remembers anything, and we have several minutes yet before the sylphs get bored of shielding this place."

"All right." Sam shook his head and pushed himself back up, wincing and letting a small groan escape his lips. "I guess we need to get back home. Where the heck are we, anyway?"

"In Los Angeles, of course." Gregory bent down to the floor and picked up some of the scattered napkins. He handed several to Satan and began patting his hands with the rest. "The demon was enjoying himself in your body and thriving on the attention he was getting."

Satan limped toward Sam, wincing as she put weight on her right foot. "Gregory's car is right outside. We should go before the spell breaks and the authorities arrive."

Gregory nodded and slipped an arm around her to brace her steps. Sam felt an urge to separate them, but fought it back.

No, it's fine. He's not the enemy anymore.

"My spells are probably not as strong as yours, Sam. I haven't used them in over two years and I didn't have the book to reference."

Sam nodded and walked to the door, his shoes crunching glass underfoot with each step. The EXIT sign hung by its wires, and he ducked to avoid hitting his head.

"Are you all right?"

Satan turned her face to his. "Yes. The demon was hard to hold down, and I forgot, for a moment, that I do not have my Angelic strength anymore. I miscalculated and he threw me."

Sara pointed. "She slammed into the wall and left that huge dent." The party looked where Sara indicated, at a network of spidery cracks and a splintered table.

Sam's gut surged. *God, I did that.* "I'm...I'm so sorry." He hung his head. "I don't know what to say."

Satan laughed, then winced and held her hand to her ribs. "This was not your fault, Sam." She reached out, her hand moving toward his face before it changed course and landed on his upper arm. "Saints and prophets alike have been taken in by Pride."

Gregory turned his face away at her comment, and the group made it over the threshold and across the street to his car. With intermittent hisses of pain and ginger movements, they piled into the vehicle.

"Fantastic." Sam rubbed his temples, where a small ache was blossoming. "I need to talk to the Angels..." He snapped to attention. "Damn it! Where the hell is he?"

The other three looked between each other before Sara spoke up. "Who?"

"Osiris sent an Egyptian sorcerer back with me, to help me figure out how to break into Heaven." Sam leaned back out of the door, looking up and down the street.

"Sam?" Satan pulled herself out the other window so that he could see her. "There is no Osiris."

Sam blinked, looked into her eyes.

She believes that.

"Then who was it I saw? Was I dreaming?"

She lowered her eyes. "I don't know. You were possessed. You could have been speaking to part of the demon, as he was trying to deceive you. It could have been a hallucination. There are any number of possibilities."

"You..." Sam closed his eyes, calling up the memories from the Duat. "How long have you existed? How long have you been alive?"

Satan creased her brow. "Why? How is that relevant?"

"I just want to know, so I have all the information." He opened his eyes again. "How long?"

She shrugged. "Since before mankind. I saw the world forged from nothingness by His Word, saw Him speak everything into existence." Her gaze became distant, misty. "Things were simpler, then, as we toiled to aid Him in creating the world."

"That's what I thought." Sam sighed. "That's what I thought."

"What do you mean?"

"What he means is that you should not believe everything you hear."

Without warning, Jambres materialized on the roof of Gregory's car. He was dressed in a swirling cloak, his face marked by tattoos much like those on Sam's hands but with different images. Around his neck swung the heavy gold pendant with the sapphire in the center, and he carried Osiris's scepter in his right hand.

Satan recoiled, almost falling out of the window onto the street. "You!" She looked to Sam. "What's going on?"

Sam met the Egyptian's eyes. "Are you going to ride on the top of the car, or are you coming in?"

Jambres laughed. "I prefer not to be trapped, if you please."

"Suit yourself." Sam slid back into the seat, and, after a few more seconds, Satan followed suit.

Sara looked up at the roof. "Is there someone on top of our car?"

"Yes." Satan was staring at Sam like he was crazy. "What is going on, Sam?"

Sam leaned forward to where Gregory sat in the driver's seat, watching them in the rear-view mirror. "You're taking all this well."

"I've learned that, when dealing with you, the best idea is to just wait and see what happens until told otherwise." They both smiled. "So, what now?"

"Just drive us home. I'll explain on the way."

~~~

"I can't believe that the cops took all of them." Sam raked his hand through his hair as he sat on the edge of the hotel bed. "I mean, why? What are they going to do with them?"

Satan came out of the bathroom and took a seat next to the tiny table, reaching for one of
~~~

the remaining slices of supreme pizza. "This is fantastic! The combination of flavors is just…"

She stopped as all eyes in the room turned to her.

"Yahweh has done you no service by keeping you from experiencing Earth." Jambres took a drink of water from a paper cup, crumpled it in his hand, held it aloft, and spoke a single word. The whole room watched it as it folded itself into a small bird with a long neck, flapping away until it slammed into the window and fell.

"Please don't speak so of my Lord." Satan's face lost its enjoyment of the food and she slumped in her chair. "He has a purpose in everything He does."

Jambres opened his mouth to reply, but Gregory cut them off. "It doesn't matter." He turned to Sam. "Is there anything that I can do to help you? Because I want to, if I can."

Sam could see the intense desire for redemption in the other man's eyes, and it tore at his heart. *He would jump at this chance, were it given to him.* He shook his head. *Maybe it should have been.*

"Sam?"

"It's nothing." Sam took a deep breath and turned to his daughter. "Sara, I need you to stay with Gregory for a while."

"Why?" Sara cast her gaze toward Satan, then back to Sam. "...Am I getting in your way? I thought you made a promise to me. You promised to show me, to tell me everything."

"I know I did, but things have changed." Sam walked over to her and looked into her eyes. "Listen, if something goes wrong, I'm going to need you and Greg to figure out how to finish what we've started."

"What?"

Sam smiled. "I know. This is a huge deal, and it doesn't all seem real yet. But here's the thing, Sara: I could die, or get possessed again, or worse. And if that happens, it's going to be up to the two of you." Sam reached into his bag and removed the great silver tome which held the Seals. "So I'm giving this to you."

Satan stood up. "Sam! Are you sure –?"

"Shhh." Sam held the book out to his daughter. "Sara, I name you, my daughter by rite of adoption, as my heir. If I fall battling the forces of evil, then you will take up where I left off. You will fight the enemies of Heaven until you pass the responsibility to your own heir." He took a deep breath. "In the name of God, it is so."

The room trembled, the lights dimming to the barest flicker, casting the room into darkness except for the inner luminescence of the Seals. A pure silver light encompassed the book and, as Sara took the tome from her father, the light spread out over her, wrapping itself around her from head to toe.

And then it was gone.

"What...what just happened?" Sara's eyes were wide and the book shook in her trembling hands. "What –?"

"Just one more thing." Sam reached out and opened the tome to the front cover, the front page. On that page was a long list of names, some circled, most not, that blanketed the samite. The last two were Mary Elizabeth Buckland and Samuel Laurence Buckland.

"That was my mom." Sam's eyes filled with tears, but he made no move to wipe them. "She tried to tell me what this was about, but I didn't want to listen to her."

No one spoke.

"She wrote my name on here when I was born, and I circled it when I took up the mantle. Now, I didn't know you when you were born, Sara, but I do now. Your name belongs here." He brought a marker to the cloth and inscribed the words Sara Imani Hammons.

"Okay, now that's that." Sam handed the book back to Sara, who was gaping at him like a fish. He leaned down and embraced her, and whispered in her ear. "It'll be okay. Gregory will take care of you, all right?"

After a second, Sara dropped the book and hugged her father tight. "You'd better be okay, Sam. I don't want you to leave me, okay?"

Sam laughed. "Me? Don't you worry about me. I've got plenty of backup." He detached himself from the hug and turned to Gregory, who nodded.

"I won't let anything happen to her."

Sam took a deep breath and closed his eyes. His fingertips moved in an intricate dance. When he opened his eyes again, Gregory was no longer looking at him, but at the message the sylph had spelled out in the air under his command.

The message that read, "If I don't make it, take her and hide until she's ready. Promise."

Gregory read the words, and Sam saw his throat move as he swallowed. "I promise."

"All right, then." Sam dug into his wallet and pulled out several hundred dollar bills, handing them to the other man. "She's going to need new things while she stays with you. I have no idea how long this is going to take."

Gregory took the money and put it into his own pocket, then extended his hand. "God bless you, Sam."

They shook, then Gregory turned to Sara. "Come on. We should go now."

Sara held back for a second, holding the Seals to her chest, then she ran out of the door, sobs coming through the thin window and cheap walls of the hotel room. Gregory looked at each of the remaining people in the room, nodded, then closed the door.

THE SORCERERS

Silence held the room for several moments before anyone spoke.

"You made the right decision." Jambres leaned forward from his perch on the bathroom sink and grabbed another water cup. "She would have slowed us down, and was not likely to have survived."

"I know." Sam stared at the door, and he rubbed his upper arm. "Still doesn't feel good, though."

Satan put a hand on his shoulder. "She'll be a lot safer this way, Sam."

He turned toward her and put his hand on hers. "Yeah. Thanks."

Another few seconds of silence.

"Can we begin?" Jambres leapt down. His dark eyes burned as he advanced on Sam. "I want to get this done as fast as possible so I can return to my reward in the Duat." He passed Sam and peeked out of the blinds. "The world is much less pleasant than it was when it was all I knew."

"I'm sure that's a fascinating story, but we need to get started." Sam pulled over the legal pad and pen left by the hotel staff. "So we have to find something representing Divine power, a mortal soul, and the spell incantations to make this work."

"And we need to move quickly." Satan shuddered as she took a turn at the window, looking up at the sky. "The heavens seem angrier and angrier every second. It even looks bad to me now."

Sam moved up behind her. The clouds had changed from the stratus covering to dark cumulonimbus, and they were moving so fast that it almost made him dizzy. "What is going on up there?"

"Jannes is battling the Voice of Heaven." Jambres sighed and took another drink of water. "And this time, he expects to win."

Satan shook her head. "No one can defeat the Metatron. He speaks with the Word of God. It's not possible."

"Then you can sit back and let him try." Jambres crossed his arms. "If you're that confident, then why am I here? Just wait until the skies clear again."

Sam stifled a smirk. "We can't do that. Soon enough, normal people are going to start noticing. I'm not an expert, but I know that, eventually, magic spills into the world people see—the effects, if nothing else." He gestured to Satan. "She couldn't see it with her human eyes before, but it has obviously changed already."

Jambres nodded. "I have observed the same. Mortal man may not be able to see the clouds overhead, but the gloom will permeate their hearts in time."

Satan rubbed her face. "So where do we go? What sort of incantation are we looking for?"

Jambres laughed, low and deep. "My brother spent over two thousand years seeking those spells, and then more time before he could cast them. We'll be lucky to obtain half of it."

"Your brother was alone." Sam wrapped his arm around Satan's shoulders as he opened his hand toward the Egyptian. "We're a team."

Satan looked up at Sam and her lips moved.

"Of course we are." Jambres waved his hand like he was swatting at a mosquito. "Just like the United States and Russia during the Second World War."

"Weren't you dead for that?" Sam's curiosity got the better of him. "How much were you aware of, that was going on?"

Jambres leveled his gaze on Sam. *There's power there.*

"The incantation is not a simple spell. It requires experiential knowledge. The spell is distilled from trials that the sorcerer must undertake. That was what made it take so long for him to accomplish."

Satan shook her head as if she had lost her train of thought. "He...he had to find the experiences first, didn't he?"

"You haven't lost all of your intelligence, Servitor." Jambres grinned and Satan recoiled at the epithet.

That must mean more than it seems. "So what's the first 'experience,' then? Where do we need to go?"

Jambres shrugged.

"Why are you even here, if you can't help us?" Sam tried to conceal his rising anger.

"I can tell you what my brother did, so long ago." He sat down and held his hand out for the pad of paper. "It is up to us to determine how to translate that to today, when so many things no longer exist."

Sam took a deep breath. "All right." He sat as well, and Satan followed. Handing over the pad and pen, Sam tapped his index fingers together. "So what did he do first?"

Jambres closed his eyes. A white glow crawled from the tattoos on his face, swirling down his body like a centipede climbing down a tree trunk, until it reached his hand. The pen moved, sketching a scene on the paper.

"Jannes finds an oracle, a seeress, who sets him on the path to enlightenment. She tells him that he must see the future reflected in the past." The figure in the drawing held a knife over the oracle's head. "He slew her and coated a mirror with her blood. Thus he learned the first part of the spell."

"Wait, what?" Sam looked at Satan, whose eyes were as wide as his. She shook her head and shrugged. "How the hell did that teach him anything?"

"The second portion of the spell is learned through pain." Jambres's hand moved, drawing the ice-lined peaks of a mountain. "Hot pain, and cold pain. Jannes climbs to the top of a volcano with no protection. No spells or clothes guard him from the snow as he reaches the top. He then shoves his right hand into the dormant lava flow after enchanting it to burn again."

"My God." Satan grabbed Sam's arm as she stared at the picture of the Egyptian sorcerer with his arm half-buried in lava. "Why would anyone do this?"

"The third portion of the spell, he learned through happiness." A village began to appear underneath Jambres's hand, filled with happy, smiling children. "He watches them for years, watches them grow up, have children, and die. This is the hardest part of the spell for him to understand, as he cannot remember what it was like to be happy."

Sam nodded, his hand moving up to hold onto Satan's. "How much more?"

"The final part of the spell, my brother learned by forgetting." Jannes's figure knelt in front of a crystalline structure, in which a perfect image of him stared back. "He gives his memories away and lives for a lifetime." Jannes was now an old man, sitting before a fire, surrounded by children and young adults, all smiling. "When it is time for him to die, he comes back to himself and makes an offer." Jannes clutched at his blanket as he stared at the specter of himself, still young, standing beside his bed. "The memories return, and he has the choice—pursue his revenge or allow his family to prosper." A rejuvenated Jannes stood over the bloody bodies of the children who had surrounded him before.

"He chooses revenge."

"Wow." Sam brought his hands together in front of his face. "And we need to do that? How does that have anything to do with the spell?"

Satan answered, but her voice was low, quiet. Sad. "Because those are what you go through to get to Heaven."

"What?" Sam turned to her. "What do you mean?"

She took a deep breath and rubbed her arms. "The first thing that happens to a soul bound for Heaven is that they watch their lives. They see every good thing they've ever done, and every evil thing. But this time, unlike when they were alive, they are given full knowledge of the consequences of their actions. They see who died because they decided to run that red light. They see who was fired because they swiped that soda from the supermarket."

Sam whistled. "They see the future from the past."

Satan nodded. "Exactly. A terrible interpretation, but true."

"What about the rest?" Sam leaned in toward her. "The pain?"

"Do you remember in the New Testament, where it talks about the fires, the gnashing of teeth?"

"You mean Hell?"

Satan winced. "Not exactly. Hell is different...and much worse. In Heaven, we don't punish anyone for what they've done, but many of them punish themselves. Some reject the Light of Heaven, running from it, always alone. Afraid."

Sam's eyes were wide. "Cold pain."

"And others burn in the Light, refusing to accept it but unwilling to run. They are angry at God for allowing them to make these mistakes, so they bear what they think is His punishment."

"Hot pain." Sam sighed. "I'm almost afraid to hear the rest."

"When the soul overcomes this, accepts that they did what they did and takes blame with understanding, then they join our community in Heaven where they can find happiness." A smile touched Satan's face and her gaze became wistful. "All the comforts they wish, all the joys they remember are amplified and made better. They find the people they wish for perfected in all their aspects. Life is wonderful."

"And then they forget?"

Satan nodded. "They forget what life was like on Earth. They become so immersed in their new lives in Heaven that Earth fades from their memories until it surprises them when mentioned."

"What about the last part?" Sam stood and walked away from the gathering. "The remembering?"

Satan hesitated. "I...I don't know. I don't know what that part refers to."

"And it doesn't matter." Jambres stood as well. "We know what we have to experience. Now we have to find them."

"Find an oracle? A real one? And then bleed her out? I don't think so." Sam leaned back against the wall. "We're going to have to find a different way to do this."

"There are few oracles left today, so that may be closed to us anyway."

Satan was quiet, her eyes low, her lips moving as if she were reading to herself. Sam came over and lifted her chin with his forefinger.

"What's wrong?"

"None of it makes any sense, Sam." She sighed. "There are holes in my memories, yes, but I know that I have never seen another god, never seen another kind of true magic, and yet, right now, an Egyptian sorcerer is using powers from all over the world to invade Heaven and challenge the Metatron, something that should be impossible." Her voice quivered and she looked up at him with teary eyes. "What is going on?"

"I don't know." Sam glanced up at Jambres, who was digging through the mashed potatoes from KFC. "When I was...when I was with Osiris, I didn't believe it either. But he showed me what happened on the day that Azrael killed the firstborn of Egypt. He saw Michael, and Michael..." Sam shook his head. "Michael told Osiris that it was *him* that made the decision, and not God."

Jambres threw the Styrofoam container into a trash can. "Is this necessary? Can we have the soul-searching later? If my brother succeeds, then the entire *world* is going to pay witness to the things you're whimpering about right now."

Sam rose to answer, but Satan beat him to it, slamming her hands into the Egyptian's chest and pushing him against the sink. "I don't care *who* you are or how important what you know is, you will *not* treat me as if I were some sort of whining child. I am SATAN, the Accuser of Man and Advocate of God, and I will not suffer your foolishness."

Shit. Sam glanced back and forth. *Who do I save?*

Jambres grabbed onto Satan's wrists and smiled, leaning in close.

His lips approached hers.

Sam clenched his fist.

Jambres glided past her and whispered into her ear. "Hold onto that anger. You may need it as we move ahead."

He released her, sending her back a step, and grabbed his scepter. "Time is growing short."

Sam took a second to collect his thoughts. "You're right about that. Okay." *Come on, Sam. What do you do?*

He exhaled. "I think we should split up, Jambres. Each of us should take one of these things and—"

Jambres shook his head. "That's impossible. The spell must be experienced by the wielder, as I said. One person must learn all of it."

Sam smiled. *It feels good to know something he doesn't.* "No. If one of us knows it, that's going to be enough."

"How do you know?"

"I don't." He smiled. "But I have faith."

Jambres cocked an eyebrow, but said nothing.

"Does it matter which one you go for first?"

"No, it doesn't."

"Okay. We'll go after the oracle or whatever. Will you be all right with the volcano?"

The Egyptian laughed. "I have fought against the serpents of Ammit as they sought to devour the great solar barque. I do not need to visit a volcano to solve this riddle."

"Okay." Sam picked up his bag. "When you figure out the first part, then let me know." He blinked. "You *can* let me know, right?"

Jambres arched an eyebrow, and Sam put up his hands in surrender. "Okay, okay."

"Then let us move." Jambres pushed toward the door. "We can solve the rest of it on the way."

Sam looked toward Satan. She squared her shoulders and nodded.

"Let's go, then."

THE INTRUDER

"I would say that it is pleasant to see you again, but it is impossible to lie in Heaven."

Jannes laughed, wiping angelic blood from his coat. His crimson pendant gleamed in the ever-present radiance, catching the light and sending it in red streamers around him.

"I'm actually very pleased to see *you*." He waved his hand out, forcing a look of sadness onto his face. "What's wrong? No tea this time? Where is your hospitality?"

The Metatron stood his ground. "You are the intruder here, not I. I do not need to answer to you, sorcerer."

Jannes began to pace around, keeping one hand clutching his medallion. "You know that I've been waiting a long time for this. Planning it, working out the logistics, the necessary spells."

No answer except the suppressed anger in the Angel's eyes.

"But it got me wondering—why didn't your God stop me?" Jannes opened his arms to encompass the room. "When my brother and I were here, I thought that maybe it was because of the Compact, that he couldn't interfere with another god's servant directly."

He brought his hands back before him, centering them over the medallion, almost like a prayer. "But I serve no god now. Where is yours?"

The Metatron smiled. "That is what I hoped you would ask."

THE ORACLE

Sam stepped out of the Sylph's embrace into the ancient theater of Delphi. The Grecian sky, blotted out as it had been in California, was a sharp contrast to the strong sunshine beaming over the ruined structures. The light cast long shadows, exaggerated shapes of pillars and half-destroyed benches. The air whipped around them, a chill breeze that forced him to retreat into himself.

Satan set down a moment later, squinting as she looked around. "Strange, but I would expect people to be here. Tourists. Sightseers." She shivered. "I feel cold."

Sam nodded. "This place was truly...I don't know. Something." He waved his hand in a wide circle, and the Sight dropped over his vision; he watched as echoes of ancient rituals played out before him in shadow and mirage, layered over one another thousands of times over so that he could make out no specific image. "If the oracle here wasn't legitimate, someone sure had some sort of power to make it seem like she was."

"Do you think this was home to a prophet? A seer of..." Satan swallowed like she had tasted something distasteful. "Of a god?"

"I don't know." Sam concentrated, trying to filter the information that his mystic vision was giving him. One after another, reenactments began to disappear, cellophane peeling away. "I just know that this was the most famous oracle I've ever heard of, so it was the first place I thought to go."

Satan rubbed her arms and pulled herself further into her jacket. "I wish I'd brought a bigger coat."

Sam didn't respond. *This must have been her.* He watched as the Oracle of Delphi delivered a hundred prophecies. The flesh was different, dozens of women in the role, but he could see something in the eyes, a burning, golden presence that marked them as the same.

"This is incredible." Sam listened to the lilting sound of her voice. "I don't know what she was saying, but it was magic, powerful. I can feel it, even now."

Satan's shivering intensified. "S-S-Sam. S-s-something is w-wrong."

Sam turned around and his heart slammed against his chest. Satan was covered in tiny spirits resembling snakes, slithering and hissing. They were already red, fat and sated from her heat, and she fell to the ground, lips moving but soundless.

"Oh my God!" Sam extended his hands in a gesture of protection. "Begone!"

A blast of power, a metaphysical hurricane, tore at the snake spirits, scattering them to the aether, end over end as they dispersed. Sam tore down the steps to where Satan lay.

"You...oh, God, you're so cold." Sam looked around for any source of heat or fire, but there was none. "Hold on, I need to summon a fire creature, something for warmth."

Satan shook her head, but it took Sam a moment to realize that the gesture was deliberate and not the result of tremors. "C...C...C..."

Sam took a step back, knelt onto one knee, and began drawing the summoning sigils in the ground. His finger moved in the dirt, gouging out soil and pebbles as it carved the symbols to conjure an efreet. Satan's shivering hand reached out for him, and her head continued to shake.

He finished inscribing the circle, and stood to invoke the spell.

Satan winced, squeezing her eyes shut and lying face-down.

Sam spoke the first word of the incantation.

A blinding flash, brighter than fifty suns, burst in front of his face and threw him backwards. His back slammed into one of the old stone benches, knocking the wind out of him and driving him to the ground.

Swirling winds spiraled inward, and a form took shape at the center of the vortex. Sam turned his eyes as the light brightened, coughing and gasping as he tried to bring in air.

"You dare?" The voice coming from the light washed over Sam's consciousness. "This is my holy sanctuary, and you invoke another within? Sacrilege!"

Sam fought to his feet, still unable to look toward the light.

"Mortal man, you stand before Phoebus Apollo, giver of life and of death. Kneel, or I shall destroy you!"

Sam forced the words from his throat. "You can't. The Compact—"

Before he could finish, the light exploded in a thunderclap, with the afterglow still burned into the back of Sam's eyelids.

Wait. I think that... He peeked open one eye, just a crack. When he was not rewarded with searing blindness, he risked a better look.

Sheathed in golden silks and linens, the Greek God of the Sun stood before him. Easily ten feet tall, he was in full splendor, his skin luminous and his hair waving in the winds created by his power. In one hand he held his golden bow, and his head was crowned with leaves forged from the same metal.

Sam's eyes drifted behind him. Satan's were closed, and she had stopped moving.

"No!" Sam dashed past the god, who watched him with a mixture of anger and confusion. The solar fire lashed out, seeking to drive Sam away from him, but he ducked under the blast and grabbed Satan in his arms.

"Oh, no, no..." She wasn't breathing. He put his fingers to her carotid artery.

No pulse. "God, no, please!" Sam laid her on the ground and tipped her head back. He pinched her nose shut and gave her two deep breaths, then started chest compressions.

"Come on!" It came out with each thrust, like he was pushing the words out of his own throat rather than forcing her heart to beat.

"She is beyond your ability to save, mortal." Apollo's voice vibrated Sam's eardrums, but he kept up his efforts. "My guards have drained the heat from her body. Her blood is cold within her now, and you cannot summon anyone here, in my sanctuary."

Sam kept trying, leaning in for more breaths then resuming the chest compressions. The woman under his hands was pale white now, with blue touching her lips and ears. Her body flopped a little with each thrust, a rag doll in a game of pretend.

From his peripheral vision, Sam could see the shining golden god kneel down close to Satan's body. His glow tickled Sam's skin and his aroma, cinnamon and honey, filled the air.

"She was beautiful, though, wasn't she?" Apollo caressed her face with the backs of his fingernails. "It is truly a pity that—"

A concussive blow across his jaw silenced him, but the scream that propelled that blow had already drowned him out. Apollo fell backward on his haunches, then rose up, his light echoing his motions as it burned ever brighter.

"You won't touch her." Sam extended his hands. "I'll die before I let you."

"*You* think to command *me*?" Apollo laughed, but the smile did not spread to his eyes. "You stand in my sanctuary and think to threaten *me?*" The god drew back his golden bow and a gleaming arrow appeared within, dripping orichalcum flames, leveled at Sam's chest.

God and man stared at each other. The red haze of anger burned Sam's eyes, calling for blood, calling for revenge.

Apollo pulled back farther on the bow. "Deliver my wrath unto him."

Wrath.

The god's voice was only a whisper, but hearing it deflated Sam like a pin to a balloon. He lowered his hands.

"What will it take?" His voice quivered, but he held his gaze steady. "I know who you are, Phoebus Apollo. I've read the stories. You were once the great god of healing, teaching your son everything, even how to raise the dead." He pointed back toward Satan. "She was innocent. She and I are trying to prevent an apocalypse, something that threatens all of us, including you." A tear ran down his face and his other hand shook from the strain of the emotion burning him.

Apollo's grip loosened but did not falter. "What are you asking? Say it plain, that the world may bear witness."

"Save her." Sam let himself fall to his knees. "Save her, Apollo. She isn't beyond your reach yet. Save her and I..." Sam's forehead touched the ground. "I will do whatever you want."

Apollo brought the bow down; the arrow misted away. "Swear it by the Styx, mortal. Swear that you will serve Apollo and the Olympians, from now until we release you."

Sam took a deep breath. *I'm sorry, Gabriel.*

"I swear it, by the River Styx."

Sam felt the world shift, felt something new latching onto his very being, a bond on his soul. Searing pain burned into his hand, and, when he looked, he saw that the mark the Archangel had left was replaced by a sunburst.

"Stand aside." Apollo advanced on Satan's cold body. He knelt beside her and, as Sam had done, pressed his lips against hers and exhaled.

This time, though, coruscating light pulsated through the gap, like an overpowered strobe.

Through his Sight, Sam could see the energy flowing from the god into the woman. His heart loosened in his chest. *She looks better already.*

Apollo drew back as Satan began to cough, her eyelids fluttering as she spasmed on the ground, chest hitching and muscles seizing. Sam started stripping off his coat.

"She needs something under her head before she cracks it on the stone!"

Apollo tipped a smile. "Watch, mortal. Be silent and watch." He stretched forth a golden finger and tapped it on Satan's breastbone. A hot-white pulse spread through her body and faded, and the spasms went with it. She took two ragged breaths, then opened her eyes.

Sam's were waiting. Three heartbeats passed as they stared at one another. Then she smiled.

"Good to see you, Sam."

He shook his head, laughing as he fell back onto his haunches. "That's something you say when you run into someone in the morning, not when you've just been brought back from the dead."

Satan coughed, rolling herself over onto her side. Sam's hands leapt out to steady her, and she managed a weak laugh. "I hope never to experience that again."

The tension washed away from Sam, and he sagged onto the ground. "I...I was..." The overwhelming emotion manifested itself in stubborn tears that fought their way to the surface. "I thought you were gone."

Satan rose to a sitting position, but, as she did so, she caught sight of Apollo, still standing nearby, and her eyes narrowed. She backpedaled, trying to get her feet under her.

"It was him! I saw him!"

Sam blinked. "Wait, what? What are you talking about?"

Apollo turned away, walking toward the edge of the area as Satan stood.

"As I was dying, Sam. He was watching. Waiting for you to do something—I saw his face when you began drawing your spell in the dirt.

He was smiling, waiting. He wanted you to try casting it." She rubbed her arms again, an echo of the draining she had suffered. "He was speaking to the snakes, too. When you blew them away, they dissolved and their essence flew back to him."

Sam turned to look at the god, who was still ignoring them. "Is this—"

"Is it true?" Apollo turned, his smile mocking, his arms crossed. "Of course it is, Samuel. I knew you were coming, have known it since before you became Keeper of the Keys." He raised his arms and celestial torches lit around Delphi, bathing the place in eerie light, even through the sunshine. "I have been waiting for a very long time so that you would be here, with her, that I could bind you to my service."

"You son of a bitch!" Sam stood and tried to raise his arms to fight, but they felt as if they were weighed down, bound by the same chains that had latched onto his spirit. "You almost killed her so that I would follow you?"

Satan's eyes widened. "Sam? What are you talking about?"

"Ah, yes." Apollo favored her with a grin. "The Keeper of the Keys is now a servant of the Dodekatheon, and of me, personally. My new High Priest, as it were."

"Sam!" Satan was panicked now. "You...you can't worship another god! It's against the Commandments! It—"

"It was the only way to save your life, is what it was. Exactly how he planned it." Sam took a deep breath, then looked back at the shining Apollo. "Fine. You got me. But I swear to God, if you try to make me do something that's going to hurt someone that I care about, I will fight you with everything I have."

Apollo chuffed a laugh. "Absolutely. Spirit is a wonderful thing in a servant. And I applaud your conviction to protect those you love...but I have no desire to possess an unruly prophet. As useful as you may be to me, you are less so if you are actively subverting my commands. Therefore..."

Sam rolled his eyes. "Therefore, you're going to offer me another deal in exchange for my cooperation. How unexpected."

Apollo didn't seem to notice the sarcasm. "Indeed I am. You do as I ask, without question, and, at the end of your assigned task I will release you from my service to return to your God...if he will have you."

Satan ran up. "Sam, you have to stop this. If you get caught, if God—"

Sam shook his head. "If God finds out? He's supposed to already know. If He doesn't, then all the more reason for me to do something about it, find out what's going on, maybe put a stop to it. And if He does..." Sam slumped a little. "Then hopefully good intentions don't *always* lead to Hell."

He looked up again. "All right, I'll—"

"NO!" Satan jumped in front of him. "Apollo, release Samuel Buckland from your service, and I will enter it instead."

Apollo smirked. "Why should I do that? He is the representative of Yahweh on Earth. You are no one."

As he spoke, Sam turned her around. "What are you doing?"

Satan looked into his eyes for a moment, then brushed her lips against his. "Saving your soul, like I'm supposed to." She turned back to Apollo.

"You are mistaken." Satan shook her head. "I am Yahweh's advocate, charged with testing humanity for Him and bringing them closer to Him through trial. When the Keeper completes his mission, I will be restored to my full angelic form...and I will be yours to command."

Seven heartbeats.

Say no. Please say no.

"I accept your offer." Apollo raised his hand. "The mortal is no longer bound to me."

Indeed, Sam could feel the obligation lifted from him, the bonds which encircled his soul loosening until all that remained was the ache of a memory. Sam looked at his hand, but the mark of Apollo remained, overlaying the crescent moon and blotting it out.

"So, *oracle,* I don't suppose you know why we're here?" Sam's brow was a mountain range, furrowed and wrinkled with restrained anger.

Apollo waved his hand again, and lyre music began to fill the area. "Yes. And I will tell you this, Samuel—if you fail to defeat your enemy, you fail the entire world."

Satan licked her lips. "Is the situation that dire? How long do we have?"

Apollo squinted, looking up into the ethereal cloud bank. "Even I cannot know. In the Realms Beyond, including your Heaven, time turns differently depending on the will of the ruler. I know that time is short, for I have seen the sorcerer's victory before the stars change positions."

"That's helpful." Sam kicked at the ground as he pondered.

"But I also have what you seek—a vision of the future from the past. Or, rather, you already have it, but you do not know how to catalyze it, to form it into the knowledge you need."

Sam took a step forward, some of his anger fading in the wake of Apollo's words. "Have we given you enough? Will you give it to us, give us the secret?"

Apollo nodded. "You were correct before, Samuel, that this threatens me and mine as well." He stepped forward once more. "Accept this gift, then, and go forth as we cannot."

He leaned forward and breathed over Sam's face, and a light, shimmering mist washed over it. Sam winced, coughed, and felt his eyes cloud over.

No, not again. The world below him burned as the servants of the gods, all of them, were attacked, tormented. Sam could smell the smoke and blood as his perspective soared over the agony and the joy. *How do I find the spell? If this is the future, where is the past?*

He came up next to the old man, shoving the child back into the fire with his cane. He watched as the man's face contorted in near-rapture at the screams his action elicited. Watched as the man turned and raised his walking stick like a gold medal from the Olympics.

"We are free!" The words echoed in Sam's ears. "God is dead! We believe in nothing!"

The crowd responded. "We are our own masters! We are the new gods!"

The chant repeated, point in counterpoint, as Sam curled in on himself, covering his ears as the sound grew louder and louder.

"Stop it!" The repetition grew, jarring his eardrums, shaking his hands, churning his gut. "Stop! No more! Please!"

Silence.

Sam blinked, his hands still on his ears. He craned his neck.

Everyone was gone.

The street was empty, and the rubble of the house oozed smoke into the air. Discarded rakes and shovels lay scattered on the remnants of the lawn, stuck in the dirt or tossed aside.

Sam stood, looking up into the sky. The clouds were familiar, the signs of Heaven's separation from Earth, but now they blotted out the sunlight. The entire street labored under the heavy greyness, weighed down by the dim.

He took a step.

His foot slipped on a small piece of roof tile, the loose fragment flying behind him and sending Sam face-first into the dirt.

"*Ow.*" He put his hands under him and raised his chin.

Blue eyes met his.

They were under a section of wall, leaned over and fallen down against an inner beam, attached to a small head and blonde hair, wearing Winnie-the-Pooh pajamas stained by smoke and blood.

In a flash, Sam was up, but he stopped himself from rushing over to the girl. He reached out one hand, trying to be non-threatening.

"Hey. Come here. Are you all right?"

She shook her head and took a step back.

"They killed my sister, and my mom, and my dad."

Sam felt tears prick his eyes. "I know, honey. I want—"

"When they put the knives in my Momma, she was begging for God to help her." She shook her head. "He didn't. He didn't help any of them."

Sam's hand faltered. "But He didn't let you die, right?"

The girl looked down. "If God was real, He wouldn't have let those people kill my family." She turned her gaze toward the sky. "They were coming for me, you know. I could hear them. They knew I was there, calling me 'little whore of Christ.' I could hear them in the house."

Sam felt like he had when Apollo had thrown him across the amphitheater. The wind seemed to abandon his body, and he could not speak.

"The fire didn't hurt them. It was so hot, it burned me, burned my sister, but it didn't stop them." She was on the verge of hyperventilation, breaths coming between almost every word. "They just laughed and laughed and laughed."

"I..." Sam tried to say something. "I don't—"

"Momma and Daddy used to tell me that God would protect me, but I knew then that He wouldn't. I knew He wasn't real, or if He was, that He didn't care about me." She raised her chin, tears sparkling as they fell. "When I knew that, when I got that, the fire stopped being hot. The people who killed my Mom and Dad went right by me on their way to cut up my sister. One of them patted me on the head."

Sam reached for her again. "I'm so sorry, honey. That must have been terrible."

From beneath her hair and tears, a sickle-grin appeared, slicing across her face like a blade.

"I'm not."

Sam recoiled. "W...what?"

"My sister screamed when they cut her apart. She tried to run, but an old man shoved her back in here with his cane. They tore her into little pieces and threw them in the fire." The smile widened. "I loved watching her suffer. She deserved it. They all deserved it, you know. They put their faith in gods instead of doing things themselves. They were weak and they died for it!" She put her hands on her hips and laughed. "The gods don't care about us. They never did, if they were ever real. I don't care about them, and anyone who does should die."

The scene around Sam began to fade, with only the young girl's voice left. "Faith makes you weak, like they were. You can only believe in yourself if you want to be strong. Are you strong, Sam?"

316

THE SUNRISE

The Solar Barque approaches the exit. Before, great Ra would have been welcomed on the other side of this portal, resurrected to resume his rule over the Egyptian gods.

Now, I look over his sarcophagus. Empty. Barren, like my heart. I run my hand over the wood, and a tear drops from my eye. I make no attempt to wipe it from my face, because that would dishonor the reason I weep.

I have lost my gods, and my brother. Both to hatred and despair.

I look up as the waters become choppy. The portal is fast approaching now—I can feel the magic that will bring the ship from the great River into the world of men once more. Amazing that the old magic still holds, even in this age of unbelief.

I bow my head to pray.

"Please forgive my sacrilege."

I climb within the coffin and, with a quick spell, seal myself within. The cedar is cold, and the interior dark.

Why has my brother done this? Why must I fight him? Can I? Will I?

I wipe sweat from my brow. The sarcophagus has warmed within, and I feel the imminent transformation upon me. I close my eyes and center myself, protecting my inner core, my very being, as I learned so many centuries ago.

The pain begins.

My bones scream within my body like hot lances impaling a leech. My muscles convulse and I cannot hold back my shrieks. My teeth burn, scarring my tongue, and my eyes boil within their sockets.

There is no word for the agony.

Every part of my body, every element within me, is broken down into its parts. I am rendered down to base material, slag from steel, twine from cloth. My consciousness remains, suspended in awareness, and I know that my khat is gone. Only my soul, held together by my will from fragmenting into its components as my body has done, bears witness to what has happened.

Have I made a mistake?

Have the gods passed judgment on me for my blasphemy?

...Am I glad?

The next part happens slowly, a sunrise creeping over a hill and advancing inch by inch over the grass. I am aware, again, of my toes, feet, and ankles. My muscles stretch forth, and I can feel them connecting to my physical brain once more. Every second brings more of the warmth back to me, brings more of my khat into existence.

Then it is done. I stand outside of the Gate, which closes to me, as it will remain until this time tomorrow.

With my new eyes, I look out on the world. I see forever and far away, but it is fading quickly. My heart aches at the glory that calls to me, the hidden fabric of the world that I walk upon without seeing.

How blind we are, even I, when compared to the gods. How can we question those that see so much we do not?

I look to the sky. Sam will need to know what I know. I hope that he has been successful.

My hands move, almost on their own, and I am gone.

THE BELOVED

"I think he's coming back."

Sam fought to open his eyes, but they were slow to respond.

"Sam? Sam?" *Satan's voice.* "Are you all right?"

Sam put all of his will into raising a hand. It lifted about a foot off the ground, trembling and shaking, before gravity brought it back down.

"Why is he so weak?"

Apollo's deep, sonorous voice came from the other side of Sam's head. "He was trapped in an oracular vision. Some mortals can handle that more easily than others. The fact that he was not bleeding from his eyes is encouraging."

"Nope...no eyeball bleeding here." Sam rolled over and pushed himself up into a sitting position. "And my muscles are starting to work again, it looks like."

His eyes fluttered open. He was sitting on the ground at Delphi. The Shadows were longer, and the sun had darkened since Apollo had set him on his path.

"Did you discover what you sought, Samuel?"

Sam nodded and put out a hand; Satan grabbed hold of his wrist and helped him stand, where he wobbled only twice before steadying. "Faithlessness."

Satan crinkled her nose, but Apollo nodded. "Interesting. And logical."

"How do you mean?"

Apollo opened his hand. "Faith identifies you, defines part of you, makes you who you are." A ball of sunfire appeared. "If you believe in a god, then your soul responds to that god, can be affected more easily. You are bound by that god's rules."

Apollo extinguished the ball and looked up toward the sky. "All gods are bound by the Compact; we may not enter each other's sancta. Heaven belongs to Yahweh, and not I, nor my father Zeus, nor Odin may enter, with very few exceptions. We could act to protect an appointed emissary of ours, or to retrieve something stolen from us, but, otherwise, no. If you hold faith in us, you are bound the same as we. That is why a soul may come to our paradise instead of Yahweh's. That is why the fates of our worshipers and our own are intertwined."

"But you!" Apollo spun and pointed at the two others. "Faith in Yahweh binds you to his rules. A soul may not enter the afterlife without permission or death. There are none on Earth to give permission, as they are all trapped. You are not dead." He held both hands in front of him, palms up.

Satan nodded, understanding creeping over her face. "The only way to enter alive and unexpected is to not believe in any gods, then, so that none of their rules apply?"

Sam sighed. "Exactly. And I'd wager dollars to donuts that is why Jannes is going after *all* the faithful, not just Yahweh's."

Satan ran both hands through her hair. The fingers got caught in snarls at the ends of the strands, and she winced as she pulled them through.

"OW!"

Sam glanced over and smiled. "I guess you'll need training in how to brush your hair, won't you?"

Satan glared. "I hope not. You're supposed to fix this so I can go back to my perfect Angelic form, as I recall."

"Heh." Sam refocused on the problem. "So we've got the first piece of the spell." His smile faded and he shuddered. "As difficult as it may be to *use* that information, at least we found it. I sure hope that Jambres has been able to get the second."

"Of course I have!"

The Egyptian sorcerer's voice boomed out of the swirling vortex that appeared moments before he stepped out of it. His hands were covered in hieroglyphs, and he smiled as he emerged.

Apollo's hands moved, his bow reappearing with golden arrow nocked.

"Whoa, whoa!" Sam ran forward, waving his arms. "It's okay. He's with us."

The Sun God's eyes narrowed. "Then why didn't I see his approach?"

Jambres appraised Apollo, looking the god up and down. "An oracle? Perhaps your sight is clouded; I am not truly part of this world, by virtue of my long stay in the Duat, Great One. "

Apollo hesitated, then nodded. "Perhaps. If you are working with Yahweh's servant, then I welcome you to my sanctuary. You are safe, as long as you remain here."

"Safe?" Sam spun around. "Is something after us?"

Apollo licked his lips. "I cannot know. It is best to be cautious."

Jambres bowed. "With your leave, Divine One, we will discuss amongst ourselves what we have learned in preparation for our next actions."

"Very well." Apollo turned. "Do not leave these grounds unless you are ready to be heard once again. As I said, you are safe here."

Jambres nodded and waited for Apollo to walk away before turning back to the others and sitting down, cross-legged on the ground.

Satan sat next, with Sam following. She cleared her throat. "So...did you find anything?"

Jambres scratched at his stubble. "It was actually easier than I thought. Do you know anything about passing through the gates of the Duat?"

They both shook their heads.

"At first, you have nothing. You are cold, you are isolated, you can't see. Tormented by constant hunger, thirst, and fear, you press on, and the only thing you can hold to is your faith, your memories."

Satan's eyes brightened. "That's similar to what I was talking about! The isolation from God."

Jambres acknowledged her comment by opening his hand. "Exactly. Cold pain, as it were. Easy. Hot pain was more difficult, until I remembered the Solar Barque."

Sam shook his head. "I don't understand. How is that pain?"

Jambres laughed and sat back. "The God Ra, when he still lived, was reborn at the beginning of every day. Each night he would die to be resurrected, like the benu."

"Benu?" Satan tilted her head.

"A bird that would erupt in flame and be born anew."

"Oh. A phoenix."

The Egyptian shrugged. "Names change over time. Regardless, using my magic I rode the barge and, as it was about to cross over into day, I lay in Ra's coffin."

He smiled. "It was so much pain. Such searing, searing pain...but there was something else with it, the knowledge of forever, of life eternal, of everything that was and will ever be." He clenched his fist, still lost in the memory. "It's gone now, but the impression remains."

Sam nodded, looking away. "I think I have an idea of what that must have felt like."

Jambres came back to himself. "I now understand the key that Jannes learned through his experience. To enter Heaven, you must come neither too close nor stray too far from the Light, lest you burn or be frozen."

"A truth that has many reflections." Apollo's voice startled Sam, causing him to jump. "My own son fell to such folly trying to reach Olympus."

"I think I've read that story." Sam turned at the waist. "I thought that you had promised him anything, and he chose to drive your chariot."

Apollo winced, his glow dimming as he turned his face away. "Mostly true. What the myths do not say is that Phaeton knew the secret you have discovered, but was unable to keep himself on the right path. He strayed, and, by straying, brought himself to my father's attention. Zeus struck him down for attempting to enter Olympus."

There was a moment of silence.

"So if we make a mistake, God strikes us down?" Sam shook his head. "That doesn't sound like a good time."

"What choice do we have?" Satan sighed. "If we don't try—"

"Heaven falls." Sam nodded. "I know. I just don't like the way the odds keep piling up. This is a real bitch of a spell."

Jambres grinned and held his hand forth. The image of a set of scales appeared on it, with one plate holding a feather and the other a heart. "My brother and I were the most powerful sorcerers in Egypt, until Moses arrived. After his departure, we spent years improving our mastery with magics from all over the world." He closed his fist. "He has only gotten stronger since my death. His skill is incredible. He would not have made a mistake."

"Obviously not." Sam pointed upward without looking. "So we have two more parts of the spell?"

"Happiness and forgetting." Satan scratched at the ground with a stick and brought her legs in. "And I don't think that those are going to be so easy, honestly."

"Why not?"

Satan looked to Jambres. "Didn't your brother take years to get through these? He raised an entire family after forgetting who he was, didn't he?"

Jambres nodded. "Yes. He subsumed his identity to become something else, and he did not learn the secret until he regained his memories."

"The River Lethe in Hades provides forgetfulness." Apollo paced around their impromptu circle, caught up in their discussion now. "But there is no easy way to regain memories once lost."

Sam turned to Jambres. "Your brother cast a spell to remind him of who he was, to give him his own memories back. Could you do that?"

Jambres shook his head. "I told you that he learned many things that we had not known when we challenged Heaven."

Satan held up her hand. "It has to be me."

Everyone turned and looked at her, various forms of confusion on their faces. Sam was the first to speak. "What has to be you?"

"If I..." She shook her head, started again. "If I am still truly the Angel that I was, then Sam can help me remember after I've forgotten. He can use my Name to bring me back to myself."

"And what if you aren't?" Jambres appraised her, looking into her eyes, examining the way she sat. "You have been in a human body for quite some time now, Servitor. You may be entirely mortal."

Satan bit her lip and nodded. "And I would as soon forget the glory of Heaven, if that is true."

Sam glanced over at Apollo. He nodded.

"Are you sure?"

A smile. "Yes, Sam. I don't think we have another choice, do you? None of us can bring back mortal memories...but you might be able to bring back mine." She stepped up to Sam and leaned into his ear, whispering the syllables of her True Name.

Sam hesitated, then sighed. "Okay. Give her the water."

Apollo reached out his hand. A crystal decanter appeared, filled to the brim with a dark liquid. He handed it to Satan, who took it into her hands and gripped the handle. Her nostrils flared as she considered the flask before tipping it into her mouth.

Sam watched her throat move, swallow after swallow, until she brought it away. He watched her eyes for any sign of the magic working.

She stared back at him.

Then she sighed.

"Do you know who I am?" He moved closer, examining her with both mundane and magical Sight. "Do you know where we are?"

"Yes." She shook her head. "It didn't work, Sam. I'm sorry."

Sam nodded. *Great. Now what?* "Okay. What else can we do?" He turned to Jambres. "What about the spell that the two of you used before? Why can't we do that?"

The Egyptian scratched at his nose and shook his head. "One of the first things that Jannes tried to do after I died, when Anubis refused to bring me back, was to try to reenter Heaven." He shrugged. "I think he intended to bargain for my life with the Archangels."

"And?"

A slight upturning of his lip. "He didn't make it. It was...painful."

Sam turned back to Satan. "Can the Archangels do that? Maybe the Metatron, since he got the most chance to watch their magic before they got kicked out of Heaven?"

She raised an eyebrow. "I don't know, Sam. You're the expert on Angels."

Sam blinked. "I don't know what their exact powers are. You'd know better than I would."

Satan stepped closer and put a hand on his brow. "Are you all right? I know you've been under a lot of stress." She smiled. "After this is over, we're going to need to take a long vacation."

His forehead knotted. "I don't—"

She leaned in and kissed him. Her lips moved against his for a few seconds before she withdrew, affecting a pout. "You're always so proper when there are other people around. One of these days I'll break you down."

Sam's cheeks burned, and he took a step back. A snicker from the side drew his attention back to Jambres. The sorcerer was shaking his head.

"It worked, Sam."

He rolled his eyes. "You think?" Then, to Satan: "Um...can I check your memory? We think maybe the water did actually work."

She nodded.

"How did we meet?"

A tolerant smile. "I was working as a bicycle telegram attendant. I brought you a telegram a couple of years ago." She snuggled under his arm. "You thought I was cute."

Despite himself, Sam grinned. "Well...you were."

"I *was*?"

"All right." Jambres broke in. "Let's move on. Cast the spell."

Satan looked between the two of them. "Why? I haven't forgotten anything."

"Actually, you have." Sam took both of her hands in his. "Now hold on a second, okay? This shouldn't take too long."

He did his best to ignore her look of confusion as he set up the casting circle. "All right. Stand over there."

Satan moved into the indicated portion of the diagram. "Sam? Aren't these symbols for Angels? Why are you—"

"Because you're an Angel." He stepped into the center of the circle. "The Accuser. Satan."

She crossed her arms. "That's not possible, Sam. If I were an Angel, I never would have fallen in love with you."

Sam's body and mind both stopped moving.

"I mean, you told me yourself, right? An Angel can't fall in love with a human. They can't desire them, lust after them. It doesn't work that way." Her eyes half closed and she raked her eyes over Sam's body. "And believe me, Mr. Buckland, I certainly don't have any problem desiring you."

Sam looked to Jambres for help, but the Egyptian raised his hands and backed away. Apollo shook his head when Sam turned to him, motioning with one hand toward the woman in the summoning circle.

She loves me...or at least she thinks she does. The thought warmed Sam's core, a pleasant happiness spreading out from his heart before his next thought crushed it. *But I have to bring her back, or we'll never get to Heaven.*

"I..." His voice was thick, and he had to swallow to get the words out. "It won't hurt, either way."

Satan narrowed her eyes. "You..." They widened and she looked at the decanter on the ground. "No. No! You can't!" She stepped out of the diagram. "If you're right, Sam, then..."

"Then you won't love me when you're an Angel. I know." He took a shuddering breath. "But we don't have a choice. If we don't...if I don't bring your memory back, then Jannes starts his war against the gods. Remember?"

Satan shook her head, tears forming. "But...but I don't want to be an Angel. Not if it means we can't have one another."

Sam tiptoed over the lines he had drawn, moving toward the young woman. Satan's jaw was trembling as he ran his thumb across her cheek. She turned her face and kissed his palm, sending warm shivers down his arm.

"The world is more important." Satan smiled, although she was still crying as she looked him in the eye. "That's what makes you the hero, Sam. Always willing to sacrifice your happiness to save everyone else." Before he could respond, she took her place in the circle. "Go on, then."

Sam resumed his place as well. "Please don't be angry with me. I..."

"Don't say it." She shook the hair out of her eyes. "And I'm not angry, Sam. Just sad."

That's worse than being angry. Sam nodded, not trusting himself to speak, and instead focused his mind on casting the spell. He spun his hands in the air, intoning the power of Satan's True Name, as spirals of golden and green light followed his fingertips and the air around them trembled with his song. The sparks gathered around the waiting woman, suffusing her skin with their power, sending shadows out from the circle. He was caught in the spell, the magic pouring from his soul, from his voice as he sang.

Then it was done. Sam stumbled as he was released from the magic's hold, then ran over to where Satan stood, head down.

"It is done, Keeper." She looked up, and her eyes were still wet. "I am once again myself. You have done well."

"Do you...do you remember? What happened while—"

"Yes." She sighed. "But we have more important things to deal with right now. We can discuss this another time, Sam."

He hesitated, then nodded. "All right." He turned to Jambres. "Is that enough? I think we're done."

Jambres barked a laugh. "What about happiness? True happiness. The last piece of the puzzle."

Sam tapped his head. "Two years ago, Gabriel showed me true happiness. She showed me what the world looked like from God's perspective, and I felt His joy."

Jambres looked impressed. "I think that should be sufficient, then. Especially since we seek to enter that particular god's sanctum." He gathered himself, clasping his sapphire amulet.

"If the two of you are ready, I will cast the spell to bring us to Heaven." He glanced skyward. "I hope that we're right." He looked back to his companions. "But if we're not, we won't have time to worry about the barrier that eviscerates us."

"Evisceration is low on my 'want' list." Sam smiled.

Heaven. Holy shit.

THE TRAVELERS

"You must cast your spell outside the borders of my domain." Apollo walked to the edge of the area. "The Compact forbids magics that will link the realms of two different pantheons."

Sam sighed. "You know, I need to get a copy of this Compact at some point and find out what the heck it is."

"Later." Jambres's humor had left him, and his voice was gruff and serious. "We have no idea what will happen once we get there."

Satan hung back.

"Sam?"

Sam turned. "What's wrong?"

"I...I don't think I should go."

Sam's brow furrowed. "Why not?"

She hung her head. "Because I..." Her tongue licked out and ran over her lips. "Because I don't belong to God anymore."

Sam glanced at Jambres before stepping toward her. "Listen. You know Heaven better than either of us. We need you there."

Satan looked into his eyes. "I..." She breathed out. "I'm afraid."

Sam hesitated, then wrapped her in his arms. "I know. That's new to you, isn't it?"

She nodded in his embrace.

"Would it help if I told you that I was, too? I mean, anything could happen. We could be set upon by crazy Egyptian spirits, or the Powers could be corrupted and attack us, or—"

Satan laughed. "You're not actually helping, Sam!"

He released her. "I think I am."

Her laughter stopped, but a smile remained at the corner of her mouth. "All right." She stepped out of the border demarcating Apollo's sanctuary, and she took another breath.

"Let's go, then."

Jambres nodded and motioned for the two of them to link hands. He grasped his amulet and stood between them; Satan and Sam put their free hands on his shoulders, closing the circle.

The Egyptian began to mutter the words of his incantation, calling out in his native tongue. Even with the aid of the Keys, Sam could not make out the full meanings of his words.

Although the sound was not overloud, Sam felt assaulted by the force of Jambres's magic. *How did Moses ever defeat these two?*

He felt gravity loosing its hold, felt his heels lifting off the ground. The same happened for the other two, bringing them up into the air. Their flight was slow at first, but came faster and faster until they were blazing through the sky toward the firmament.

"Can we let go?" Sam's voice fought against the onrushing wind.

"Not until we cross the boundary!" Jambres held his amulet between both of his hands now.

Sam nodded and held onto Satan's hand. He looked over Jambres's shoulder and saw her staring at him.

She nodded, her face set, then looked up again.

"Brace yourselves!" Jambres freed one hand and held it out, where it burst into blue-green flame. "We're almost there!"

"Is it going to—"

They crossed the border between Earth and Heaven.

THE VOICE

"What the hell was that?" Sam released his grip on Jambres's shoulder. "You had me thinking that there was going to be some crazy transition, like we were going to be turned inside out or something, but—"

Sam stopped when he realized that neither Jambres nor Satan paid him any attention. He turned to look in the direction they were looking. Toward Heaven.

Or what was left of it.

"My God."

Stairs of white alabaster led up to a pair of pearlescent gates, decorated with gems and gold. Those gates hung from their hinges, smashed aside. Beyond, thousands upon thousands of Angels hung from weapons—spears, swords, pikes—, moaning and writhing in agony. Glowing blood ran down the hilts, and their perfect faces were contorted in suffering, and Sam could see how close they were to dissolution.

But it was what was beyond them that terrified him.

Satan lunged, but Jambres held her back with a hand on her shoulder.

"No. We can help them later. We need to move on." He pointed at the stairs.

Sam shuddered, then looked around. "I don't see him anywhere."

Jambres hesitated, then shook his head. "If he were defeated, would Apollo have still seen danger?" He gestured toward the impaled celestials. "Why haven't they been taken down already?"

Sam looked around a moment, then sighed. "You're right. Something is definitely going on." He put his hands up in a defensive posture. "Be ready for anything."

The trio began moving toward the stairwell.

"Those are Powers." Satan's whisper was eerie in the otherwise-silent Heaven. "Look at their hands and their wings."

Sam did. "Black. Both of them black."

"Exactly. With gold, to remind them of the reason they exist—to fight against the darkness with the grace and power of God." She put a hand on Sam's elbow. "The front line in the War."

"Okay." The group slowed their pace as they came within thirty feet of the stairwell. "What do the black tear-streaks under their eyes mean?"

Satan stopped walking and looked over at him. "What?"

The other two stopped as well, and Jambres pointed. "I see them too. They look like ink."

Satan peered forward. "I...I don't know what that is. I can barely see it, but, no, the Powers aren't supposed to have anything on their faces."

"Then let's agree that it's bad." Sam looked over at Jambres, then motioned toward the stairwell. "Do we assume the worst?"

Jambres grinned, brandishing his amulet. "I thought you'd never ask, Sam."

"One."

Sam and Jambres set their feet, tensing their muscles in preparation for the sprint.

"Two."

They brought up their hands, ready to summon their respective magics.

"Three!"

The two sorcerers began to run, pumping one foot after another into the indeterminate surface that was Heaven. Sam called up a protective spell, ready to complete the incantation and ward off any attacks he received; Jambres had summoned ghostly khopesh sickle-swords that spun around him in an expanding wall of death, whirling to catch anyone who dared attack their creator.

No attack came.

"Nothing?" Sam glanced around. "That just makes me more suspicious."

"You don't attack someone who doesn't pose a threat." Jambres inclined his head toward the spiraling gold and alabaster structure. It spun upward for about twenty feet, then disappeared into nothingness. "And Jannes obviously doesn't feel we are a threat."

"What's up there?"

Satan smiled. "The Heaven of Generosity, where all is provided but nothing is needed. Souls need only ask their fellows to receive whatever they wish."

"Osiris's palace." Jambres nodded and smiled. "The gods are more similar than they would have us believe."

Sam put a hand on the banister and began to pull himself up the stairs. "Well, we know that Jannes isn't going to be hanging out with the souls. He's obviously looking for something, for someone."

"The Metatron. For revenge." Jambres followed close behind. "He would mention it often when he made prayers and offerings for the dead.”

“You could hear those?”

“Of course.” Jambres laughed. “Does Yahweh not permit the dead to hear the well-wishes of those they leave behind?”

“I wouldn’t know.” They were about halfway up the stairs; they had already passed the place where the spiral had disappeared into the air, but the first level was still visible to them. “I haven’t ever been—”

“The dead can hear the prayers, but they are forbidden to answer.” Satan’s breath tore its way into and out of her throat as she tried to keep up.

“Why?”

“God didn’t want the dead to consort with the living. He declared that the two realms were separate, except that the dead relied on the living to get here and so it was proper for offerings to come this way.” A glittering, shimmering disturbance appeared above them, higher on the stairs.

Sam pointed and began to speed up. "I think that's our exit."

"Thank Heaven!" Satan gulped air. "I don't know how much farther I could have gone."

"Before you go through, catch your breath." Jambres slowed down, forcing the other two to match him. "It makes no sense to run into a possible battle exhausted if you have any way to avoid it."

Several moments of heavy breathing followed, slowing and slowing until the sounds resumed their normal rhythm.

"When my brother and I attacked, we had to fly to the next stair." Jambres spoke while facing the entryway. "If they do decide to attack us here, we need to be ready. It's a lot of open space and they'll have complete freedom of movement. It's the perfect environment for them."

Sam grimaced. "Fantastic. Another place to lay a trap. If there's an ambush, it'll be right on the other side of this portal."

"Move fast and turn around to face them before the attack comes." The Egyptian cocked an eyebrow. "Should you or I go first?"

Sam considered. "I think it should be you."

"Of course you do."

"No, listen. You know the spells to fight Angels—you've done it before. I know how to bind them if necessary, but it takes time and effort. If all Hell breaks loose in there, you can fight them off while I work on locking them down."

Jambres's smile turned from mocking to genuine. "Well said, Sam. I'm pleased that you know your craft so well. I had thought you too young."

Sam waved off the praise. "I don't feel young right now." He moved to one side of the portal. "Are we ready, then?"

Satan stepped up. "Remember that there will be human souls here. I don't know if you can harm them, but be careful."

"They were here before, but none took to the sky. If we keep aloft, we should avoid any risk of injuring them." He turned to the portal. "Let us move."

Jambres dove through the entry, hands aflame. Sam counted to two in his head before stepping out and moving to the side.

There were no Angelic armies awaiting them. There were no weapons leveled.

The two of them stood amongst a great city. The buildings resembled marble, white with pink veins throughout. Many of them towered overhead, but the space between was open and pleasant. Greenery grew in many places, beautiful trees, bushes, grasses and vines, always present but never obtrusive or obscuring. Fountains poured crystalline water into the air, and the entire area was fragrant and clean.

"Where are the souls?"

Satan had stepped through the gate and strode in front of Sam. "They're gone. They're gone! How could—?" She shook her head. "This city should be teeming with them. Millions and millions of people! Where are they?"

"I remember." Jambres waved his hand. "Even then, when my brother and I were here, they watched us as we fought with the Angels. Not as many as you say, but..." He took several more steps; the echo of his feet against the pathways heavy in Sam's ears.

What the hell is going on here?

"Could the Angels have evacuated them?" Sam's head pivoted right and left, looking for any sign of movement. "Is that something they would have done?"

"I...I..."

Sam put a hand on her shoulder. "You need to focus. We need to figure this out before not knowing gets us killed."

"Yes." Satan made a visible effort to compose herself. "I don't know. We've never been invaded before—"

"Yes, you have."

She glared at Jambres. "Except that time, and I was not in Heaven when that happened. If you say that the souls were there for that, then..." She shook her head. "It's not like we have some sort of emergency preparedness plan."

"Noted." Sam took one more look around. "Do we go on? Retreat? Option Three?"

Jambres stepped forward. "Jannes! Where are you?" His voice carried far, rebounding on the group as it reflected from smooth marble walls. "Are you afraid, brother? Come out and face us!"

In a burst of red flame, another man appeared. His resemblance to Jambres was strong, but his face was more weathered. The amulet he wore held a red stone rather than a blue one, and his eyes swept over the gathered three.

Then the fire was gone, and he swept his cloak outward and laughed.

"I truly did not think that you would dare show yourself here, little brother. You have grown much since your death."

Jambres stepped forward and laid a hand on his brother's shoulder. "And you have fallen much since then as well, Jannes. What are you doing here? Attacking Yahweh's realm again. Why? What purpose does it serve?"

"Why do you care?" Jannes pushed the other man away. "You've been happy in the Duat for more than three millennia. You haven't had to watch as the world forgot you, forgot your gods, watch as those very gods turned away from you." The sorcerer laughed. "Fortunately, that isn't going to be a concern much longer. We've already defeated the Angels, and the other gods are too weak to interfere in Earthly affairs anymore."

Jambres seemed floored by his brother's words. He stumbled backward and rubbed the place where Jannes had pushed him.

"We?" Satan came around Sam, moving up to the brothers. "Who else is with you, sorcerer? Who else seeks to overthrow the Throne?"

Jambres turned his eyes on her. "The little Angel. The Accuser. Perhaps you should have turned your gaze toward your own, rather than mankind."

Her eyes narrowed. "Still your tongue and return what is mine, and I shall pray to the Lord to forgive your trespasses." She took another step. "You have violated me, stolen the essence of my very being, and I will have it back, one way or another."

Jannes waved his fingers in front of her. "Oh, you will, will you? How will you manage that?" He leaned into Satan's face, spittle flying as he spoke. "You have no power now, Angel. Even if you did, what could you do to me? What could you use to defend yourself against my magic?"

Sam interposed himself between the two, his hands already raised. "Step back, Jannes."

The Egyptian cocked his head. "You. You interest me. I have seen your ancestors' actions, but I avoided them. Is it true that you can command the servitors of Yahweh as well as those of the Earth, so long as you know the incantation, the True Name?"

Sam held his position. "I'm not really in the mood to have a conversation with you." Sam's hands moved, tracing sigils in the air, leaving afterimages and sparkling contrails. "Honestly, I'm kind of looking forward to kicking your ass."

Jambres moved into a flanking position, holding his amulet in front of him. "We won't let you do this, Jannes. I'm sorry."

Jannes laughed again, erupting into flame and vanishing in a gust of wind. He reappeared on a nearby balcony, wreathed in fire. "If you can kill me, Jambres, then you have fallen even farther than I have." He mirrored his brother's actions, brandishing the glowing ruby necklace. "Let us test your strength against mine, then."

Jambres intoned words which darkened the Heavenly sky. His amulet seemed to absorb the light, pouring it forth in a stream of sun-fire that forced Sam and Satan to avert their eyes. The power enveloped Jannes, wrapping about him like molten fabric.

"The Spear of Ra!" Jannes's voice rang out from within the fireball. "We mastered that when we were still at Pharaoh's court!" Dark blotches appeared in the sphere, spreading, blotting out the light until it dissolved away, leaving the sorcerer untouched.

"Is that really the best you can do?" He opened his arms. "Have you truly become so soft in Osiris's realm?" Jannes tilted his head and cocked a sly smile. "Or perhaps you have been spending your time in the arms of his wife, and that is why you have let yourself become so weak."

Jambres laughed. "A test, brother. Merely seeking to know the depths of your power. It has grown since we parted." Thin strains of music began to float over the battlefield, *a capella* but deep and powerful. Jannes paid it no mind.

"You mean since you died, and Anubis refused to bring you back." The amulet on his chest burned a deep crimson. "The gods turned their back on me, forsook me." Jannes held out his hand, and a swirling grey disk appeared above. "So I learned different ways to do what needed to be done." The disk expanded until it hovered over his head, crackling with black lightning."

Jambres gripped his amulet more tightly. "What is that? Its power comes from no god. It's...it's a blasphemy."

Jannes snapped his fingers and the disk lashed out, stretching tendrils of itself toward Jambres. He fired energy at the encroaching power, but the blasts did nothing to deter its approach.

"It's only a blasphemy if you follow the dictates of a god." The grey plunged into the other sorcerer, into his arms, his chest, his legs, pouring itself into him as he stood, shuddering and shaking. When it was done, Jambres collapsed on the ground.

Jannes coasted off of his perch, arms spread. "Do you still have any fight in you? Or are you done?"

Jambres got back on one knee. "What...what did you do? I can't—"

"You can't feel your gods anymore, can you?" Jannes shook his head. "Your dependence on them is a weakness. A weakness that I have overcome."

Jambres stood. "There is no magic without the gods. Not in the history of the world."

"Is that was Osiris told you? What Isis told you as you feasted in the paradise of the Duat?" Jannes raised one hand, black lightning coursing through his fingers. "There is power untold of in the souls of men, regardless of their belief in gods."

Jambres reached for his amulet, but the metal crumbled under his fingers, corrosion and rust spreading out from his touch. The gem detached from the gold and fell onto the marble streets.

"The gods want to control us, Jambres." Jannes's feet touched ground in front of his brother. "I finally learned how not to let them."

Jambres lunged, swinging a fist at his brother, connecting across his cheek. "The gods created everything that we are! We owe them our lives, our civilization, everything! Without their guidance—"

"We'll never know, will we?" Jannes straightened back up. The red mark on his cheek melted away. "We never had the chance to find out. They took that away from us." He stepped up to Jambres and backhanded him, sending the other man spinning through the air until he landed face-first on the ground.

"You forgot, didn't you?" Jannes followed his brother to where he lay. "This may look like me, but it's an Angel's body. You're a man. Returned, yes, but you're still just a man, Jambres." He knelt down and ran his hand through his brother's hair, the echo of the older brother car-ing for the younger. "At least your being dead means that I don't have to kill you after all."

"That's what we were waiting to hear." Sam's voice caught Jannes's attention, and the Egyptian's head snapped around to where the other two had been hiding amongst the buildings. Glittering circles and sigils danced around Sam, obscuring him from view, pulsating with power.

"Angel body." Red chains began to form, dancing up Jannes's arms and legs. The sorcerer struggled against the binding, but his limbs would not move.

"If that was *your* body, I think I'd beat the shit out of you for a while before I finished this." Sam moved in front of Jannes, with Satan beside him. "But since it actually belongs to her, I think I'll just banish you and be done with it."

Jannes ceased his attempts to escape. "I misjudged you, Keeper. I did." He moved his eyes toward his brother, then back. "And I misjudged Jambres. His attack was the diversion, not the real thing. Well played." His face donned a mask of curiosity. "How did you get the name? Only a mortal can speak one."

"You gave me a mortal body." Satan crossed her arms and raised an eyebrow. "And who knows my name better than me?"

"Of course." Jannes sighed. He opened his mouth again, but before he could speak, Sam interrupted him.

"I think that I'm just going to get you out of there, now." He leaned in close. "I hope that it's painful, Jannes."

"Go ahead!" The ferocity of Jannes's outburst startled Sam. "What do you think will happen? Do you think I can't figure out some way to survive? It's what I've been doing for millennia!" His eyes narrowed. "Do it, then. Do it and you'll never be rid of me."

"Sam." Satan put a hand on his shoulder. "He might be right. In an Angel's body, you can trap him, bind him forever if you have to. If you exorcise him, then who knows what he's going to do?"

Sam turned to her. "What are you saying? If I do that, you'll be trapped in a human body forever. You can't seriously be suggesting—"

Her eyes dipped. "There...there are worse things." She straightened. "Like someone like *him* running wild over the Earth! Think about this."

Sam grimaced. "Well, I suppose we have time to figure it out. It's not like you're going anywhere, anyway." He flicked a finger and Jannes slammed into a nearby wall, the red chains digging into its surface, locking him down.

The sorcerer laughed once, then relaxed, allowing his muscles to go limp inside the chains.

"Jambres?" Satan knelt down beside the fallen Egyptian and shook him. "Are you all right?"

"I...I don't know." He groaned as he got to his feet, clutching the fallen sapphire in his right hand. "I still can't feel the gods, but I'm not as off-balance because of it."

Sam scanned him with his Sight. "It looks like there's some sort of dam or something, between you and your power—but it's wearing away." He nodded and looked in Jambres's eyes. "I don't think it'll be very long."

Jambres returned the gesture, sparing his brother a single glance before looking away. "That was well done, Sam. I will never doubt what the magic of Solomon can do again."

"To be fair, I wasn't sure I could do it myself." Sam gestured toward Satan. "We didn't know if he was still in her body or not. If he had switched, even to another Angel—"

"Still a worthy gamble. There were really no other choices." Jambres stretched and looked at his gem; the sapphire pulsed once, a royal blue. "I can feel the barrier beginning to falter. Thank the gods."

He strode over to where Jannes was trapped. Two pairs of dark eyes locked...and Jambres's fist flew out, striking his brother in the stomach, forcing a gasp and a grimace.

Satan tapped Sam on the arm, causing him to turn around. "Sam...something's still wrong. Something is *very* wrong."

Sam's nerves jolted back to full awareness, and he and Jambres scanned the nearby environs. The city was quiet, unmarred, empty.

"What? What's wrong?"

"Jannes is beaten." She pointed at the sorcerer, still bound by the Keys. "His power is restrained until you release it...and yet, where are the Angels? The Archangels? Why has no one come to find out what happened, to see if we're all right, to question us, *anything*?"

Sam nodded, his mind trudging through the implications. His eyes narrowed and he stormed up to the trapped Jannes, slapping him across the face.

Jannes's head rocked, and, after a moment, his eyes came up to meet Sam's. He was still smiling.

"Where are all the Angels?" Sam gesticulated with one hand while holding the other ready for spellcasting. "Where'd they go?"

Jannes's smile widened, showing his teeth like a shark might. "Gone with their leader, I should expect."

Satan gasped. "The Metatron. Is the Metatron gone?" Her voice rose to a panic pitch. "Without him, we don't know the Word! We don't know what God wants! We—"

"Calm down." Jambres stared at his brother for several seconds, then nodded. "Leave him here. We should investigate the upper Heavens to see if what he says is true."

"Leave him, hell!" Sam shook his head and beckoned with one hand, causing the bonds to release their hold on the wall and wrap wholly around Jannes once again. The Egyptian floated in the air, controlled by Sam's magic. "That's like one of the major no-nos in the Evil Overlord List."

Satan and Jambres shared a glance.

"Never mind. You two seriously need to spend some quality time alone with a computer and a high-speed connection. Anyway, I'm not going to leave him because then someone will come and set him free."

"Ah." Jambres nodded. "His accomplice could circle around us. I understand now." He held up his sapphire and a blue-green light covered all of them. "Let's move, then."

Time for more flying. With a thought, Sam followed after Jambres, keeping a corner of his mind focused on bringing Jannes along for the ride.

Within seconds, the group had breached the barrier into the Third Heaven. This realm took the form of a vast library, bookshelves and scroll repositories stretching into the sky, into the clouds, beyond the reach of eyesight. Ladders and card catalogs shared space with state-of-the-art computers and search technology, suitable for whomever might make use of them. The smell of paper was strong but not overpowering, bringing happy memories to the forefront of Sam's mind.

"I remember the first time I was in a library." The words came out without Sam's direct command, but he made no effort to fight them. "The librarian came down from a ladder just like that one, leaned down, and asked me what kind of books I liked to read."

A tear formed in his eye. "I didn't answer at first. My mom...my mother told me not to be afraid, that the librarian just wanted to help me. I wasn't afraid, though."

He laughed. "I was in awe. I thought that the librarian was God."

Jambres chuckled. "Really?"

"Yeah. The way he came down, the knowing look in his eye, the calmness of his voice. Even right now, if I were told I could pick anyone from any time to play God in a movie, it'd be that guy."

Satan smiled. "That sounds like a beautiful memory, Sam."

"Yeah..." Sam's voice began to trail away, before his eyes regained their focus and he shook his head. "Holy shit. I could barely hear you or see you anymore, like—"

"This is Adam's Library." Satan took a deep breath. "All memories of all humanity, living or dead, past and present, are written here. Their dreams, hopes, wishes, fears...everything."

Jambres cocked an eyebrow. "Is it truly *all* humanity? Or just the worshipers of Yahweh?"

Satan smiled. "Everyone, as best as I can tell."

"Is it always empty, then?" Sam looked around. "Or is this abnormal, too?"

"Unless you intend to meet someone, or desire to have a conversation or discussion with those of similar interests...yes. The Library ensures that you have whatever level of privacy you desire, defaulting to aloneness."

"Then where is everyone?" Jannes chuckled. "I know you're looking for them. Where did they go?" Everyone turned back toward him. "I'd be more worried than you're acting if I were you, is what I mean."

Sam's face drew into a frown. "You're right."

Satan narrowed her eyes. "Why do you say that?"

"It's not just the Angels and Archangels that are missing. It's the souls. It wasn't just the Second Heaven—if this is any indication, it's all of them."

"We need to find the Metatron." Satan picked up the pace, moving through the stacks. "The entrance to the next level is this way."

The group followed. *This doesn't make any sense.* Sam turned a sharp corner, moving more quickly to keep Satan in view. *Who could have done this?*

"No other god could be responsible." Jambres had come up on Sam's flank, speaking as if he had read the other man's mind. "The Compact forbids the poaching of souls once they have reached their proper resting place."

"I seriously need to read this damn Compact sometime."

"It took me three hundred years to get through the whole thing, on and off."

"Fantastic." Sam ducked through a wide wooden doorway. "I'll get right on that."

"Right here." Satan pointed up at a hatch that looked like it was leading into an attic. The wood was cherry, red and warm, and the trapdoor was emblazoned with Angelic runes.

"No human souls are allowed past this point." Satan reached for the chain, but it passed through her fingers. "Damn it!"

"You shouldn't blaspheme in your Heaven, you know." Jannes shook his head, left, right. "It's in very bad taste."

Sam's fist clenched at his side. *God, I want to knock his fucking head off.* "Shut up, asshole. We're dealing with something right now."

"Are you really?" Straining, Jannes turned his gaze on Sam. "It doesn't look like you're dealing with *anything* very well right now."

Sam brought a hand up, and it flared with a transparent flame, like a heat-haze distorting the air around his fingers. "Why don't you open it for us, then?"

"Oh, I'd really rather..." Jannes's hand began to move, despite the muscles fighting to hold it back. Disquiet passed over the sorcerer's face, but it dropped away, replaced by another smile. "But if you insist, I suppose I could."

Sam answered the other's fake grin with his own. "So kind of you."

Jannes's hand clenched around the chain, and a musical note rang out through the entire Library. The trapdoor opened, and a ladder slid down.

"Well, that one looks a hell of a lot better than the one at my house." Sam tested his weight on it; it held without buckling or bending.

"It will let us up now, Sam." Satan ran her fingers over the beams. "The restriction is for opening it, to keep unescorted souls out."

"We're losing time." Jambres scowled at the back of his brother's head. "Go on through. If we're attacked, just move Jannes in front to take the blow."

The other Egyptian laughed. "I don't expect that we will be set upon, but your concern for my well-being is noted, brother."

Sam began climbing, followed by Satan, then Jannes floated up the ladder with Jambres behind him. A cool sea breeze blew through the tunnel.

"Why are there tunnels and stairs in Heaven?" Sam turned back to glance at Satan as they climbed.

"There aren't. Your mind is assimilating the fact that you're moving through a...a dimensional barrier, I suppose, and translating it to something that you understand. Angels don't see things this way."

"What about you?" The sound of crashing surf echoed down the passageway, but there was no light yet. "I know you're in a human body, but your mind is still Angelic, isn't it?"

Satan slowed, chewing her lip and glancing here and there until the floating Jannes bumped into her from below.

"Are we stuck?" His voice, mocking, was very loud in the tunnel. "Because I didn't know it was even possible to get stuck in here."

Satan planted a foot on his shoulder and used it to push herself up, drawing forth a small yelp.

"I can't really say, Sam. Yes, I see the tunnel we're in right now, but the fact you brought my memory back with the Keys contradicts the idea that my mind is truly human. Perhaps it is a limitation of the body. I can't know."

"Right. Ow!" Sam's head bumped into stone. "What is that?"

"Uh-oh." Jannes laughed again. "It looks like we really *are* stuck."

Satan pushed her way up the ladder, forcing Sam to move to the side. "This doesn't make sense. There should not be a barrier here."

"Nothing about this makes sense." Sam flicked his hand and a small aura of bluish light surrounded it, illuminating the slab above. "It's solid, looks like granite."

"What's the problem, Sam?" Jambres's voice came from below his brother, floating up through the near-darkness. "Why are we stopped?"

"Oh, we're just trapped in here, possibly for eternity." Jannes swayed back and forth in his bonds. "Nothing for you to be concerned with— isn't that the way you've spent the last few millennia?"

"There's Angelic script written on it, Sam." Satan drew her finger across the surface of the stone, bringing Sam's attention to the faint impressions upon it. "But why are they so weak? It's like someone wasn't pushing hard enough on one of those carbon copy papers."

Sam repressed the urge to roll his eyes at her lack of cultural savvy. "Let's clear it up a little bit, then." Tracing his own finger across each letter, Sam poured a little bit of the light he had conjured into the grooves, drawing them in blue fire for all to see.

"This...this was written by Archangel Gabriel!" Satan's eyes widened as she read the runes aloud.

Do not pass, for we have chosen our doom.

"That doesn't sound good." Jannes's voice was filled with his unseen smile. "Will you save them, Sam? Or will you turn tail and leave the Archangels to whatever fate?"

"Don't listen to him." Satan turned toward Sam, their faces almost touching in the narrow space. "You can't lie in Heaven, Sam. Not even in writing." She touched the runes on the slab. "Gabriel meant this when he wrote it. He doesn't want us to go by."

Sam winced at the use of the masculine pronoun for the Archangel. "But what if they're all in danger? What....what if Jannes is right, and we could save them?"

"What if he's right? What if he's wrong! Sam, we have no idea what's on the other side of that stone. We can't know without bursting in there and doing exactly what Gabriel told us not to do!" She ran her hand through her hair. "I know that you want to help, but listen to reason for a moment!"

Sam stared at the stone. Time drew out so that each thud of his heart seemed to take several seconds to finish. He pressed his forehead against the rock.

"God, I don't know what to do. Please, give me guidance. Show me the right path."

"Oh, I don't know how helpful that's going to be, Sam." Jannes's mocking laughter grew in volume. "Your God is—"

His words were cut off, descending into muffled garbles.

"Shut up."

Sam didn't turn. "Thank you, Jambres."

He closed his eyes.

Gabriel? Michael? Are you there? Are you safe?

The aroma of roses welled up, permeating the rock, filling Sam's nostrils.

His eyes shot open, but what he saw was not through them.

~~~

Michael lies in chains, his weapons tossed aside and his armor rent in many places. His head is unbowed, but, despite his might, he is imprisoned, trapped.

"Blow the horn, Gabriel."

The voice susurrates, whispering, caressing my ear. The trump is at my side, waiting for my command. My entire being demands that I submit, that I obey.

"I will not." I stand, and fire fills my hands once more. "I will die before allowing you to visit this evil upon the sons and daughters of God."

He moves, terrible and quick. "There is no one to save you, you know. Not even the Almighty."

A tear falls from my eye. "God help me, I hope that you are right."

~~~

Sam's head snapped backwards, almost sending him tumbling down the ladder. Satan reached out to steady him.

"Sam? Did He answer? Did God answer you?"

He shook his head. "No, but I saw Gabriel and Michael. They're fighting something, something powerful, but they're losing. Michael is already trapped, and Gabriel's alone in there." He fought to remember the details of his vision. "She's afraid that whatever it is wants to do something terrible to humanity."

"Could you tell what it was?"

"No." Sam squared his shoulders. "But they're both going to die if we don't do something about it."

"Sam." Satan put a hand on his chest, drawing his attention back to her. "Angels are willing to die to save humanity. God set you above us. Those that weren't—"

"They Fell. I know." Sam grimaced, then set his shoulders and laid both hands on the granite. "And that's exactly why I can't let them do it. We need them too much."

With practiced hands, Sam drew a series of concentric circles on the stone—the depressions too slight to see, microscopic, but sufficient to the task. The spirits of the stone itself stirred, then shifted, responding to his commands.

"Fly." He clenched his fists, and a burst of light punctuated his words. "To the four corners. Fly away."

The spirits broke away, fleeing in all directions. The stone followed suit, blowing apart into tiny pieces of shrapnel that thudded into the people below. Sam threw his hand up to cover himself and turned away as a razor-sharp piece bisected his right earlobe.

A rush of power, a metaphysical burst, flew outward from the new opening as if it had been a cork holding it back. The attic setting dissolved, leaving the group staggering, blinking in the sudden bright light.

Sam put a hand up to shield his eyes, scanning the blurred shapes and waiting for them to resolve.

"Sam!" Jambres pointed to a disturbance in the starlit sky above. "That is where the entrance to the next Heaven lies."

"Okay, then. If we're going to find them, find the Metatron, that's where we need to be."

Sam began to run, turning his head back to address his comrades. "Let's go!"

He slammed into solid stone, tumbling backward and landing on his ass.

"Were you looking for me?"

Sam glanced up to see that the thing he had run into was not, in fact, stone—instead, he had struck a ten-foot tall Angel. His shimmering samite robe caught the ambient light, and his purple wings glistened, almost as if they were moist.

Satan fell to her knees.

"None of that, please." The Metatron reached out, bringing her back to her feet. His smile was smooth and pleasant, but not dazzling like that of Lucifer. He turned to Sam, Jannes, and Jambres. "I was once human, and I remember still what it was like."

Jannes choked a laugh from behind his brother's hand, and Jambres tightened his grip.

"I am sorry to see the two of you fighting, though." The Metatron approached the pair, looking down on them a moment before turning back toward Sam. "But I suppose there are more important issues."

"Do you know what's happening?" Sam looked around, but he couldn't see anything except for the ambient glow and a faint mist obscuring the surroundings. "Where are Gabriel and Michael?"

"Safe, and recovering, although displeased by their defeat, I should imagine." The Metatron shook his head with a small chuckle. "I have taken command of the situation."

Satan burst into a smile. "Thank God!"

"Indeed." One side of the Metatron's mouth curled up in a wry smile.

Sam stared at the Metatron. *Something's wrong. What's...*

"Is everything all right, Sam?" The Archangel's pleasant voice cut through Sam's thoughts. "You seem distressed."

"I..." He shook his head then inclined it toward Jannes. "What should we do with him?"

"I will take him with me." The Metatron extended a hand, and Jannes floated through the air. "I wish to know what has transpired since last we met."

"Of course." Satan nodded her head, almost a bow. The Archangel turned his gentle smile toward her.

"Accuser. Once I have finished with the sorcerer, I will return you to your proper body." He laid a hand on her cheek, and her face moved into his palm as if it were magnetized. "You have done well, given the circumstances."

"Thank you." Her eyes were locked on the Metatron's face. "It wasn't as difficult as I thought it would be."

This isn't right. Sam felt confusion, annoyance, anger bubbling under the surface of his mind. *Or is it me?*

The Archangel laughed. "While there are many things about being human that I don't miss, I still find myself reminiscing now and then." He looked at the assembled company, at Sam and Jambres. "You are, both of you, strong and amazing examples of humanity. Learn to trust in yourselves and you will do great things."

He turned, his wings extending, and Jannes floated up to his side.

"Farewell."

"Wait."

Sam stepped forward, The Metatron paused, his head turning toward the group again, looking down at Sam.

"What is it, Keeper?"

Sam licked his lips. Everyone was looking at him now, curious. *What am I doing?*

"What about...what about the fallen angels?" He waved his hand at the ground, indicating Earth. "They were taken from my house by a demon. What's going to happen to them?"

The Metatron smiled again. "You need not worry. They have not been further harmed." His head began to move again.

"No!"

Another pause. "I'm sorry?"

Satan came up to Sam's shoulder, laid her hand on it. "Sam? What's going on?"

Sam ignored her. "Tell me how. There are others, angels that are trapped below. What's going to happen to them?"

The Archangel turned full toward him. "Why do you ask these questions of me? I am—"

"The Metatron. I understand." Sam rubbed his cheek as he kept his eyes on the Archangel. "But—"

"Sam!" Satan pulled on him, trying to make him face her. "Why are you questioning the Voice? He is the direct link to the Almighty! It..." Her face fell. "It sounds like you're accusing him of something, even though I'm not sure what."

"Yes, Keeper." The Metatron folded his arms in front of him, and his wings made a single beat. "If you wish to make an accusation, do so. My patience is beginning to wear thin, even for the Creator's favored earthly servant."

Sam took a deep breath. "Before all of this happened, at the start of it all, the first thing was the falling of the angels, all over. I saw dozens of them myself, and I know there were more." He turned his head to look at Jambres.

"Is there any spell you know, anything you can conceive of, that could have done that?"

Jambres hesitated before shaking his head. "...Nothing. Not even to one, let alone many."

Satan nodded. "It's never been done before. Angels have only fallen by being..." Her mouth gaped, and she turned back toward the Metatron. "...by being cast out of Heaven."

Sam counted three heartbeats.

"Did *you* cast them out?"

The Archangel stared down at him, then laughed. "I do not answer to you, mortal man, or to you, Accuser."

Sam raised his hands, and Jambres began to radiate a blue-white aura.

"I don't care who you are." Sam began to trace a circle around himself, and the runes on his arms shifted and glowed. "If the truth will not damn you, then speak it. Answer the question."

Instead, the Metatron waved his hand, and a burst of golden flame erupted from his fingertips, flying toward the three. The fire burst on the protective circle, crackling and snapping at

Sam's face. He took a half-step back, shielding himself from the heat.

Jambres held his amulet up once again as the firestorm flowed away from him like a river down the mountainside. "You haven't tricked me this time, Angel. I am still protected from your magics by the will of Osiris."

"So you are." The Metatron's lip curled. "But she is not."

Both Sam and Jambres turned, their mouths opening in shock. The flames still raged, covering Satan's body, covering her flesh and hiding her from view. The only indication that she was there was the general humanoid shape curling in on itself as the fire burned in a smokeless conflagration.

She didn't even have time to scream.

"Why...why would you do that?" Sam stepped toward her, but the heat was too intense for him to approach. "She couldn't hurt you, she..."

"Sam!" Jambres's voice trembled with urgency. "Get back in—"

"Too late." As Sam's head came up and his eyes began to widen in comprehension, the Metatron brought his fist up and clenched the fingers together. Another eruption of the angel-fire formed around the Archangel's hand. "Goodbye, Keeper."

Sam's eyes locked onto the onrushing doom.

Well, shit.

THE COMMANDERS

Burning doesn't hurt nearly as much as I thought it would. Sam looked down at his body, covered in golden fire. *Maybe I'm already dead and just don't realize it.*

The flames snapped, hissed, and burned on his skin, but the heat did not reach him, the light did not harm him. He extended a hand, curling the fingers in and out. He couldn't see his own flesh, but the digits still worked.

He turned his eyes back toward his enemy.

The Metatron's face was furrowed, his eyes uncertain. "How are you doing this? You are unprotected by the Keys of Solomon."

"So he is." A deep, rich voice burst from the Heavenly silence. "But he is not alone."

The ambient light brightened, and the sheer intensity of it overshadowed the fire, blowing it away as if the radiance were a physical force. Sam blinked, turning to the source of the brightness.

A flash, and Apollo appeared, stepping out of the glow and striding toward the Metatron.

"You are a fool, godling." The Metatron flared his wings out. "You are not welcome in Yahweh's domain, by virtue—"

"Yes, the Compact." Apollo reached out his hand, and his orichalcum bow materialized, arrow nocked. "But you have attacked my chosen prophet, Servitor."

Confusion returned. "No...no. What do you mean? He is—"

Movement near Sam's feet caught his attention.

She's alive!

Satan had brought herself up to one knee before rising. "No. Apollo marked us before we came here." She turned her eyes on the god. "Did you intend for this to happen?"

"If a prophet is attacked by the servants of a god, it demands a response." Apollo laughed, his teeth brighter in the luminescence he gave off. "And when you're this badly outmatched, you play fast and loose with the rules."

The Metatron took a step back, his eyes flicking back and forth between the individuals assembled in front of him.

Sam moved back into the circle he had drawn, still glittering just above the ground. "Submit, Archangel. Explain yourself and stop this, so we can repair the damage you've already done."

The Metatron slammed his fist into his chest and advanced on Sam, stopping just at the edge of the circle. "The damage *I've* done?" His face fell, and his voice cracked, the music in it hitting a discordant note. His eyes blazed blue, leaking gold. "Ask him! Ask him why I've done this!"

The sheer violence of the emotion in his cry gave Sam pause. "What? Who are you talking about?"

"Who am I talking about?" The Angel drew himself up, then raised his hands above his head as if making an offering to the sky. "Him! The Almighty! Lord of All!" The fire burst into being around his hands again.

Satan stepped toward him, reaching out a hand. "I don't understand. What has the Lord done to anger you so?"

"Nothing!" The Archangel waved her away, causing her to step back to avoid being struck. "He has done nothing, don't you see? I was his Voice, his Word. He spoke to *me*, and I to the world for Him."

He hung his head. "And now...nothing. Nothing for so long. The Creator has not spoken to me for over two thousand years."

Sam almost moved forward, but stopped himself before exiting his protective circle. "You mean...Christ?"

"Yes." The Metatron's eyes came back up, wet with golden tears. His wings faltered, folding behind his back. "The birth of Jesus Christ. Since then, I have not heard the Almighty."

Apollo lowered his bow. "How is this possible? Yahweh's influence has done nothing but expand since then, under the influence of Christianity. The Catholic Church alone—"

The Metatron shook his head. "He told me nothing about the new faith that was spreading in His name, but Gabriel had delivered the revelation. I did my best to help it thrive..."

"But the saints? The miracles? What about those?" Satan's head moved back and forth in an unconscious negation as she spoke. "Are you saying that you...you made those things up?"

"Is it so hard to believe?" Sam's voice was hard, cutting. "What other explanation can you have for all the factionalization, all the splintering? How many denominations of Christianity are there, anyway? And the rest, too. Because you didn't know what to do?"

The Archangel turned away, leaving only his profile visible. "You don't understand. Everyone looked to me, wondering what the

Almighty wanted, what He needed us to do. What was I supposed to tell them?"

"So what about now?" Jambres shook his head. "What is the purpose of all this? Are you trying to take over Yahweh's position?"

"...No." The Metatron sighed. "Lucifer tried that, and his pride condemned him. I have no desire to Fall into Hell."

His eyes turned to Sam, Angelic boring into man. "You were supposed to be the catalyst, Samuel. The Accuser came to me, asked me for permission to tempt you, to test you."

Satan's eyes widened, and she backed up, pivoting to face both of them. "Sam, I..." She closed her eyes, reopened them, addressed the Archangel. "I thought I was speaking to the Creator."

"I know." He didn't turn, but kept looking at Sam. "You were not worthy, Samuel."

Sam fought to keep his countenance still; even though he knew that this Angel was his enemy, the words still came with the air of God's judgment, spoken by his Voice.

"You were eminently flawed, completely unsuited for the task at hand...but I called you because you had a quality that I needed—disbelief." The Metatron looked into the distance. "But I could not have anticipated how strongly the experience would affect you."

"Why did you let Satan test me, if you thought I was such a failure?" Sam's voice was strained, holding back his emotion. "If I had failed, wouldn't I have lost the power?"

"Yes. Unfortunately, the Accuser was appointed by the Almighty. I could not deny the right to test. If I had, it would have given me away."

"But I found him worthy." Satan moved backward, closer to Sam. She was crying. "I knew he was worthy!"

"And so he proved to be. Once again, Accuser, you fulfilled your duty, bringing a man closer to the Creator through temptation and trial. You took him away from me, so I had to improvise." His head dipped again. "And then there was Gabriel."

The mention of the other Archangel brought Sam out of his injured pride. For just a moment, he thought he could smell honeysuckle. "What about Gabriel?"

The Metatron smiled, but it was sad, almost a weak laugh at himself. "Gabriel is gifted above all of us—above myself, above Michael, Uriel, above even Lucifer before his Fall. Gabriel receives the Divine Revelation."

Sam licked his lips. "She told me about that, how God's thoughts, His knowledge, consume her sometimes, take her over."

"If I were gone, Gabriel would step in to guide Heaven in my place." The Metatron turned back, facing the others fully once more.

"And the Angels would follow the Divine Fire." Apollo nodded, his fingers twitching on his arrow. "I understand the visions now. You hoped she would be trapped forever, to remove her from Heaven."

"But why?" Satan screamed, crying freely now, anger and fear and sadness all mixed together in her face. "We trusted you! You were the Word of God! Why would you do this to us?"

The Metatron looked at the weeping Angel and put his hand on her head. "How could I do otherwise, Accuser? If the Almighty no longer speaks, what is Heaven?

"I had hoped it was a...a hiatus. That the Lord would return. Decades passed, and nothing. No change at all. I started to search for Him...but I could not leave Heaven. If I had told the Host, we would have fragmented for lack of authority. So I made a decision. When the Byzantines fell, I knew that Yahweh had abandoned us.

"So I abandoned Him."

Stunned silence.

"When His servants are gone, will He return? Will He come looking to see why we no longer answer?" The Metatron held his hand out toward Apollo. "When He has no more worshippers, will He come to find out why? When His power begins to wane, will it concern Him?"

Apollo was as shocked as the rest. "You...you have betrayed your Creator. He invested his power into you, and—"

"And yet, He has done nothing about it!" The Archangel clenched his hand again, and the bonds on Jannes shattered, splintering into thousands of fragments of light. "He allowed this sorcerer to storm Heaven, to defeat His Angels. He did nothing!"

"Maybe Yahweh is dead." All eyes turned to Jambres. "It is possible. Many of my own gods live no more."

Jannes brushed himself off, shaking the remaining runes off of his clothes and sending them dissolving into the air. "Don't be foolish, brother. Yahweh is not a member of a pantheon—there is no one who can provide power to his followers if he were to die."

"And Gabriel still receives the Revelation." The Metatron shook his head, closing his eyes. "No, the Lord still lives, but He has abandoned us. Ignored us for too long." Light, blue and gold, surrounded the Archangel. "And I will not allow it anymore."

At once, everyone was battle-ready again—Jambres and Sam prepared with spells, Apollo drawing his bow. "We won't let you get away, Metatron. What you're planning is wrong."

"What I'm planning?" The Metatron laughed. "Keeper, do you truly believe I would reveal my *plans* to you? I just hope that, as you watch what follows, you understand why I do what I do." He raised one hand. "Good-bye."

Apollo's arrow fired in concert with Jambres's bolt of electricity, but neither found their mark; the Archangel and Jannes were both gone—no fanfare, no explosion, no sparkle, just winking out of existence as if they had never been there.

"Damn it!" Sam stormed over to where the two had stood, as if he could trace their departure. "Where did they go?"

Apollo dipped his head and closed his eyes. "I...I cannot see them. Not yet. Their future is not set firmly enough to be writ by the Fates."

"Sam."

He turned to the woman, the Angel. She was standing, looking away from him.

What have I done? Sam stepped up to her side, put a hand on her shoulder. *She could have been killed. I never should have brought her.*

"Are...are you okay?" *God, did I really just ask that?*

"I...I want to kill him, Sam." Her voice trembled, and Sam could feel her muscles vibrating, tense, under his hand. "I feel...horrible. Angry, but..."

"You feel betrayed." Sam glanced back at the others; they had withdrawn, giving a respectful distance to the pair. "You trusted him. He violated that trust."

"Is it always like this?" The question held new meaning for Sam now as he looked into her eyes, saw the confusion, the pain swimming within. "Does it stop?"

Sam licked his lips. "Eventually. But it can take a long time."

Satan's eyes danced from one to the other of his. "How long?"

"That depends." He couldn't break away from the deep pools of brown in front of him.

The two stood there a moment, breathing, staring at each other.

Then Satan's feet moved, standing on her toes, bringing her face up toward his.

~~~

Heaven split open with a stroke of lightning, the thunderclap booming, driving the mortals present to their knees with its sound.

What the hell was that? Sam blinked, trying to dispel the dots floating in his vision. "Jambres? Satan? What's going on?"

A warm hand touched Sam's face, sending soothing warmth through his body. His vision cleared, and he saw the loving smile of the Archangel Gabriel.

"Hello, Samuel."

Sam stood back up, and the Archangel withdrew to allow him room. He looked around; the others were rising as well, except for Satan, whose head remained bowed.

"I did not expect to see you this soon." The new voice came from the sexless form of the Archangel Michael, whose hands gripped his two blades as he stepped out of the mists near
~~~

Gabriel. "I am sorry it is not under better circumstances."

Apollo raised his hand. "Forgive me, Servitors. I mean no trespass in your realm."

"You are welcome here, Apollo." Gabriel turned to the god. "You saved the lives of the Keeper and the Accuser. You helped reveal the nature of the threat against us. We are in your debt."

Michael glanced sidelong at the Greek divinity. "But that debt does not extend far. Remember that, godling."

"There isn't time for that!" Sam's shout drew the attention of the Archangels back to him. "What are we going to do? The Metatron has betrayed God!"

"He has forfeited the office, and the title that went with it, but, yes." Gabriel hung her head, her gold-tipped wings sagging behind her. "I tried to seal him within Heaven so that he could not escape to work his mischief, but you broke through my barrier, Samuel."

Sam felt some of the anger drain, replaced by shame. "I...I'm sorry. I was just—"

"You were trying to help. I know." She reached out for him again, this time brushing his hair back from his eyes.

"Did you know?"

Satan stood, wiping her eyes. Her face was filled with leashed fury, and she repeated her question, advancing on the glorious Archangels. "Did you know?"

Gabriel said nothing. Michael came forward, sheathing his blades. "Yes, Accuser. The Archangels all knew."

She stepped backward, her hand going to her heart. "Wh...why didn't you tell us?"

Gabriel tried to take Satan's hand, but she shook it off. "We could do nothing else, Satan. What would we have said? That the Creator was gone, but we knew not where?"

"Yes!" Satan waved her arm in front of her, snapping it in a wide arc. "We could have looked for Him, tried to find Him! Hell, at least we could have decided what to do about it, together!"

Michael shook his head. "It was too dangerous. The Archangels decided to investigate the

Creator's absence for ourselves before making the Host aware."

"And did that work?" Satan spat the words into Michael's perfect face. "Maybe if you had enlisted the rest of us, we could have found Him!"

Sam put a hand on Satan's shoulder; she glanced over at him.

"You're letting your anger get to you again." He inhaled through his nose. "Deep breaths. Calm down."

For a moment, Satan's eyes danced in her head, the skin surrounding them twitching with muscular tension. Then she nodded, bowing her head and beginning to breathe.

"There will be time for recriminations later." Sam extended a hand toward Jambres and Apollo. "I think it's time you told us the truth. What's going on? What is the Metatron planning?"

Gabriel gave a sad smile. "Enoch. Enoch has lost faith."

Jambres snorted. "That much was obvious."

Michael cut the air with his hand. "You don't understand. Angels cannot lose faith. We are creatures of it, forged from it. Without faith, we are nothing."

Gabriel nodded. "Your brother has learned to do magic without faith, without a connection to his gods. We think that he taught, or changed, Enoch to make it possible for him to exist without his faith."

"But for what purpose?" Apollo motioned to Sam. "The Keeper of the Keys saw a terrible vision, one that I have seen myself. Yahweh turning his back on the faithful of the world, and the unbelievers rising up to destroy the ones who held the gods in their hearts."

"Of course." Sam's voice was low, but Apollo turned to look at him. "It was the Voice of God." He looked up. "Don't you understand? The Metatron is the Voice of God. It was never God at all."

Jambres considered. "Then, if we are to believe him—"

"Falsehoods are impossible in Heaven." Michael did not turn to address the Egyptian. Jambres returned the favor.

"—then we have to accept that his plan is to eliminate those who believe, trying to draw Yahweh out of wherever he is."

"That's not great." Sam shook his head, then looked back to Gabriel. "You have no idea where God is?"

"None, Samuel." Her wings beat twice. "What I showed you two years ago was true. It came from the mind of the Almighty, from His heart. But I cannot find His consciousness. It is as if it is...masked, or dispersed, or..."

"It doesn't matter now." Michael pointed at the skyline, and the air wavered, until it showed the Earth. "Enoch and his servant are free. We must find them, capture, contain, or destroy them, and prevent this atrocity from occurring." He paced back and forth, then stopped in front of Satan. "Accuser, we will need your help."

Satan recoiled, looking between Michael, Gabriel, and Sam. "Wh...what do you mean?

"Not as you are." Gabriel stepped toward her. "But Enoch is not the only one who can return you to your Angelic form. We have spoken with Uriel, and he agrees—we need an Archangel to replace the Voice. We want that to be you."

Satan gasped. Sam blinked. Jambres narrowed his eyes.

"As the Accuser, you are the perfect counter to whatever Enoch plans." Michael drew his sword, which burst into flames, and he swung it in the air to punctuate his sentences. "You understand the hearts of mankind more than any member of the Host. You can help us ensure that, whatever his exact plans, he cannot take faith away from humanity."

Satan stood, her hand on her chest, absorbing the impact of the Archangels' words. Her face began to turn to the left, toward Sam, but stopped before it had moved more than two inches.

"I..." She shook her head. "I don't know. I've never wanted to...I mean, I..."

"Satan." Gabriel's musical voice brought her face to the front again. The Archangel laid her hands on the woman's shoulders. "We need you. Without you, we may not be able to confront Enoch. He may succeed." Blazing blue eyes met dark brown. "You love the Lord. You love mankind. You have heard the consequences, from the Keeper of the Keys himself. Will you allow this to happen, without doing whatever you can to stop it? Can you?"

Still she did not respond. Her eyes flicked back and forth. Sam could see the emotions warring in her face.

What do I do? Sam tried to speak, but the words died in his throat. *Do I tell her to accept? Does she want to? What if she wants...what if she wants to stay?*

Nothing.

"We are wasting time!" Michael drove the sword-tip into the Heavenly landscape and advanced on Satan.

Gabriel put a hand out to stop him, but Michael brushed past it, coming right up to her, invading her space, nose almost touching hers.

"Accuser, Heaven has need of you. As the Commander of the Hosts, I demand that you submit, that you serve. Will you take up the charge, or will you be cast out, as was Lucifer, for disobedience, for the sin of Pride?"

"You're going to kick her out of Heaven because she's hesitating?" Sam threw his hands in the air. "I thought this was Heaven, not some sort of tyrannical government where people get told what to do all the time!"

Gabriel put a finger to her lips. "Heaven *is* an autocracy, Keeper. We all serve the Lord."

What the fuck? Sam's thoughts stuttered under the weight of the shock. "You mean...you mean that, if you needed to, you could go tell the human souls that they needed to help you invade, like, Duat or something? And that if they didn't come with you, they'd be kicked out of Heaven?"

Jambres crossed his arms. "Why did you have to suggest that they invade *my* realm, Sam?"

Sam ignored the Egyptian. "Well? Is that right?" He looked back and forth between the

Archangels. "Because that sounds like bullshit to me."

"No, Sam." Satan's voice was a whisper. "Humans are different. The Creator says we are not to infringe upon human free will, but..." She swallowed. "We serve. Angels serve. We don't have the same freedoms that you do."

Michael nodded. "We are the Almighty's instruments, nothing more. Our existences are at His pleasure, and we must follow His commands."

"But He's not even here!" Sam held his head in his hands for a moment. "Whose orders are you following?"

"Mine." Michael turned. "As the Commander of the Hosts, appointed by God Himself, I am the highest-ranking Archangel left in Heaven. It falls to me to make the decision of what assets to use in the upcoming battle, and those orders will be followed...or there will be consequences."

Sam sputtered. "You're seriously conscripting her? The punishment being falling to Hell? I don't believe this!"

Satan nodded. "The last time it was neces-sary, there was War in Heaven. Michael won that war for us, and earned the right of com-mand from the Almighty. We all knew it, we all accepted it." She sighed.

"Very well, Commander. I submit. I will obey." She turned away from the Archangels and stepped up to Sam.

"I can't believe this." Sam's face flushed with his anger and frustration. "I know you want to be an Angel, I understand, that's fine, but to force you into this, to threaten you with –"

"Please don't be angry, Sam." Satan put on a brave smile, but tears sparkled in the Heavenly radiance. "We can't help it. It's the way we were made, what we are. We serve."

"But..." Sam deflated. "If this is what you want, then all right. I just wish that it was your choice, not theirs."

Satan embraced the Keeper, wrapping her arms around him. He felt the warmth of her still-human body against his, allowing himself to reciprocate, holding her close to him.

"It isn't what I want, Sam." Her whisper tickled his ear. "But it's what I have to do. I'll miss you."

Sam recoiled. She let him go, the smile still on her face. "You...you..."

Satan nodded, and the light of Heaven shone in her tears. "Goodbye, Keeper."

Her flesh turned to light, sending out pulses of power. Jambres averted his eyes to avoid the outpouring of radiance, but Sam stared into it, his eyes burning, searing inside his skull.

He raised his hands.

Traced a circle around himself.

"Fuck you all."

THE LIGHTBRINGER

Sam materialized back in his living room, falling to his knees as soon as the power he had summoned had released him. He stood, skin hot, boiling within.

"Goddamn it!" He swung his fist, smashing it into the nearest wall, putting his hand through the plaster.

"Goddamn it!" He reached out, pulling the bookshelf off its rivets, sending tomes tumbling onto the ground, splintering the wood.

Sam stumbled with the effort, colliding with a glass cabinet, shattering it, sending sharp slivers falling to the ground.

There he sat, crying, screaming with no words.

Why? Why did she say yes? How could they? A piece of glass stuck out of his palm; he pulled it, not feeling the pain, watching as his blood dripped from the wound.

"Sam?"

His face came up. Sara was standing at the entrance to the hallway leading to the bedrooms. Her eyes were wide, and she was clutching the Keys to her chest. A moment later, Gregory's head rounded the corner, above Sara.

"My God." He pushed past the girl and knelt down next to Sam. "Are you all right? What happened?"

Sam kept looking at his daughter. *Get it together!*

Who the fuck cares?

You do! He wiped his eyes with the back of his hand. His voice shook, and his face began to ache. "Hey, Sara. How you doing?"

"Are you serious? You just show up after you leave to do some crazy magic shit, start smashing up the place, and you're asking *me* how I'm doing? What the fuck is the matter with you, Sam?"

Sam started to chuckle, then snort. All the injuries—his hand, the bleeding wound, his back—hurt, but it did nothing to dampen the laughter.

"Well, he's not possessed, if that helps." Gregory shook his head. "But I think I recognize the symptoms of a breakdown when I see one"

Sam nodded, wiping his eyes again with his thumb. "Yeah. Yeah, I guess. It's just..." He looked up at Gregory. "Two years ago, I found out about God. And Angels, and demons, and everything. Changed my whole world, you know?"

Gregory smiled. "I remember, Sam. Very well."

"Yeah. It was like, the world may be hard, it may suck, there might even be demons crawling around trying to tempt you into Hell and all these terrible things...but there were these amazing, divine beings that were looking out for you. And they were everywhere. I mean, seriously everywhere. They were there when the Twin Towers fell. They're at every car crash, every time someone has a dead baby. Always there."

Gregory nodded.

"But it turns out that they're just as bad as the fucking demons!" Sam shoved a still-standing pane down to the ground, where the shattering sound made Sara jump. "If you're an Angel, you can't even say no—they say jump, you say how high. What the hell is that? How could God set it up that way? How could He ignore His own creations like that?" He looked back down. "If He really loves us all so much, why doesn't He love them enough to give them freedom, too?"

"Funny." A smooth, suave voice startled them all. "That's exactly what *I* said, once upon a time."

The trio turned to see a dark-haired, dark-eyed gentleman in a white suit and red tie standing at the door. He winked at Sam.

"Long time no see, Keeper. How've you been?"

Sam shook his head, as if to banish a hallucination.

"Lucifer?"

Gregory recoiled, backing up to the wall and raising his hands. "I banished you once, monster, and I can do it again!"

Sara stared. "Is that really...are you really the Devil?"

Lucifer flourished his hand, materializing a top hat and placing it on his head. "Indeed I am, lovely miss, although that name means different things to different people." He turned back to Sam. "But I heard you were having some difficulties of your own, Keeper, and thought that I might be able to help."

"As if we'd ever accept *your* help." Gregory's face was etched with anger and hatred. "You ruin everything you touch, bring darkness into the hearts of good men. You—"

"Yes, yes. Granted." Lucifer shook his head, then brushed off his shoulder as if some insect were crawling on it. "You see, I think we got off on the wrong foot, before. All that business about trying to kill people and take over the world, and all. But that's not what this is about."

Sam brought himself back to his feet. "He's right, though. Why should we trust you? I should just send you away, back to Hell, right now."

Lucifer laid a finger on his nose. "And yet, you haven't. Because you know I'm right." He rolled the top hat down his arm, making it vanish as it reached his fingers. "God, or the Almighty, or the Creator, or whatever they're calling Him in Heaven nowadays, gave you humans more rights than he had us, his first creations. I called Him on it, and I was banished for it." He raised a finger to forestall interruptions. "Now, to be fair, I did then lead an army against His, and I got beaten. Michael booted my ass out like a...well, anyway." He laughed. "So I agree with you, for one thing. Why, what good would it do me, to betray you when you're actually on my side?"

"We're not on your side, demon." Gregory began to move his hands in a spell.

Lucifer ignored him.

"But then there's what's going on with the Metatron and everything."

Sam's voice worked of its own volition. "Enoch."

"Oh, so they've officially exiled him, too, have they? They take your title when they do that, start calling you by your name." He nodded. "Anyway, I don't know everything, but when my princeling was stuck in your head, Sammy, he got to see what you knew, and told me." Lucifer smiled. "That vision you had? I recognized the voice straight off. Definitely the...definitely Enoch."

"So why does that affect you?" The sound of Gregory's incantations caught Sam's attention. "Hey, I don't like him either, but I think we need to hear him out. Just...just wait a minute before trying to exorcise him or anything, okay?"

Lucifer's grin grew at the hurt look on Gregory's face. "It affects me because...well, now you know about the other gods, right? The other afterlives? They all have their versions, and their faithful go there, that sort of thing?"

"Sure."

"Where do you think I get my followers? My souls? I can only get them from people who believe in God, and that they need to be punished. If someone is guiltless, I can't touch them." He opened his hands. "So, this whole 'let's kill the faithful thing' may sound great to a lower-ranking soldier demon who doesn't know spit from shit, but that's only because he doesn't understand the drawbacks."

"Enlighten me."

Sara spoke up. "You mean that, if they don't believe in God, then it doesn't matter what they do, they won't go to Hell, and you won't get new souls?"

Satan turned to Sara, raising an eyebrow and clapping his gloved hands; she blushed and retreated against the wall. "Got it in one. You're exactly right." He addressed Sam again. "I can't let this happen any more than you can, but the Angels sure as Hell won't work with me." Three heartbeats. "Pun intended."

Sara snickered.

"But you think I will."

"I have a lot to offer, you know." Lucifer straightened his suit coat. "I am an Angel, albeit Fallen, and I command an awful lot of demons. The souls in Hell span the entire history of mankind." He winked again. "And, in my exile, I learned many secrets about the universe that even the Archangels don't know."

Sam said nothing.

"You're not seriously considering taking his offer, are you?" Gregory came up to Sam's side. "He's *Lucifer.* Have you forgotten what he tried to do? What he *did* do? He almost—"

"He almost killed me. Several times. But it didn't work then, and I think he knows it wouldn't work now." Sam inclined his head, looking at the Devil. "Right?"

"Unfortunately, yes." He sighed. "While I would still prefer to have control of the Keys myself, it isn't worth the effort right now to try to corrupt you or to kill you and take them. It wouldn't help me, and it wouldn't help stop this."

Sam nodded. Gregory looked back and forth between the two of them.

"If you do this, Sam, I'm leaving. I will have nothing to do with him, and I pray to God that he doesn't lead you to ruin as he did me."

Sam nodded again. "Noted." He turned to Gregory. "I'm sorry. You get to be free, Greg. I have to be the Keeper of the Keys, and do what I need to do." He glanced up at the ceiling. "Just like the Angels."

Gregory scowled, then stormed to the back door, avoiding coming anywhere near Lucifer. Sara watched him go, her eyes clouded, worried.

Sam squared his shoulders. "If we do this, we do it my way. I'm in charge, and if I think for a second you're trying to pull something, I send you straight back to Hell for the next thousand years."

Lucifer nodded, still smiling.

"All right." Sam extended his hand. "You're in."

ABOUT THE AUTHOR

Jason Patrick Crawford is a father of three rambunctious boys and has been happily married for over ten years. He lives in sunny California, where he constantly laments the lack of rain. He welcomes your feedback and hopes you will take the time to review this novel. Thank you for reading!

More from Jason P. Crawford

Chains of Prophecy: Samuel Buckland is a young man who has it all and is planning for the future. Gregory Caitlin is a businessman and politician. He has designs to bring hope back to a world in need...and he'll be damned if anyone gets in his way!

When the two cross paths, even the angels tremble.

An ancient magic has been rediscovered. Sam must overcome his lack of faith and accept his destiny, or the world he knows will suffer the consequences. .

A skeptic who must harness the powers of demons and genies. A zealot who has begun to walk a darker path. Bound together by a stolen secret. Can any of them escape the Chains of Prophecy?

The Drifter: The drifter is a man out of time. Plagued by visions of historic events he never could have witnessed, he struggles to understand the strange abilities that seem so natural. When Death comes for him, he has no choice but to run. He must find allies who can protect him until he learns why he is being pursued.

The keystone of a terrible plan. A society of demigods buried in the rolls of history. Deadly schemes older than man. Welcome to the world of The Essentials.

Cycles of Destruction: A relic of unknown origin appears on Earth . . . and, through a series of coincidences, falls into unexpected hands.

A hidden organization guards the secret of the relic and will do anything to retrieve it.

Still grieving the loss of his wife, Army Veteran Cameron Mitchell must call on his military experience to piece together the mystery of the Alien relic before time runs out. all while protecting his greatest treasure - his son.

Seeking the Sun: Daphne Gianakos begins having strange dreams as she prepares for college life at the University of Florida. A chance encounter with a striking young man triggers conflicting emotions within her, but his identity challenges her entire worldview - he is the last surviving Greek god.

When he goes missing, Daphne must learn who she is, who she was, and the truth about what has happened to the gods...or the world will pay the price.